PROPER ROMANCE

THE LADY

AND THE

HIGHWAYMAN

SARAH M. EDEN

SHADOW
MOUNTAIN

Library of Congress Cataloging-in-Publication Data

Names: Eden, Sarah M., author.
Title: The lady and the highwayman / Sarah M. Eden.
Other titles: Proper romance.
Description: Salt Lake City, Utah : Shadow Mountain, [2019] | Series: Proper romance
Identifiers: LCCN 2019016912 | ISBN 9781629726052 (paperbound)
Subjects: LCSH: Women authors—Fiction. | Women teachers—Fiction. | Man-woman relationships—Fiction. | Penny dreadfuls—Fiction. | Nineteenth century, setting. | London (England), setting. | LCGFT: Novels. | Romance fiction.
Classification: LCC PS3605.D45365 L33 2019 | DDC 813/.6—dc23
LC record available at https://lccn.loc.gov/2019016912

Printed in the United States of America
Lake Book Manufacturing, Inc., Melrose Park, IL

10   9   8   7   6   5   4   3

To Lisa,
who trusted that I could take the
seedling of a story idea and grow
something other than weeds

CHAPTER 1

London, 1865

Rumor had it, Fletcher Walker wasn't born but had simply appeared one day, swaggering down the streets of London. He hadn't any better explanation for his origins, so he embraced it. He'd been a very confident four-year-old pickpocket. At ten years old, he'd strutted into a ragged school, no matter that he was the kind of no-account urchin who didn't belong in any school. He learned to read, learned to write, and learned to saunter his way through doors that ought to have been permanently closed to him.

No one seeing him now, casually tossing and catching a penny in his finely gloved hand as he strode down Bedford Street near Covent Garden, would ever guess he'd started in the ditches. Nor would anyone feel the need to ask him where he was headed or what his business was. Everyone assumed he belonged and knew what he was about.

Cries of "Flowers for sale!" and "Eel pies!" and "Ginger beer! Penny a bottle!" filled the air as they did all day long on the streets of Town. He'd money enough now to be the hero to many of those desperate for a coin here and there. But he needed to go unremarked. Generosity always drew notice.

He reached the corner of King Street, still tossing his penny, still pretending not to notice every person and cart and white-knuckled grasp on baskets of goods. More than anything, he made a point of not noticing the gentleman approaching from Garrick Street, tossing a penny in just the way he was. The man made no acknowledgment of him, either.

A group of grubby street boys leaned against a building, all clamoring for a glimpse at a well-worn softcover publication. The size made it easy to identify: a "penny dreadful." The cheap serials were popular among the laborers and mongers and poor children of London. For a penny, they could enjoy a weekly installment of any number of sensationalized stories featuring criminals and monsters or grand adventures and daring heroes. They were everywhere to be seen around London.

A costermonger began his bit of puffery. "Got peas, guv. Greenest, snappiest peas in all the—"

Fletcher's quick glance, amusement and annoyance mingled in just the right amount, changed the man's tone to one of deference.

"Peas, sir."

If the bloke was still there when Fletcher walked past again, he'd buy something off him. He didn't dare risk drawing attention now. Secrecy was of the utmost importance.

The costermonger tugged at his cap as Fletcher continued on, not slowing his step, not pausing in his coin tossing. It pained him turning down these struggling people, but his clandestine work did the lot of them vastly more good than a trickle of pennies ever could.

The other penny tosser turned onto King Street. His hair, the color of sunset against the industrial skies of London, made him an apple in a basket of spinach: there was no missing him. Theirs was the same destination, but Brogan Donnelly always entered through the back. He drew too much notice. Fletcher knew how to draw none at all.

Fletcher paused on the walk, a bit in the shadows. He slipped his penny inside his watch pocket, then pretended to shake dust off the brim of his silk hat. He didn't meet the eye of anyone passing by, but he also didn't make a show of avoiding doing so.

Once Brogan had disappeared from view, Fletcher popped his hat on his head and casually continued his unhurried ambling. His steps took him up to and through an unassuming blue door. The entryway beyond looked bang-up to any number of plain, respectable spaces throughout London: an improvement over a poor piece but falling short of the splash of aristocratic homes.

The butler sat on the cushioned bench near the door, his eyes closed and chin pressed against his chest, back bowed, shoulders rising and falling with each heavy, buzzing breath.

Fletcher pulled his penny from its place in his waistcoat pocket as he stepped to the dark wood table across from the slumbering man. Fifteen other pennies sat on the tabletop. He set the coin on its edge and, with an expert twist of his fingers, set it spinning.

Nothing about the butler's position or posture changed except for the movement of a single arm. He reached out and pressed the circular center of a carved flower in the molding. The click of a lock sliding open echoed from the right side of the entryway.

Fletcher touched the brim of his hat and dipped his head in the butler's direction. The man simply returned his arm to his side, neither speaking nor opening his eyes.

While the entryway wouldn't've grabbed anyone's notice, the secret room beyond the mechanical door would've brought anyone up short. It wasn't a parlor or dining room in most homes in Town, but rather a smaller version of the House of Commons.

Fifteen men—as familiar as they were varied—stood about the room, chatting. Fletcher set his hat on a hat rack. He slipped off his jacket and gloves. Devested of those bits of discomfort, he undid the buttons of his waistcoat. He was no longer a player on a stage clinging to a role; the men in this room were frauds in their own rights. They'd not begrudge him being one as well.

He sauntered down the wide aisle separating the two sets of facing benches, past the lectern, and to the ornate chair that was his at each of these meetings. A throne, really, but one that had been left behind by the house's previous occupant. If history had taught the English anything, it was that a throne left empty would be claimed by someone. And poverty taught a man to do what he could to make sure that "someone" was himself.

Fletcher plopped himself down on the throne. "Time to be outstandin' but not upstanding, lads." Eye rolls and chuckles met the declaration. The others moved to their usual spots.

"You are late," his friend Hollis Darby observed.

Fletcher leaned against one arm of the chair. "Meeting don't start 'til I get here, so I'd say it's more a matter of you lot arrivin' too early."

Hollis made a cheeky bow. "Yes, Your Majesty. I will strive to be less punctual in the future."

He and Fletcher got on well, no matter that they were as different as coal and water. Hollis's people were aristocratic types, the kind with old bloodlines and older money. He'd taught Fletcher how to swagger like a gentry cove rather than an overgrown street urchin.

Fletcher looked over the men, not all of whom were sitting yet. "Order, mates!" he called out. "Order."

They took their seats, a proper roughs-and-toughs version of Parliament.

"With me, then, men."

In near unison they offered the oath that opened each meeting. "For the poor and infirm, the hopeless and voiceless, we do not relent. We do not forget. We are the Dread Penny Society."

Fletcher sat with either elbow on the chair arms, his fingers entwined. "Penny for your thoughts, gen'lmen."

Hollis Darby rose from his place on the middle of the long bench to Fletcher's left. "I've secured invitations for Fletcher and myself to attend a political salon toward the end of the week, one that will be patronized by many with known interests in both education and the betterment of the poor. We can covertly ascertain who among them might be open to the idea of contributing to Mr. Hogg's ragged school."

Nods of approval from the other men matched Fletcher's.

"Has anyone had any luck sniffing out the bally cod who's undermining Hogg's work?" Fletcher didn't bother hiding his contempt. Mr. Hogg's school was the only one open to the lowest dregs of London street children. Some blackguard was trying to shut him down.

No one seemed to know. Leastwise, not yet. Fletcher had no doubt they would eventually. One benefit to writing the sensationalized penny dreadfuls: there were few villainous plots—outlandish or otherwise—that they couldn't dream up and sort out.

"We'll see his school made right-tight," Fletcher said. "This society won't be best pleased with anything less."

The air filled with echoing declarations of "Hear! Hear!" and "Righto!" and a few other phrases exclaimed in languages other than English—they were a varied group.

Fletcher repeated the call for business. "Penny for your thoughts, gen'lmen."

On the bench to Fletcher's right, Stone rose to his feet. They knew him only by the one name and knew better than to press the matter. He kept mum on near everything but did not for a moment give the impression of timidity. Indeed, Fletcher suspected, should it prove necessary, Stone could thrash the lot of them in a bare-knuckle fight and wouldn't hesitate to do so if it needed doing.

"We've a new monarch growin' mighty comfortable on the throne." Stone's accent had taken some getting used to when they'd first met. The man had lived his early life as a slave in America's South. His escape was the stuff of legend amongst the Dread Penny Society, in large part because Stone refused to tell them how he'd managed it. When it came to

Stone, no one asked for information he hadn't already provided.

"Our Victoria's not stepped down or stuck her spoon in the wall," Donnelly's Irish lilt was more familiar to English ears. "And I'll not be believing the ol' girl would let someone else borrow her crown."

"I reckon your Queen's safe in her claim." Stone looked to Fletcher. "But someone's fixin' to toss you off your high seat."

Fletcher eyed the crowd. "Is one of you aching to dance this jig?" He tapped the arm of his chair.

"Not *that* throne," Stone said.

Ah. Fletcher had been the top-selling writer of their brand of low-literature serials for more than two years, but someone had been inching ever closer to his position. He'd not heard there'd been an official changing of the guards.

"Mr. King has surpassed me, has he?"

Stone nodded. Expressions of understanding filled the other faces. They had all taken note of the rise of the mysterious Mr. King. His work was different than any of theirs. It had elements of nearly everything: adventure, nearly always involving criminals or otherworldly apparitions, sometimes both; a desperate love story; a mystery. Someone was forever being kidnapped, robbed, or forced on the lam. King's first story had seen more than one poor soul shot and left for dead. He was, slowly but surely, claiming an ever-larger slice of the penny-dreadful pie.

Stone retook his seat. That he'd said as much as he had spoke to the seriousness of the situation. They weren't worried for Fletcher's sake. He was far from wealthy, but neither was he an in-and-out pauper making his home on the steps of the poorhouse. Fletcher's earnings helped fund the efforts of the Dread Penny Society: saving working children from abusive masters, feeding poor families, finding work for those searching, rescuing far too many women held against their will in places of ill repute, finding better situations for children in the most desperate of circumstances. His place at the top of the penny dreadfuls was what kept the society afloat. Without his monetary contribution, they couldn't do half of what they did.

"What do we do about it?" Fletcher asked. The group always made these decisions together.

"We need to find this Mr. King and decide what game he's playing." Dr. Milligan spoke without rising. Once they had a topic to chew on, things weren't so formal. "If he's the sort to take up our cause, so much the better. If not . . ."

He didn't finish. Didn't have to. If this Mr. King undermined their work, they'd have no choice but to find a means of knocking him out of the top-sellers position. Too many lives depended on what they did.

"There will be writers at the salon Fletcher and I are attending," Hollis said. "Perhaps we might find someone among them in possession of clues as to King's identity."

Brogan shook his head. "Silver-fork writers, yah? Highbrows? They'll not be deigning to admit they've heard of the penny dreadfuls, let alone know those who write 'em."

Fletcher shook his head. He had rubbed elbows now and then with those who wrote for the more well-to-do. They'd no interest in the work he did, but they knew of it. "Someone'll know something."

"Agreed," Stone said.

Fletcher nodded. He and Hollis would dig for information at the upcoming function. He'd have to put on his "society" airs.

More points of order were raised: a charity they'd helped, a young girl they'd rescued from exploitation, the possibility of admitting a new member. They hacked it out, made plans, and then Fletcher adjourned the official portion of the gathering.

The group mingled once more, some remaining in the Dread Penny Chamber, others wandering out.

Stone made his way to where Fletcher sat. "Do you really reckon King's not worth more worry? He'll be your undoing if you ain't careful."

"I'll worry when I've no other choice," Fletcher said. "His stories are interesting, I'll grant. But he'll not steal all our readers for good."

Stone's expression didn't lighten. He reached into the inner pocket of his jacket and pulled out a folded booklet, then held it out to him.

Fletcher accepted it, curious. The purple cover was unfamiliar, as was the title, *The Lady and the Highwayman*. The author's name, however, was well-known to him. "This is King's newest, i'n'it?"

"It is." Stone tucked his hands into his pockets: not a posture of defeat, but one of confidence. "Blast if there ain't somethin' in it, Fletch. I think it'll catch fire. He's grabbed on to something none of us has."

Fletcher met his eye. "You think he's a threat to the society."

"He's an unknown. When a feller's work is dangerous like ours, he cain't have question marks."

As Stone walked away, Fletcher rose and flipped to the first page of Mr. King's latest offering. He walked slowly toward the door, meaning to read in the privacy of one of the upstairs chambers. Stone was not one for exaggeration. If he said King was encroaching, he most certainly was. And that spelled disaster for all of them.

For the first time in memory, Fletcher's swagger held an unnerving degree of uncertainty.

THE LADY
AND THE
HIGHWAYMAN

by Mr. King

Installment I,
in which our admirable Heroine finds herself
at the Mercy of a dastardly Highwayman!

On a dark, windy night, hours after the sun had slipped
below the horizon, its warmth little but a memory to the
poor souls left to brave the thick chill left in the air by that
amber orb's departure, an ancient traveling carriage, its ill-
kept wheels screeching with every revolution, flew at tremendous speed down a road most people avoided toward an
estate no one had lived in for decades. Inside the dilapidated
vehicle, Lucinda Ledford sat with clasped hands pressed to
her breaking heart.

She had long since resigned herself to this fate. All her
life, she'd known that, upon her parents' deaths, she would
be sent to live on this obscure family holding, far from every
person or place she had ever known, alone, grieving. As she
moved ever closer to her unavoidable future, the prospect
weighed ever more heavily upon her.

"Oh, that Providence would choose to smile upon me!"

whispered she, expecting no answer beyond the forlorn howl of the unfeeling wind. "I, who have been the recipient of nothing but Her cruel frowns!"

No matter that she was no longer a child, she was now an orphan, relegated to the loneliest corner of the kingdom, without a soul to care what became of her.

She sighed, blinking back the tears taking up residence in her eyes. How very unkind Life had chosen to be.

A voice carried on the ceaseless wind, its words indistinguishable. Hands still clasped over her breast, she listened, straining to hear this unexpected evidence that another human life existed in this abandoned corner of the world.

The carriage shook to a stop. Had they arrived so soon, so quickly? Perhaps her unasked-for new home was not so isolated as she'd feared. Oh, hope! Oh, blessed fortune!

The tension lessened in her tightly woven fingers. She lowered her clasped hands to her lap, the smallest whispers of cheer restored to her aching soul.

Outside in the darkness that same voice called again, this time discernible, clear, and sharp. "Stand and deliver!"

Those three words struck cold fear into every knowing heart. To hear them shouted on a lonely and isolated road could mean but one thing: the travelers were soon to find themselves dependent upon the questionable mercy of a ruthless highwayman.

"Oh, dear departed Father," she whispered. "How I need you here with me."

His absence—his permanent absence—was the very reason she was on this dangerous road bound for a home she knew not. Her only hope lay in the knowledge that the would-be thief of the night would discover his prey had nothing of value with which he could abscond. His nefarious efforts would be thwarted by her poverty.

She closed her eyes and forced a slow breath as she counted deliberately. The driver could surely make this highwayman aware of her state before she reached the number ten. Surely.

Her fortune ran short before she'd whispered, "Six." The handle of the carriage door turned, protesting the interruption to its rest. The coachman had never, during their two-day journey, failed to knock first before opening the door. Highwaymen possessed no such commitment to civility.

Cold, biting air rushed inside. A wide silhouette filled the empty space beyond the open door.

"You'll be stepping out, miss," a gravelly voice declared.

A shiver of apprehension slid over her from her hair to her boots. "No, I thank you." She kept her voice steady despite the tremor inside.

"I weren't askin' for your thanks. I'm requiring your cooperation."

"You will have only the former," she insisted.

To someone farther in the darkness, the man said, "We've a stubborn one this time, cap'n."

"You, Smythe, don't know how to talk to ladies." The courtliness of this new voice surprised her. Whoever the second man was, he did not seem to be the rough and uncouth villain his comrade was.

The first man stepped aside, and the shadow of a tall, lean figure assumed his place.

"M'lady," came the graceful voice once more. "I would be

most obliged if you'd step from the carriage. You've my word no harm will befall you."

"Of what value is the promise of a criminal?" Fear made her bold, though her bravery was unlikely to last. If only this dastardly duo would hastily retreat before the danger of the moment overwhelmed her fragile fortitude.

An extended hand entered the carriage, lit by the dim spill of light through the opposite window. He wore no glove. No matter that he spoke with propriety, here was a reminder that he was not, in fact, a gentleman. That he currently demanded she step out into the cold night air whilst he pilfered whatever he chose from amongst her paltry belongings served as a strong indication as well.

"You'd best do as we bid, m'lady," the man behind the hand said. "Your carriage'll be ransacked with or without you in it."

Alas, she hadn't the slightest argument against that logic. Stubbornness was insupportable when it simply added to one's suffering.

"I will alight," she said, "but without your ungloved assistance."

He laughed, the sound deep and rumbling and warm. Oh, the sinister pitfalls that awaited the unwary. Such a laugh might convince the ill-prepared to think well of a man with such contemptible intentions. She was not so easily deceived.

Hand pressed to her heart and head held high, she slid to the end of the bench. She set her free hand on the doorframe and took careful step. Despite her care, despite the fortitude with which she maintained her dignity, her ankle proved fickle. She stumbled.

An arm slipped about her, keeping her upright and unharmed. "Forgive my ungloved assistance," the gallant thief said with another of his rich laughs.

Lucinda pulled free. She turned slowly, assuming her most disapproving and regal expression. No matter that she was afraid, no matter that her ankle ached, no matter that the cold of the late autumn night sent frigid shivers over her, she would prove to this vagabond that she could be strong.

Her assailant wore a broad-brimmed hat, set so low on his head as to cover all his features except his mouth. Despite herself, her heart fluttered. His smile, not subtle in the least, produced a pair of dimples one could not help but find fascinating. She would do well to focus on his dastardly undertaking lest she be fooled by him.

"Proceed with your pilfering," she said. "Your efforts will yield you nothing beyond wasted effort and time."

He appeared not the least admonished. "That is a risk I embrace, my lady." He removed his caped outercoat.

She gasped, hand pressed once more to her heart. Did highwaymen regularly undress whilst undertaking their robberies? Surely not! With a flourish, he spun the coat around and rested it on *her* shoulders.

"What are you doing?" she demanded.

"Perhaps November is a warm month in the area of the kingdom you've called home, but in this corner, the weather is bitter."

"I do not need your coat," she said.

"Alas, my lady, I suspect what you mean is you don't *want* it." He turned to his shorter comrade. "Do not neglect to maintain the watch. I will search inside."

Weapon drawn, Smythe eyed the road, the cluster of nearby trees, and Lucinda herself. As the highwayman climbed into the carriage interior, Lucinda cast her eyes, now adjusted fully to the dark of night, about the area. They were not so alone as she'd believed. Several mounted men watched the encounter, though they were just far enough away that she was afforded no more details. Despite the warmth of the highwayman's unwanted coat, she shivered.

Oh, the cruelty of Fate to take away her home and parents only to send her to this dark and dangerous roadside. Was it not misery enough that she should be alone and in so unfamiliar a place? Must she also be thus accosted?

The highwayman emerged from the carriage, his face still hidden. "It ain't in there," he told his associate. "Best let the lady be on her way."

An odd turn of events to be sure. "*What* isn't in there?" Clearly, he sought something specific.

"Never you mind, miss." He produced another of his dimpled grins.

"You have importuned me and slowed my journey," she declared. "I will indeed mind."

He stepped nearer her. "You are new to this area, my lady. You know not the dangers that reside here."

"I have been made intimately aware of one local danger," she insisted, eyeing him with pointed accusation.

Did all highwaymen laugh as often as he? She would not have assumed them a jolly sort. Neither would she have assumed this road to be a path through treacherous waters.

"I am not the danger you should fear," he said. "On the

contrary. I am all that stands between this neighborhood and a fate far worse than any of its residents comprehend."

This was not a declaration one wished to hear upon arriving in one's new home.

The highwayman took back his cloak and handed her up into the carriage. "You'd best not stop again until you are safely arrived at home."

"I had not intended to stop *this* time," she tossed back with greater courage than she felt.

Again, he laughed. She liked the sound, despite herself. Oh, the fickleness of a heart, finding pleasure in the warm sound of an unwanted laugh.

He slipped something into her hand, closing her fingers around it. "I found this during my 'pilfering.' Guard it, miss. It wouldn't do for you to lose it."

The door was closed. After a hard rap against the side of the carriage, the team of valiant steeds resumed their journey. Lucinda opened her fingers. A necklace lay inside, one upon which she had never before laid eyes. Had it once belonged to the distant cousin from whom she'd inherited her new home? Likely the jeweled pendant was merely paste and not an actual gem. Otherwise, the highwayman would most certainly have kept it.

She sighed, closing her hand once more. Life had too often been like this bit of worthless jewelry: the promise of something beautiful that proved nothing but an illusion. How was she to endure it?

CHAPTER 2

Elizabeth Black, headmistress of Thurloe Collegiate School, was a lady of birth and relative standing, versed in the nuances of the upper class. She had several well-received novels to her name, the kind which appealed to and earned the approval of Society. She oversaw the very proper education of the daughters of both long-established and newly elevated families. She was the very picture of respectability and all that was proper and refined.

She was also lying through her teeth.

Her particular flavor of dishonesty was nothing truly exciting. She wasn't secretly a spy, nor did she have any nefarious ne'er-do-wells hiding in a secret passage in her school. She didn't even have a secret passage.

No. Her deception was comparatively boring, more was the pity.

She stood beside her desk looking over the few measly paragraphs she'd managed to eke out while waiting for Mr. Headley to arrive. He would be her escort to that evening's political salon. She hadn't as much time for completing new chapters as she once had.

Were this the latest in her silver-fork novels, she could have worked on it openly, without fear of reprisal. Writing books for the fine ladies of the upper class was considered an acceptable endeavor for the headmistress of a girls' school. But this was her secret project, her lie . . . her lifeline.

She took hold of the topmost page and read aloud, "Little beyond the nightly howl of the wind broke the silence of her new home." All the wind ever seemed to do was howl. She needed a new descriptor. *Whistle?* No. Readers of these particular tales preferred something more jarring, more ominous. *Shriek?* That wasn't terribly different than *howl.* There had to be something else. *Moan.*

"The nightly moan of the wind." She was getting closer.

The sound of the front knocker stopped her contemplation. She swiftly slipped the stack of parchment in her desk drawer. It clicked closed just as Mrs. Hale, the school's housekeeper, inched open the door to Elizabeth's office.

"Mr. Headley, ma'am."

Elizabeth smoothed the front of her sapphire-blue evening gown and straightened the string of pearls hanging over her clavicle. While she enjoyed the lively conversation and thought-provoking topics of the London political salons, she was keenly aware of the fact that the impression she made directly impacted the success of her school. Disapproval from this set could result in students being withdrawn or new students not applying. She needed their acceptance if she were to stay afloat.

Alistair Headley stepped inside her office. His golden hair was combed, as always, to perfection. His clothes spoke both of significant financial comfort and an eye for fashion. He cut a dash everywhere he went, and she had been told they made quite the sight when they traveled together with her arm through his. The declaration was both flattering and vaguely annoying, though she could not explain the latter reaction.

"Always at work." Mr. Headley dipped his head. His manners were always impeccable. "I do hope you don't intend to change your mind about tonight."

"Of course not." She stepped around her desk. "I have been anticipating this evening all week."

"Ought I to be flattered, or is your enthusiasm in spite of me?"

She knew well how to respond. He quipped this way often. "My eagerness is for both the evening *and* the company."

He offered his arm, and she slipped hers through it.

"I understand a number of this evening's attendees have an interest in education," she said as they passed into the entryway and through the front door. "I always enjoy conversing on that topic."

"Then it *is* the evening that claims your interest after all."

She looked back at him, allowing her features to turn in lighthearted scolding. "It is *both*, as I said."

He did not tease her further as the carriage rolled down the London streets toward their destination. They spoke, instead, of her writing—the bit he knew about. As *that* endeavor was not looked down upon nor required the upmost secrecy, she could answer truthfully.

"I am not progressing with my latest novel as quickly as I would like. Too much presses on my time, but I do hope to have something ready soon."

He nodded in approval. "A great many people will be

pleased to know you mean to produce another offering. Few write with the sophistication you do."

Elizabeth turned her head to the carriage window, needing to hide the laughing grin that rose at his words of praise. "Sophistication" was not the word one would use to describe her most profitable works. That, though, was what made them so vastly diverting to write. Excesses of emotion. Dastardly villains. Daring escapes. Sword fights. They were exaggerations of the most delicious sort, exciting the senses, palpitating the heart, offering an escape from the doldrums of life.

It wasn't that she didn't enjoy her more sedate stories. Indeed, she deeply enjoyed writing her more "sophisticated" works. But when one spent one's days in the sameness of a well-ordered school, presenting a façade of perfection to one's potential benefactors, a bit of an invisible, scandalous escape was a wonderful and needful thing.

A hired hackney flew past theirs at breakneck speed.

"Shocking bit of driving, that," Mr. Headley said, clearly disapproving.

What had the hack in such a hurry? She watched for something, someone, in pursuit. Nothing. Had the passenger been rushing to someone's deathbed? A detective hot on the trail of a criminal? Or a criminal hot on the trail of his next victim? The possibilities were practically endless. She made mental note of as many as she could think of, in case she decided to add a carriage chase later in the story she was writing.

Only when Mr. Headley took her hand in his did she recall her company. "George can be depended upon to drive us safely to our destination, regardless of the dangers we encounter."

That was a pity. She'd have far rather followed the speeding hackney to whatever its seedy destination might be.

But, no. She was the prim and proper headmistress of Thurloe Collegiate School. She could not afford to forget that. A lady in her position could be respected or she could be adventurous. What she could not be was *both*.

By the time she stepped into the Gallaghers' parlor, her arm through Mr. Headley's, she had regained full control of her wayward thoughts. She dipped curtsies as expected, offered words of greeting, and wove through the guests with grace and graciousness.

"Thurloe School is spoken of quite highly," Mr. Gallagher said after the appropriate greetings were exchanged.

"I am pleased to hear that. I work very hard to make it an exemplary educational institution."

Mrs. Gallagher nodded. "Such effort is rarely made on behalf of a girls' school. Too many feel it is wasted on the fairer sex."

Elizabeth had heard the argument too many times to be offended by it. "You and I must stand as proof that a female mind can, indeed, receive education and be improved by the effort. The girls at my school are no different."

Mrs. Gallagher agreed, as Elizabeth had fully expected her to. She had made the point for the sake of the others listening in. More people ought to see value in the minds of women.

"Do you feel the same about schools for the poor?" a nearby gentleman asked.

She turned toward the speaker, a gentleman she did not know. "I do, indeed." She looked to Mr. Headley, hoping for an introduction.

He obliged. "Mr. Darby, this is Miss Elizabeth Black, head-mistress of Thurloe Collegiate School and renowned novelist. Miss Black, this is Mr. Hollis Darby, of the Nottinghamshire Darbys."

"A pleasure, Miss Black." Mr. Darby offered a respectful bow. "May I make known to you my friend?" He motioned to a gentleman on his other side, one who stepped forward in that moment, coming into view for the first time.

Elizabeth's breath caught. Here was a man a woman could not help but notice. His dark hair, though neatly combed, had something riotous about it, as if barely tamed by his ab-lutions. The beginnings of stubble darkened his jaw and chin. And those dark eyes beneath thick brows watched her in such a way that she could not be certain he didn't see more than she realized. Here was the perfect model for a penny dreadful hero—or villain.

"Fletcher Walker," Mr. Darby said, completing the intro-duction.

"Pleasure, miss." Mr. Walker dipped his head, an accept-able motion of greeting but one that felt the tiniest bit au-dacious. He seemed to know his mannerisms and speech re-vealed him to be a bit below his company and that he found the arrangement amusing.

"Fletcher Walker?" Elizabeth hoped she kept her interest at just the right level to not draw too much scrutiny. Fletcher Walker was the name of a very successful author of penny dreadfuls. "Your name is very familiar."

"I've a propensity for scratching pen to paper," he said. "And I've been told I spin a good tale." His was not a voice borne of an upper-class rearing. There was something of the middle class in his tenor, but it felt acquired. If she had to guess, she would say he'd come from the lowest dregs of society but now occupied a higher rung. "Perhaps you know my work."

Mr. Headley nearly snorted, a moment of unexpected incivility. "That is unlikely." He looked to her once more. "Mr. Walker dabbles in the . . . less refined areas of, well, I dare not say 'literature.'"

"Why?" Mr. Walker asked. "Is it too difficult for you to pronounce?"

Oh, this Fletcher Walker was a dastardly sort. She liked him already.

His remark clearly caught Mr. Headley unawares, though he regained his footing quickly. "I only meant that the penny dreadfuls are not quite the same offering as those more nuanced books authors such as Miss Black produce—books which we describe as literature."

"I've heard a few choice descriptions for them highbrow novels." Mr. Walker was not the least put off by Mr. Headley's disapproval.

"You've only just released the first installment of a new 'Urchins of London' tale, I believe," she said.

Mr. Headley eyed her with something akin to horror. "Do not tell me *you* read them."

Heavens, she did far more than merely read them.

"It does not do to ignore success in one's chosen field, even if that success occurs in slightly different incarnations than one is accustomed to." She addressed Mr. Walker once more. "I believe you are by all accounts the most successful author in your particular area of literature."

"I commend you on your pronunciation of that very difficult word." He spoke dryly but with unmistakable humor. Here was a man with whom she would enjoy a verbal sparring match. She didn't dare risk it, though. Not in their current company. Prim and proper, that was the key to her school's continued success and her hard-won independence.

"Mr. Walker has recently been unseated," his friend said. "A newcomer has taken the upper hand."

"That must be a sore disappointment," she said. "I find myself forever chasing the success Mrs. Gaskell has claimed in our shared area of publishing."

"You've the good fortune of being able to name your rival," Mr. Walker said. "Mine is an unknown, as slippery as an eel pie in the summer sun."

"Is that not rather appropriate?" she pressed. "A genre so given to mystery and intrigue suddenly seized by an inscrutable phantom?"

"I'll grant you, it's fitting," he conceded. "I've my suspicions Mr. King enjoys sending us all on an endless chase."

Mr. King. How tempted she was to grin, to gloat, to do something at the sound of that name.

"This mysterious author is the new 'king,' if you will, of the penny dreadfuls?"

"He is, indeed, a rather dreadful king."

Oh, yes, he had a sharp wit. She liked that more than she ought.

"We'll run him to ground, though. Someone's bound to know who he is."

"Is it this puzzle which has brought you here this evening?" she asked.

"No, actually." He deferred to his friend, something she would wager did not come naturally to him. Fletcher Walker was quite obviously a man accustomed to taking charge of any situation.

"We understood the focus of tonight's salon was to be education," Mr. Darby said. "That happens to be a topic that interests us."

Yes, he had said something about that when they'd first begun speaking.

"You advocate for the education of the poor, I believe," she said.

He nodded. "Ragged schools mostly. Mr. Hogg's in particular."

She was familiar with the endeavor. "Many have said he is foolish to take in students whom other schools have deemed too dangerous or too far down the path of ill repute for redemption."

"And many have said educating girls is a waste as well," Mr. Walker tossed in. "It is possible 'many' are wrong."

"It is more than possible, Mr. Walker. It is true."

Mr. Headley tugged at her arm, urging her toward a different group of attendees. She offered a quick farewell to Mr. Darby and Mr. Walker. Even as she moved about the gathering, speaking with people she knew, meeting people she didn't, her thoughts and, more often than she cared to admit, her gaze returned to the intriguing Mr. Fletcher Walker.

He was chasing down the elusive Mr. King.

What would he think if he knew he had, in fact, been speaking with . . . *her*?

THE VAMPIRE'S TOWER
AN URCHINS OF LONDON ADVENTURE

by Fletcher Walker

Chapter I

Morris Wood had clocked twelve years of life and had nothing but survival to show for it. He worked what reputable jobs he could scrounge, filling the gaps with pickpocketing and nipping second-rate bunts from unsuspecting costermongers and selling the bruised or misshapen apples for a few coins. He wasn't a bad sort, just a lad born under an unlucky star.

"Carry your parcels, miss?" he asked, his tattered hat in his hands, as a finely dressed woman stepped out of a milliner's shop.

She looked to her maid, walking at her side. They exchanged amused smiles.

He wasn't so easily put off. "You're like to be full knackered after a day of shopping. Allow me to lug your goods, miss."

Morris watched, hopeful. The younger misses and the oldest matrons were most likely to cross his palm with a farthing or more, sometimes even a shilling. He need only bow and scrape and try to look a bit younger than he was. Pity paid, after all. And little ones got a blimey lot of pity.

The fine lady motioned to a carriage two skips away. "I am going only so far as there."

"I'd carry your load that far, miss."

The gentry sorts had a way, when he'd worn them down, of dropping their shoulders and sighing like they had to empty their lungs all at once. Pity paid, but so did exasperation. He'd take the coins however they came.

The lady's parcels were carried to her carriage. Two sixpence were set in his hand. He pocketed them, along with the few other coins he'd managed to pull together that day. It was a meager pile, nowhere near the bunce he'd like to claim as his own. Still, it'd be enough to pay his daily due for the roof over his head that night. Another couple of morts out doing a bit of shopping, a gent here or there with a bit of silver jingling in his coat, and Morris'd have something left over after the Innkeeper took his share.

He walked down the street with his hands tucked in his pockets, whistling. The day was fine. He appreciated the weather for more than the convenience. Rainy days or windy days or otherwise miserable days tended to empty the streets. It was hard to go dipping when there were no jangling pockets wandering about. Honest work wasn't easier to claim either when the fine coves and morts kept to their houses.

Morris spotted his chum Jimmy standing by a fishmonger's cart. He gave a quick nod, pausing as he drew near. "Swiping?" he asked behind his teeth.

"Guarding." Jimmy's eyes pulled wide, looking as

surprised as Morris felt. Urchins like them weren't usually trusted with *preventing* a thieving.

"You drawing bunce for it?"

Jimmy nodded. "I'm to watch all these carts and warn if someone's looking to nip off with something. The lot are paying me a shilling for the day."

"A shilling?" Morris whistled in appreciation. "I ain't never pulled down a shilling in one day for anything respectable."

"Boy," a gravelly voice called. "I don't pay you for nattering."

No more chattering. Pocketing a shilling meant Jimmy'd have loads left even after paying the Innkeeper. Morris wasn't about to rob him of that. Honest work was a rare enough thing, and they needed every penny, every shilling, every guinea they could tuck away. Jimmy and Morris meant to make something of themselves. A fellow needed money to do that. Money and a whole heap of luck.

"I'm a bit short," Morris said. "May 'ave to pick a kick or two."

"Don't get caught," Jimmy warned. "Enough of us've been swept up."

Morris knew it well enough. He kept on his way, keeping an eye out for opportunities. The Innkeeper wouldn't let him stay without the daily rent. But nearly every night, one or more of the urchins that took refuge in the Inn didn't return from their day on the street. He'd guess, if pressed, that they'd been caught nipping off with coins or pocket watches or whatever else they could wrap their fingers around to bring back to the Inn. He didn't intend to take a ride in the Black Maria anytime soon.

He'd managed to earn a few ha'pennies here and there for odd jobs and tasks. He didn't have to go dipping the whole the rest of the day. Jimmy's shilling put Morris's earnings to shame, but they were a team. What one of 'em tucked away, they'd both be helped by.

With the relief that came from money in his pocket, Morris made his way quickly down the streets of London toward the slum where he spent each night. He'd not gone far when a sight caught him up short. The finest carriage he'd ever seen. Half at least was covered in gold. The rest, white as snow, hadn't even a speck of dirt on it, no matter that the streets were terribly dusty. On either side of the driver, who was wearing white livery with a three-point hat, two red flags flapped and flew.

"S'help me Baub, I'll have me a carriage like that one day," Morris whispered to himself, watching the awe-inspiring vehicle fly past. Someday. Someday he'd be out of the gutter. He'd be able to read, able to pay his own way without being beholden to a cracksman like the Innkeeper, and he'd have a carriage, a fine one like that'n.

He knew the way to the building that the urchins all knew as the Inn. Even with the rotting planks across gaps in the walk and the needed leaps to get safely over, he didn't have to think much to manage it any more. Easy enough.

He ducked through the misshapen hole in the side of the brick wall. No one knew when it had broken or if it'd once been a proper door, but it was their way in and out, and it was the reason the Inn was so blasted cold in the winter and blazing hot in the summer. Still, it was dry and better than sleeping on the street.

Morris stood in the usual line just inside the hole. The children always queued up when returning for the night. Some were a touch older than he was; most were younger. All were waiting their turn to make the daily payment.

Behind a tall, battered clerk's desk stood a grease-faced man, hair stringy and long. He eyed each child as he or she approached. His hand uncurled, palm up, gray fingernails extending like claws.

"Half farthing." That was what he asked of the youngest.

Little George set his nightly rent in the Innkeeper's hand and slipped passed. Next, a girl closer to Morris's twelve years approached the desk.

With the same extended claw, the Innkeeper said, "Ha'penny."

"I've this watch chain," Mary told him. "Worth weeks of rent, I'd say."

He examined it, that practiced greedy eye of his not missing a thing. "Bit banged up, it is." He popped it between two of his six teeth and gave it a bite. "Gold, though." The Innkeeper nodded, dropping the treasure in the box he'd lock after everyone'd paid their due. "Three weeks for you, Mary."

She'd be in fine fettle for nearly a month. Anything she earned or swiped, she could keep. Or she could give herself as close to a holiday as any of them would ever know.

Morris's turn arrived soon enough.

"Tuppence." The Innkeeper's unwavering hand waited for payment.

He set four farthings and two ha'pennies in the Inn-keeper's palm. The man counted 'em, something Morris knew wasn't necessary. The Innkeeper knew the feel of coin, knew at a glance how much he held in his claws. The coins were dropped in the locking box, and Morris was waved inside.

One more night off the street. One more night closer to the better life he and Jimmy meant to claim for themselves.

Morris grabbed a dinged and dented metal bowl from the stack in the corner and crossed to the even more dinged and dented pot hanging in the soot-blackened fireplace. He scooped out a lump of breadcrumb gruel.

Little George rose on his toes, trying to peer over the lip of the pot.

"Breadcrumb," Morris said, tipping his bowl enough to show the boy.

"Innkeeper done bobbed me." George's threadbare shoulders drooped. "Said we'd be twisting down oat gruel t'night. I like oat gruel better."

"So do I, lad." Morris dumped a heap into a bowl for George and handed it to him. "Fill up, though. It's hard to sleep with an empty belly."

He sat down on a three-legged stool, bowl on his knees, and looked out over the children, counting heads. They were two short of their usual number. One of those missing was Jimmy, but he had a longer trek back than usual. He'd be along soon, no doubt. Who else hadn't come back?

Morris caught Mary's eye. "Sally ain't back?"

Mary gave a small shake of her head, her mouth pulled low with worry. "Ain't like her to be late."

No, it wasn't.

"You don't suppose she's—" Mary didn't finish the question.

All the nearby urchins looked to him, the same nervous pull to their features. They didn't talk a lot about how many of them had simply disappeared, but everyone knew. Everyone worried.

"She'll be back soon." Morris spoke more confidently than he felt.

She didn't come back.

Even after Jimmy returned, leftover coins secreted away after paying his rent, Sally still wasn't there.

Night fell. Morning dawned. All the urchins left to make their daily silver.

And Sally didn't come back.

———✦———

In the shadowy stretch of a London back alley, a sallow-faced man watched the comings and goings of the street children. Young. Energetic. Easily overlooked. A few missing here and there would hardly be noticed. Would his master be pleased at how many he was wrangling so quickly? Just what his master needed: a fresh supply . . . of blood.

CHAPTER 3

Fletcher pulled the brim of his weather-beaten cap low over his brow, an unlit pipe hanging precariously from the corner of his mouth. He knew how to disappear into the crowds of street people, because at his core, he was one of them, no matter that he'd more money to his name now than he'd've ever imagined during his days as a shoeblack, dustman, or pickpocket. He was dressed the part with worn and stained trousers, age-dulled outercoat, and thin-soled work boots that felt at once foreign and familiar, both a costume and a second skin.

Leaning back against the lamppost sent a streak of cold through his insufficient coat. With the appearance of carelessness, he spun a single penny around the fingers of one hand, watching the comings and goings with vague disinterest. Beneath his bent cap brim, he searched the milling crowd.

A bootblack bent over a grubby copy of a penny dreadful. Two smaller boys Fletcher suspected were looking for a pocket to pick. A hansom cab driver with a folded penny serial sticking out the back pocket of his trousers. A fishmonger shouting to the crowd.

A flash of copper a bit ahead caught his eye just long enough to see who held the telltale token. Martin Afola, one of the quieter members of the Dread Penny Society, but reliable to his very bones.

With a subtle swing of his arm, Martin indicated a man—a sweep, based on the brushes he carried—with the shape and coloring of an overripe apple. Their mark. He barked something at the boy following close behind, a slight, skeletal little thing, covered in soot from his tight, curly hair and downturned eyes to the cuffs of his ragged trousers. Their objective.

Fletcher made no motions of notice or intention. He kept himself to his place in the lamplight.

Another flash of copper, this time handed to a small shoeblack who'd only just finished cleaning the boots of Hollis Darby. All was in place, then. The three of them—Fletcher, Hollis, and Martin—were fully capable of undertaking this particular rescue. They were no green branches.

Education was the topic forever caught in Hollis's craw. Rescuing London's street children was Fletcher's focus. He knew the dangerous, desperate lives they were living. He meant to help as many as he could.

Martin was particularly needed for this rescue. Those who could, upon a glance, be identified as having ancestors who'd arrived in England from the farthest reaches of the world had reason to be wary of those who didn't share that background. When reaching out to help the destitute, desperate, and frightened children of London's streets, the Dread

Penny Society had found it best, when possible, to include in the rescue someone in whom those children could see reflections of themselves. It didn't ease every uncertainty, but it helped.

"Move, boy," the portly sweep shouted at his climbing boy.

The little one rushed to keep pace with his master's long strides. It wasn't enough. The sweep grabbed the boy by his coat front and yanked him off his feet.

"If I miss this job on account o' you, I'll tan your hide 'til you bleed, hear?"

Fletcher knew well the fear he saw in the boy's eyes. That hadn't been an idle threat.

The sweep dropped the child on the ground. He landed with a thud and a whimper, sprawled in a painful twisting of his thin limbs.

Fletcher kept himself still, fighting the urge to yank the boy away and bust the man's nose for good measure. But he didn't dare risk overplaying their hand.

Hollis moved down the walk, assuming a stride that declared him the gentry cove he truly was. Sometimes Fletcher forgot how far above his touch Hollis truly was. The man was to the manor born, no matter that he now rubbed elbows with a collection of mutts and castaways and tellers of sensationalized tales.

Right on cue, Hollis bumped into the portly sweep's brushes, managing to make the collision appear unintentional. Before the sweep likely knew what had happened, Hollis's voice rang out in the street, accusing loudly and angrily that the man had ruined Hollis's clothing with the soot of his brushes. The fierce reprimand did what it was meant to: the sweep stared, shocked, bemused, upended.

Fletcher pushed away from the post and sauntered over toward the fray. "Seems ye're in bad loaf, friend."

The sweep glared. "I've done nothing to this cove. He walked directly into m'brushes, then cries and shouts that I've done him a harm."

"The state of my clothing indicates you have." Hollis could sound the puffed-chest aristocrat when he put his mind to it.

Fletcher leaned nearer to the sweep. "I'd wager you know full well how these fine gents bullyrag a fellow over every blasted thing. Best see if you can't square up with the cove."

"I haven't money to toss at a man who could buy and sell me ten times over."

Fletcher shrugged, tapping the mouthpiece of his pipe against his teeth. "Might do to brush him off a bit."

The man grumbled something Fletcher didn't try to make out; he could guess easily enough. The man produced a handkerchief, one nearly as blackened as his brushes and clothes.

"Not with that, chum," Fletcher warned. "He'll string you up." He popped a handkerchief from his own coat, one not quite so filthy as the sweep's.

As the sweep grudgingly swiped at Hollis's jacket, Fletcher noted out of the corner of his eye that Martin had secured the cooperation of the sweep's little assistant. Hollis pointed out areas where his "attacker" ought to apply greater care in undoing the damage he'd caused. Fletcher made certain to meet his pretended-friend's eye now and then with a look of shared annoyance for the absurdity of the upper classes.

Martin and the boy slipped away, unseen and undetected. Fletcher would give them time enough to make good their escape before bringing the charade to an end.

Hollis huffed and brushed the man's hand away, declaring he was helping not at all, and strode away. Fletcher remained behind.

"M'heart bleeds for that gent's poor laundry maid," Fletcher said. "He likely flies into a rage at every spot she cain't scrub out."

"Them cloddy coves'd beat a dog for havin' fur."

Fletcher bit back the observation that the sweep had tossed a child around not more than a moment earlier for nothing more than walking slower than he did. And he'd threatened to beat him if the day didn't go well. Fletcher had no doubt he beat the child often.

He tossed a mumbled agreement—his part in this theatrical called for it—and, tucking his pipe back into the corner of his mouth, sauntered off in the opposite direction Hollis had gone.

The briefest of moments passed before the sweep shouted, "Boy! You come back, boy. I'll skin you, I will. You'll sleep in the next chimney if you don't show yourself now."

Fletcher's chest seized, and his fists clenched. He had once been on the receiving end of such threats and the carrying out of them. That was life for the poor urchins of this city. But as of tonight, it was reality for one fewer than it had been. But he couldn't turn around and flatten the blackguard, couldn't draw attention.

He took the roundabout way toward York Street, making certain no one followed him or looked at him askance. Tipping his hand might help the blustering bloke find the little boy.

Fletcher doubled back a few times, keeping his strides both confident and casual. He received a few glances, but none that couldn't be explained by his swagger. His cap sat low enough and his whiskers grown in enough that the standabouts seeing him later, shaven and well-togged, would never realize he was the same bloke they'd seen before.

He slipped quietly up behind the mews not far from Hogg's ragged school. Martin was already inside, the little climbing boy with him. The stablehand, Joe, handed the urchin a bit of a sandwich. The boy devoured it in an instant.

When Fletcher stepped forward, their rescued sufferer slipped immediately behind Martin, clutching the back of his coat.

"He's one of us, Daniel," Martin assured him quietly. "He helped us get you away."

"Mr. Allen'll kill me, he will. Has been meaning to for ages."

With a flick of his hand, Fletcher tossed his cap onto an obliging nail. "He'll not know where you are, boy. We've hidden away enough now to know how to do the thing right and proper."

"Them whips there"—the boy pointed a shaking finger at the nearby wall—"what're them for?"

"Urging the horses along," Joe said.

Daniel swallowed loudly. "Whips hurt."

"Yes, they do," Fletcher muttered. He knew from vast personal experience when he had been Daniel's age.

"We only crack 'em over the animals' heads. The sound tells 'em to step livelier," Joe added.

"You don't whip 'em?" Daniel didn't seem to fully believe him.

"No," Joe said.

The boy still didn't look convinced.

"Whips ain't for hurting or causing pain," Fletcher said. "Not to people or animals."

"Are too," Daniel countered. "An' they hurt like the devil."

"I know it," Fletcher said. "I had a few masters like yours when I was a boy. You'll find none like him here. I swear it."

"Am I bein' hidden here?" Daniel slipped a little away from his protector, still eyeing Fletcher and Joe with uncertainty.

"For now," Martin said. He had a comforting way with the boy, calm and confident, soft without being wishy-washy. "And you'll have a bit of learnin' at the ragged school."

"Ragged schools don't take the likes of me," he said. "Too rough, they say. Too low."

"This one will," Fletcher said. "Mr. Hogg don't object to children what are low or rough."

Daniel looked to Martin. "Do he object to folks . . . like us?"

Martin hunched down, eyes level with the boy's. "Plenty toss us aside, don't they?"

The boy nodded.

"I'd not've let 'em bring you here if I thought anyone would treat you bad on account of your skin being like mine.

They ain't saints, but none of this lot"—he motioned to Fletcher and Joe—"will mistreat you."

Daniel turned doubtful eyes on Fletcher. Life on the streets didn't teach children to be hopeful or naïve. "You swear?"

"Frequently and fluently."

That earned him a fleeting grin. It disappeared quickly, though.

"And there'll be food?" The broken hopefulness of that simple question tore a hole clear through Fletcher. He remembered all too well what it was to be hungry. And beaten. And afraid.

"We'll make particular certain of that," he said. He pulled a silver ten-cent piece from his waistcoat pocket and held it out to the boy. "This is for you, for getting yourself a few things you need. I've every confidence you'll spend it wisely."

"Yes, sir." Daniel's eyes opened wide as he took the coin, holding it like a nugget of pure gold.

"But this'n"—Fletcher held up a penny, one etched with *DPS* in tiny lettering—"isn't for spending. If ever you're needing something, or you hear of another child or mother or person in need of saving, you bring this penny to Joe, here, and he'll fetch us."

"Is that how you heard about me? Someone tossed 'im a penny?"

"That's how we hear about most things," Martin said. "The street children know everything."

Daniel grinned, the heaviness in his eyes lifted by the change in his expression. "We hear it all, we do. And we ain't afraid to whisper it back to those what use it for helping."

"That's what we do," Fletcher said.

"C'mon, then." Martin nudged Daniel toward the door of the mews and the ladder leading up to the stablehand's lodgings. There was a small room they used for rescued children, a space where they were safe and, likely for the first time in their lives, granted a bit of privacy. Joe looked after 'em until the Dread Penny Society secured something else. Daniel would sleep and eat well that night. He'd have a bit of learning. And he'd pass a night without being beaten. Fletcher knew how rare that was for children like Daniel, like he himself used to be.

This was what he worked so hard for. He appreciated the comfort that his successes had brought his own life, but the children he was able to save was the real reward. If King kept chipping away at his profits, he'd not be able to do as much for the urchins. Finding the man and seeing if he'd support the cause, or at least not impede it, was crucial

Joe motioned for him to wait a minute before leaving. "We may have a spot of trouble."

"What flavor?"

"Ash."

He hadn't been expecting that and didn't quite know what to make of it.

"Been finding charred bits of torches and matches and such 'round the school grounds. Enough to catch m'notice."

"Children playing with fire?" The school claimed a great many children with a tendency to get themselves into mischief.

"Maybe, but I'm not finding it in places they're likely to leave it. I'm finding it under windows. Out on the walk. Even back here by the mews." Joe shook his head. "Something ain't right."

"You think it worth looking into?"

Joe nodded. Firmly.

"Hollis'll want to know," Fletcher said. The man was tireless in his fight for the education of the poor. He was the reason Hogg's school was supported so strongly by the Dread Penny Society. "We'll see what we can find out. You keep those eyes peeled as well."

The opposition to this school had been particularly fierce, but in indirect ways. Cutting off funds and support, that sort of thing. What if someone was taking more drastic measures? What if the society had rescued Daniel only to drop him into a different sort of danger?

CHAPTER 4

Elizabeth sat, as was customary on Thursday evenings, in the school's parlor, acting as chaperone while her teachers received callers. Most enjoyed friendly chats with friends of some standing, teachers from other establishments, the occasional family member. A few of the younger, prettier teachers did not pass a single Thursday without being the subject of attention from besotted men. That those younger teachers were not all that much younger than she was made her role in this weekly endeavor all the more absurd.

And Miss Beating—whose unfortunate surname had a tendency to inspire fear in newly arrived pupils upon first meeting their sewing instructor—had been a teacher twice as long as Elizabeth had been alive, yet she was not the one charged with keeping the "young people" toeing the line of propriety.

Still, the weekly calling hour provided her staff with something to look forward to and a bit of much-deserved happiness, and her presence allowed it to occur without anyone looking askance at her establishment. She did a great many things she found a bit absurd in the service of her profession and respectability.

"My dearest Miss Newport," a particularly besotted young gentleman declared upon entering the parlor and casting eyes upon the school's music instructor. Ana Newport was, without question, a veritable beauty of that delicate variety that never seemed to fall out of fashion.

Ana was only a few years Elizabeth's junior, and they had become fast friends. In Ana, she had discovered a woman who kept her inner strengths hidden from the world, while Elizabeth only ever showed the world the strengths she knew others would find most acceptable. They were both happy to have positions they enjoyed and a future they could rely upon, but neither of them were wholly satisfied.

"Mr. Porter," Ana said in a tone of gentle reproof, "you really mustn't be so familiar."

"My feelings are too ardent for prudence," he insisted, his expression that of a martyr. He spoke loudly enough for Elizabeth to overhear and, likely, Miss Quinn, the arithmetic instructor. The rest of the room took no obvious note.

"Your imprudence will end with me being censured by my employer," Ana insisted. "A teacher's position depends upon decorum."

Elizabeth managed to set her features in an expression of quiet reprimand, though she did not look directly at the couple. Ana had used this particular tactic before; Elizabeth was happy to oblige.

"Forgive me, Miss Newport." Mr. Porter pressed his hand to his heart, not tearing his gaze from the golden-haired Ana. "I would not cause you distress for all the world."

Ana had a remarkable ability to express a significant range of emotions with the tiniest lift of a brow or the smallest pull of her lips. One, however, had to know her well to see such changes in her expression let alone interpret them. Elizabeth was well able to do both.

Mr. Porter was not. He was, indeed, causing Ana distress. Not by his fervent words of delight at her company, but by his continued monopolization of her time. She was too polite and kindhearted to say as much, but he would do far more for his cause by simply leaving.

Elizabeth hid her amusement with effort. She needed to appear the staid and steady chaperone, after all. Such was her odd lot in life. Inwardly, she dreamed of daring adventure, wishing she could indulge those fantasies without losing everything she'd worked for.

Mrs. Hale, the housekeeper, showed in another caller, one that both pleased and surprised Elizabeth. Mr. Headley did not often come during the established visiting hours, yet when he did visit Thurloe Collegiate School, it was always to call upon her. This time, however, he had not come unaccompanied.

Serenity Vance was approximately the same age as Elizabeth, and like Elizabeth, had established herself as a relatively successful writer of silver-fork novels. The two of them were not rivals, but neither were they particular friends.

"Miss Vance." She offered a quickly dipped curtsy in greeting. "Mr. Headley." Another.

They settled into a comfortable seating arrangement, but Mr. Headley and Miss Vance did not prove to be particularly quiet conversationalists. It wasn't a rudeness, necessarily, more an unawareness of just how much they dominated the space upon their arrival.

"Miss Black, everyone is utterly longing for your next book," Miss Vance said. "Do tell me you will soon have something new for us to devour."

Though her choice of words was, perhaps, a bit grander than was necessary, everything in her expression and tone spoke of sincerity. Elizabeth appreciated that more than her visitor likely realized.

"My efforts are slower than I would prefer," she said. "I hope to soon find myself more productive."

Ana, either anxious to defend Elizabeth from some perceived slight or eager to escape Mr. Porter's continued attention, spoke up. "She is forever bent over her pages, pen flying with great speed."

"Oh, that is good news." Miss Vance smiled at her.

Mr. Headley offered a nod of pleased approval.

What none of them realized was that her frantic efforts to complete the necessary pages were focused, not on her next tale for the refined readers of the elevated classes, but on the daring and dastardly tale of a young damsel relegated to the misery of an empty and isolated estate and who would soon find herself at the mercy of a mysterious highwayman. Silverfork novels were an acceptable endeavor for a headmistress; penny dreadfuls were not.

"It is all too true," she said, allowing regret to touch her words. "I have put in a great deal of effort, but must admit, I do not see an ending in sight."

"We will be pleased with it whenever it is complete," Miss Vance insisted.

Elizabeth asked after her writing and, soon, their conversation took them down familiar and safe paths. She even managed to rein in the volume of the conversation, allowing the other teachers to return to their discussions. Ana managed to free herself of Mr. Porter, who, undeterred, offered a heartfelt promise that he would return next week. Elizabeth smiled as Ana sat beside her with a sigh.

"I was rather shocked to see that Mr. Darby maintains such a close association with that penny dreadful author," Mr. Headley said. "The Darbys are of good standing. And one need only listen to Walker speak to know his origins are not particularly exalted. His choice to pursue such low literature simply emphasizes it."

She, too, had noticed the telltale turns in Mr. Walker's speech: the *T*s dropped at the end of words, vowels pulled out long and produced at the back of the throat, the slight garbling of sounds and swallowing of syllables, word choices that would not be made by those on a higher rung of society.

"But that would not matter particularly to the audience of his offerings," Miss Vance said. "Indeed, it likely is part of the reason for his success."

There was likely a great deal of truth to that. Elizabeth worried over the reception of her tales, having lived a decidedly different life than most who read them. She did attempt to include some of the vernacular her readers were accustomed to but felt certain her origins showed in her writing.

"You know of Mr. Walker's work?" Mr. Headley looked to his companion with surprise.

"Fletcher Walker has been the undisputed king of the

penny dreadfuls for some time now. Though I do not read those tales, I have most certainly heard of him."

Elizabeth's respect for Miss Vance grew. Not all people from the higher echelons of literature were willing to acknowledge in any positive way the offerings from "the dregs."

"Then you have likely heard of *Mr. King.*" Ana whispered the name.

Both Mr. Headley and Miss Vance nodded. Elizabeth did as well, not wanting to draw attention to herself while such a potentially disastrous topic was discussed.

Ana looked to her. "I have heard a few of our girls mention Mr. King's stories, though I do not know for certain if any of them have read his work."

"What do they have to say about these stories?" Heavens, she was tempting fate, but her interest was too piqued to be fully ignored.

"Only that they have heard that his stories include dashing heroes and brave heroines, villains who try to thwart true love." Ana smiled. "I don't know that any schoolgirl could resist such a thing."

"Surely, you don't encourage them to read the penny dreadfuls." Miss Vance's shock was tempered by a hint of amusement.

"Could you imagine the uproar amongst the parents if we did?" Elizabeth had, in fact, imagined it many times, the certainty of the outcome convincing her to be vigilant in keeping her nom de plume a secret. "I have not heard there is anything truly untoward in King's offerings, but parents expect schools to focus on literature of higher—"

"—quality?" Mr. Headley supplied with a smile.

Elizabeth didn't argue, though she felt sorely tempted. "I intended to say 'educational reputation.'"

"One must also be concerned with the reputation of those who write these low tales," Miss Vance said.

"They aren't the sort impressionable young minds ought to be influenced by," Mr. Headley said.

The others all nodded.

Elizabeth's heart pounded even harder. These were the very arguments that kept her silent about her secret writing projects. If Mr. King's identity were revealed, she was certain that all her students would be pulled from the school.

"And one cannot ignore the questionable Dread Penny Society." Miss Vance's voice was breathless with both amazement and shock.

Mr. Headley raised his brows, not in surprise but agreement.

"What is this?" Elizabeth asked.

"The 'Dread Penny Society,'" Miss Vance repeated. "It is rumored a group of penny dreadful authors has banded together to form a gentleman's club."

"That does not seem objectionable."

Miss Vance shook her head. "Not a gentleman's club in the traditional sense. They are involved in some very questionable activities."

"Nefarious activities?"

Mr. Headley answered. "That is a point of debate."

This grew more intriguing by the moment. She leaned forward, eager to hear more. While Mr. Fletcher Walker had given the impression of being less refined than his friend or Mr. Headley or any number of fine gentlemen in attendance at the salon gathering, he had not struck her as a ne'er-do-well. Was he, in fact, the contemporary equivalent of the highwaymen of old? Harmless in the light of day but, in secret, a criminal?

"It is rumored"—Miss Vance lowered her voice further—"that they were involved in the disappearance of a child earlier this week."

Intrigue gave way to alarm. "Goodness."

"They are kidnappers?" Ana asked, shocked.

"That is the debate," Mr. Headley said. "There is no consensus as to whether the child was abducted or rescued. Some claim the master sweep from whose company the boy disappeared is, in fact, a brute of the worst sort and the Dread Penny Society somehow helped the child slip away unnoticed. Others say the man was no worse than most and that this questionable club spirited the boy away, perhaps to work as a servant at their headquarters, where, it is rumored, other children are similarly employed."

"Why does the magistrate not send a constable to their clubhouse and investigate?" A possible kidnapping seemed too drastic a situation to have been utterly ignored.

"No one knows where it is," Miss Vance said. "They are quite secretive."

Elizabeth's suspicions rose. She had not spent hours of her time concocting plots and mysterious endeavors for Mr. King in vain, after all. "If they are so very secretive, how is it you—and apparently many others—know so much of them as to discuss such details?"

That seemed to give them both pause.

Ana, surprisingly, was the one to answer. "If they are

connected to activities as noteworthy as children disappearing from the streets, whether for good or evil, the population cannot avoid some awareness of their society. That so much else is unknown only fuels speculation."

"A very sensible evaluation," Miss Vance said.

As the conversation turned to music and other, less drastic, topics, Mr. Headley leaned closer to Elizabeth. "I was reluctant for you to be introduced to Mr. Walker last week, considering he may be participating in these potentially nefarious undertakings. But Mr. Darby's association with him makes him less objectionable. I don't know that the introduction could have been avoided without causing a scene, as it was. I do apologize."

She thanked him for his concern but assured him she had not been injured by the acquaintance. Inwardly, though, something came alive.

She, who had only ever *written* about women pursuing dangerous mysteries and encountering highwaymen and villains and countless people who were not what they appeared to be, had a mystery of her own to solve, complete with shady figures, secrecy, and handsome, intriguing men.

Miss Black could not directly pursue the mystery herself. Mr. King, however, might manage the thing.

THE LADY
AND THE
HIGHWAYMAN

by Mr. King

Installment II,
in which the actions of the Dastardly Highwayman
are spoken of by All and Sundry!

The dreariness of Calden Manor, where Lucinda was to make her home now, could not possibly be overstated. The crumbling remains of long-abandoned wings of the once stately home sat in the shadow of imposing towers with parapets and arrow slits that spoke of violent days gone by. The corridors were long and winding, dark and foreboding. The staff numbered but two: a housekeeper nearly as ancient as the house itself, and the rheumatic coachman, who also served as gardener and butler. She had no neighbors near enough for spotting from the windows of the house, no promise of companionship, and little beyond the nightly moan of the wind to break the silence of her new residence.

Day after day, she watched the front drive in vain, longing with all the fervor of her tender heart for a neighbor to call. The local village must have included a church. Would not even the vicar welcome her? Had she been so abandoned by all in heaven and on earth?

"I should very much like to call upon my nearest neighbor," she told the coachman after a week of loneliness. "Do any estates lie within walking distance?"

"One mustn't walk through the forest, Miss Ledford," he answered with trembling voice. "One mustn't!"

That dastardly highwayman had undertaken his villainy on the road running adjacent to the nearby forest. Had the encounter left her coachman so rattled? Poor man. Poor, poor man!

"Have I no neighbors in the direction leading away from the fearful forest upon whom I might safely call?"

"One is not safe anywhere near the forest." The coachman shook his head as he spoke.

"Am I never, then, to have the company of a neighbor or friend? Am I forever to be alone in this place?"

The question repeated in her mind as more days passed with neither sight nor sound of anyone beyond the three unhappy inhabitants of the manor. The nights stretched long against the cacophony of the howling wind and rustling leaves of the forest.

Until finally, a fortnight following her arrival, carriage wheels could be heard. She rushed to the window of her sitting room, heart aglow with the possibility of companionship. She was not disappointed. No fewer than three coaches stopped on the drive below.

"Company!" declared she. "At long last!"

She paused long enough only to check her reflection and make certain she was presentable. A quick smoothing of her hair and a moment to straighten the paste necklace she had taken to wearing set her appearance to rights.

Excitement quickening her steps, she flew from the room to the top of the narrow front stairs in time to see a veritable crowd spill in from the cold environs beyond the front door. She had dreamed of *one* visitor; she was to have nearly a dozen!

"You are most welcome," said she, wishing her eagerness hadn't rendered her speech quite so warbly. "Please, please do come in."

A particularly beautiful lady, likely only a few years older than herself, spoke first. "Forgive our neglect of you these past two weeks. It is not safe to travel these roads alone. We have at last found a day when all of us could call at once, together."

So it was not only Lucinda's coachman who found the area too dangerous. The housekeeper pointed the newcomers in the direction of the drawing room before shuffling off, apparently uninterested in or unable to see to their needs. No matter. Lucinda would make certain of their welcome.

The drawing room, empty of all adornment other than the sparse furnishings, proved a mismatched choice for hosting so large a group. Oh, that her first opportunity for being amongst others might have been undertaken with greater dignity. The ladies occupied the chairs and sofas. The gentlemen stood. Lucinda blushed. What an impression to make on those she hoped would be friendly companions.

Miss Higgins, as she was informed the lovely young lady was called, addressed Lucinda as soon as the group was settled. "Whisper has it you endured an encounter with our famous local highwayman."

"I fear I did." She had been afforded time enough over the lonely fortnight to reflect on that interaction. She found herself less frightened than she had been at first, and increasingly confused. "He was surprisingly kind, though unsurprisingly rude."

"Rude?" a gentleman in the group asked, his voice nearly as high as Miss Higgins's. "I've not heard him described thus."

"I was afraid," Lucinda said, "trembling, even. And he laughed. To laugh at the distress one is causing is, indeed, rude."

She received a few nods of agreement.

"Are you certain he was laughing *at* you?" an older woman in the group asked, her eyes and hair the same bright shade of gray. "Our highwayman is known for finding humor in most situations. I suspect all of us have heard that deep, echoing laugh of his."

"Keeps his face covered, though," another gentleman added. "Deucedly unfair of him, that." The man met Lucinda's gaze and, with a dip of his head, said, "Forgive my uncouth language, Miss Ledford."

"Our highwayman can be a touch unsavory in his language as well," Miss Higgins said, "but never vulgar. One suspects he might be a gentleman after all."

"Or a clever mimic," another suggested.

"Have you all encountered him, then?" How odd that none of them spoke truly condemningly of the highwayman. Indeed, she sensed fondness in many of their recollections.

"Oh, yes," the higher-voiced man said. "Many times, in fact."

"Does he not feel he has stolen enough from all of you?"

What could be left to take? Were her neighbors so very well-heeled that repeated robbery could be endured with such pleasantness and aplomb?

The older woman swatted away the thought with a gloved hand. "He never steals a thing. None of us has what he is searching for."

Reflecting on her own interaction with the highwayman, Lucinda recollected a similar declaration from him. He said he had not found amongst her humble assortment of belongings what he wished to find. Indeed, he had even returned to her the very necklace she now wore, one she hadn't realized resided in her carriage. Had he shown all his victims such consideration?

"If he found what he is looking for, would he take it, do you think?" she asked them all.

A gentleman who had not yet spoken answered. "I believe he would." His deeper voice stood at odds with the other man who'd offered thoughts on the matter. This gentleman—for everything in his manner and appearance declared him as such—possessed a pair of eyes so lightly blue as to resemble ice more than pools of deep water, yet the effect was not an unpleasant one. "And I further believe he would not feel overly guilty about simply making off with the mysterious item."

She cast her eyes over the group, searching for some indication that they, as a whole, condemned such a thing. "Do you not find his actions insupportable?"

"We are of two minds on the matter," Miss Higgins said. "Many agree with me that our highwayman, in not reliev-ing anyone of his or her belongings, has shown that his motivations are not truly dastardly. He must be in search of something of great importance, something that, we suspect, is of utmost significance for the safety and well-being of us all. Though Sir Frederick"—she indicated the man with ice-blue eyes—"has suggested our gentleman of the road is in search of a fantastical treasure and that we ought to all be wary of him and his band of thieves."

Lucinda looked to Sir Frederick and saw confirmation in his captivating eyes, but no anger or bitterness. His well-defined jaw was not set with tension, but was at ease, and testified, somehow, of both strength and gentleness.

"You do not think as well of this highwayman as your neighbors do," she observed.

"It is possible his motivations are pure and philan-thropic, but one must question his approach," Sir Frederick said. "He hides his aim and his identity, causes distress to good and innocent people. That must give us pause."

"You wish to see him punished? Or worse?" No matter that she had encountered the thief but once and had, at his hand, been made to endure very real fear for her person and safety, she found she could not be at ease with the idea of him facing imprisonment or the gallows. Heaven forfend!

"If he and his comrades are doing such gallant and ad-mirable work, then why undertake it in such a way that can't help but call their admirableness into question?" he asked.

Miss Higgins answered. "Perhaps something about the object he seeks *requires* that he do so under the shadow of secrecy."

"Perhaps," Sir Frederick countered, "he is simply a vil-lain."

"You are determined to think ill of him?" Miss Higgins demanded.

"Not determined," the gentleman answered. "I am simply wary. And"—his eyes moved momentarily to Lucinda—"disappointed to know he caused our lovely new neighbor distress. I wish for all the world that he had not."

The unexpected kindness touched her deeply. She pulled from the cuff of her well-worn dress a lace-edged handkerchief, holding it at the ready should this surge of emotion begin slipping from her eyes. Too many days alone. Too many nights spent listening to the unsettling wind in the fearsome forest. How she needed his gentle words. How she'd needed this visit!

Her neighbors remained far longer than most casual calls permitted. She was grateful those particular rules of propriety were lax here in this empty corner of the world.

Some two hours later, when it was time for her neighbors to depart, she thanked them again and again as they made their way to their carriages. How she wished they could remain. She said as much, only to be met with firm and insistent imploring, that, were she ever away from home, she not remain long enough that her journeys would be undertaken in the dark of night.

"Because of the highwayman?" she guessed.

"No," Sir Frederick answered, earnest and concerned. "Because what lurks in the forest is a far greater threat than he could ever be."

CHAPTER 5

As far as Fletcher knew, no club in all of London other than the Dread Penny Society had a boxing saloon in its club building. But, then, the Dreadfuls, as they liked to call themselves, weren't an ordinary sort of club.

Fletcher tossed his shirt onto an obliging bench. He rolled his shoulders, stretched his neck.

"Limber up all you want," Hollis said. "Stone is still going to pummel you."

Fletcher smiled back at him. "'Ave a little faith in me."

"I have plenty of faith," his friend insisted. "I also have a functioning brain, one capable of predicting precisely how this is going to end: with you prostrate on the floor."

Stone's nostrils flared above his twisted mouth; it was his signature look of amusement. Fletcher didn't know why Stone's expression seldom showed anything but the slightest hint at his thoughts and feelings. He was a closed book, as the saying went. He was also a deeply good man. Brave. Unflinching. Steadfast. With a devastatingly fast and brutal fist.

"Do you mean to treat me with kid gloves?" Fletcher asked with a laugh.

"No." Stone laid his shirt over a nearby stool, the cruel scars of his former life laid bare.

"Irving would give you less of a challenge, Fletch." Hollis made no effort to hide his enjoyment of the arrangement. "I could go get him. I believe he's in the library."

A grumpy ol' codger who couldn't've felled a gnat, Irving occupied a creaky if comfortable place on the far side of seventy years old.

"I'll send you if need be," Fletcher said dryly. He rolled his eyes as he turned toward Stone once more.

The man raised his fists in fighting position. Fletcher did as well. They circled, jabbing and dodging. Hollis watched from a battered armchair in a corner. They'd placed the more undignified furniture pieces in this room, comfort trumping appearance.

"How's your latest story doing?" Fletcher asked his sparring partner.

"Publisher wants more."

Stone swung. Fletcher ducked.

"Good sign, that."

A jab. A dodge.

"Mine ain't selling like it did six months ago," Fletcher said. "But still better than a year ago." King was creeping closer to him all the time. "It's a blame good thing King weren't on the scene while we was sending funds to the Union cause back in the States. There'd not've been enough."

Stone nodded, never losing his concentration.

Fletcher's dwindling income had impacted a great many

things. He didn't live as comfortably as he had. His future was less certain. Most frustrating of all, the DPS had fewer funds to work with. It haunted him every time he passed street children he didn't know if he could save.

"The drawing rooms of the middle class are abuzz with whispers of the climbing boy who 'went missing' this last week," Hollis said. "I've heard talk of some of the things we've been involved in before, but not like this. It seems that blowhard of a sweep, Mr. Allen, is flapping his gums to anyone who'll listen to his complaints."

"We need to take more care," Stone said. "We'll have a hard go if we're caught doin' half of what we do."

Robbing a tradesman of his apprentice was a crime, and it wasn't the first the group had committed. Fletcher, himself, had broken a law or two spiriting children away from danger. He'd do it again if needed.

Stone and Fletcher circled each other, swinging and ducking. Stone landed one, sending Fletcher stumbling back a couple steps. He rubbed at his shoulder where the blow had landed. Stone waited, impatient.

Fletcher chuckled. "You that anxious to pummel me?"

"Always."

They resumed their stances and their efforts. Fletcher even managed to land a couple, himself.

"Kumar has heard rumors a coach is arriving in a few days with a couple of young women whose family has decided they're done looking after them," Hollis said. "Word on the street is Mrs. George knows they're coming."

That paused their bout on the spot. Mrs. George made her profits off the misfortune of young girls. Some she sold off to macks; some she kept in one of her many bawdy houses. If she'd sniffed these new girls' trail, they were in very delicate, but very real danger.

"A complicated rescue, that," Fletcher said.

Mrs. George and her thugs were known to turn violent when directly opposed. Drawing too much attention during the rescue might endanger the girls as it was, keeping them from finding dignified employment.

Stone wasn't shaken by the complexity. He never was. "Bring in Milligan."

Barnabus "Doc" Milligan was a physician who wrote penny dreadfuls focused on monstrous malpractices. Having a doctor looking out for the well-being of the newly arrived and vulnerable girls would not draw as much attention as any of the rest of them stepping in would. And Mrs. George's bully-boys wouldn't realize so quickly they were being thwarted.

"Brilliant."

Stone nodded, offering nothing more.

"You haven't managed to belt him a good one all afternoon, Fletcher. Are you off your feed?" Hollis could always be counted on for a spot of heckling.

"Perhaps you'd care to go a round with the man," Fletcher said

"Not on your life."

"Listen to this." Irving shuffled in with no more preamble than that. He held in his hands an easily recognizable bit of literature: a penny dreadful offering. But which one? "'If he and his comrades are doing such gallant and admirable work, then why undertake it in such a way that can't help but call their admirableness into question?'"

Stone's fists dropped, eyes focused on Irving.

"Who wrote that bit of fanciness?" Fletcher asked.

Irving held up the purple-covered circular. "Mr. King."

He should've sorted that in an instant.

"The bloke's latest installment. Not badly written. Good plot. Characters ain't a bore. Almost word-for-word the whispers surrounding the lot of us—wondering why we're so secretive if we ain't up to no good." Irving looked at them all. "What do we make of it?"

Fletcher wiped the sweat from his face with a towel. Stone stood, hands on his hips as he worked to recapture his breath after their energetic bout.

Hollis spoke up. "It could be a coincidence."

Irving nodded.

Fletcher wasn't convinced. "It's too similar, I say. This King, I'd wager, knows what we're about, or leastwise suspects. Maybe he's meaning to tell us he knows what we've been doing."

"Or who we are," Irving added.

That'd be a catastrophe. Even setting aside the trouble they'd have with the law if they were sniffed out, too much of what they did required secrecy. Being made known would keep them from helping and rescuing and doing the good that meant so much to them.

"He's warning us, then?" Hollis asked.

Stone's response dropped into the silence like a boulder. "Or he's one of us."

For a moment no one said anything. If King was a Dreadful, why hadn't the man come forward? Many published under names other than their own. But why would he keep this a secret?

The answer came in the next instant. "What if he's warning us *and* is one of us?" Fletcher asked. "He might be dangling a bone, showing us he has the upper hand and could reveal the lot of us iffen he wanted."

"Then we've a bad hat to sniff out," Irving said.

Stone moved to his neatly folded shirt on the stool. "We need to know for sure and certain."

That was as true as the day was long. "How?" Fletcher asked.

"There's a certain elevated quality to Mr. King's writing," Hollis said. "I've suspected for some time now that he might actually be a silver-fork or literary writer penning penny dreadfuls. We can start there, see what we're able to discover."

"How do we 'start there,' I'd like to know." Irving shook his head, mustache trembling. "We can't simply walk around saying, 'Hand over King or we'll keep abducting children.'"

"Miss Black showed something of an interest in Mr. King," Hollis said. "And she is familiar with the community of silver-fork writers, being one herself."

"Wouldn't pressing her for information spark her suspicions?" Fletcher didn't know her well enough to be sure.

"I'd fit the bill," Hollis said. "Except I'm not supposed to be connected to the penny dreadful authors beyond our specific friendship. But you've already broached the subject with her. She'd not think twice hearing you bring it up."

"I'd be willing." Fletcher wouldn't relish it; fine ladies weren't his cup of tea. They generally felt themselves decidedly above his touch. "But seeing as this might spin into sniffing out one of us Dreadfuls, I'll need approval from the Dread Master."

Irving and Stone simply nodded in understanding, but Hollis raised a brow. Though Fletcher served as the figurehead of the group, he was not its actual leader, and Hollis had been rather annoyed that Fletcher wouldn't tell Hollis the details of the man behind the DPS.

"Once I get direction, I'll move forward." But he knew permission would be granted. If they had a traitor in their midst, they had to know.

Calling on Elizabeth Black would be interesting at least. She'd given the impression of cleverness and hadn't been entirely snooty toward him. He suspected street urchins never fully grew accustomed to finding any degree of acceptance anywhere other than in the gutters.

CHAPTER 6

Ana was a gifted musician, far too talented to be teaching such indifferent students. Some were sufficiently grateful. Most hadn't the least understanding of their good fortune. Elizabeth stood at the door of the music room, listening to one of their oldest students work her way through a particularly complicated piece. Her skills were improving, thanks to Ana.

Elizabeth hoped Ana felt some degree of fulfillment in her work. Teaching had not been her first choice in life. It likely hadn't been her tenth or eleventh, either. Her family had fallen on difficult times, and with no dowry and very few connections, Ana had lost all hope of marriage. With her family's fortune gone, likely forever, she'd no longer had the option to remain at home, living on her father's meager income.

It was far too familiar a tale. Most of Thurloe's teachers hailed from fine families fallen on hard times. Elizabeth, herself, did.

As the pianoforte offering came to a close, young Miss

Georgiana happened to look up and meet Elizabeth's eye. Uncertainty hung there. Elizabeth had discovered early in her time as headmistress that her opinion mattered to her students. While she was often required to be the voice of order and, at times, discipline, offering support and encouragement was far more her preference.

"That was lovely, Georgiana," she said. "You and Miss Newport have certainly worked very hard."

A pleased blush spread over the girl's face.

"Play through the piece again, please," Ana instructed. "I need a moment with Miss Black." She rose and moved to the doorway.

"Is something amiss?" Elizabeth asked, keeping her voice low.

"Nothing too concerning." Ana motioned for her to step into the corridor. "The sticking keys are growing worse, and the harp has lost another string."

Something always needed repairing at a school. "Is there anything else?"

"A few of the chimneys are smoking."

While Thurloe Collegiate School was not awash in endless funds, Elizabeth wasn't overly worried about paying for the ever-present list of items. Between the income from her silver-fork novels, her students' tuition, and the contributions of a handful of patrons, she had enough to breathe relatively easily.

"Miss Black." Mrs. Hale stood a few paces down the corridor.

"Yes?"

"You've a visitor in your office."

Her office? A business-related visitor, then. "Did it seem an urgent matter?"

She thought on it. "He didn't seem worried or anxious. I'd say he was happy to be here."

"*He?*" Ana repeated with a laugh.

Elizabeth smiled at that. "Had the visitor been a woman, she would have been shown to the parlor. A man calling outside of official visiting hours is, no doubt, here on business."

They walked together down the corridor, speaking briefly of a newer student and her interest in the violin. Fortunately, that instrument was in good repair. Elizabeth would look over the ledger that evening and make certain her accounts were as healthy as she thought. And then she would spend an hour or two losing herself in poor Lucinda's adventures. "Mr. King" was her only escape from the tedium of her very respectable life.

As they reached the door to her office, they both glanced in. The man sitting inside was immediately recognizable: Fletcher Walker.

"What next and next?" she muttered.

A bit of mischief tugged at Ana's mouth. "He is very handsome."

"He is trouble."

Ana shrugged a single delicate shoulder. "Is that so bad?"

Elizabeth could not hide her amusement. "Certainly nothing I cannot handle."

Ana's laugh drew Mr. Walker's attention. He rose, as was proper, and faced them, offering a dip of his head. They responded with quick curtsies.

"Mr. Walker, this is Miss Newport, our music teacher.

Miss Newport, may I make known to you Mr. Walker, a writer."

Ana took a step toward him, her customary enthusiasm as endearing as ever. "You are a writer? Miss Black is a writer."

"I know it," he replied. "And quite revered, she is."

"Are you?" Elizabeth could not fully tell if Ana was bantering or in earnest.

Mr. Walker met Elizabeth's eye with a glimmer of amusement.

Elizabeth let her smile show. "Well, are you?"

He took it in stride, looking back to Ana. "I'd not say 'revered,' as such, though I've enjoyed a spill or two from the teapot of good fortune."

It was a surprisingly humble evaluation. Mr. Walker was, at least until recently, the *most* successful in his area of literature. He could not have been unaware of the significance of that achievement.

"I do need to return to the music lessons," Ana said. "It was a pleasure to meet you, Mr. Walker."

He dipped another well-executed bow. "Meeting a beautiful lady is always a pleasure for me. So, I thank you for obligin'."

That bit of flirting earned him the tiniest, loveliest blush on Ana's cheeks, a sight few men could resist. To his credit, he simply smiled and made no attempt to keep her from leaving the room. Too many men considered themselves fully entitled to a woman's time and attention regardless of her feelings on the matter.

Elizabeth crossed to her desk and sat. He resumed his seat across from her. Though his posture was not truly lax nor inappropriate, there was an ease to it that spoke volumes of his confidence even in an unfamiliar setting.

"Miss Newport seems a fine sort," he said with every indication of sincerity.

"She is, and she is an exceptional teacher as well."

He nodded. "That's important, that is. A good teacher is the only reason I made anything of myself. Though you'd likely argue whether or not I succeeded."

She leaned her forearms on her desk, watching him more closely. "Why do you think I so hardily disapprove of you?"

"Most above m' place in life do. And most writers have solid ideas of whose writin' is worth praise and whose is the dregs."

He wasn't wrong, generally speaking. His assessment was, however, misapplied. "I am familiar with the penny dreadfuls, and I have never offered a dismissal of them. They may not be my area of focus, and you and I don't necessarily share readers, but I have never, nor will you ever hear me, speak ill of a fellow writer simply because he does not publish silver-forks or highbrow literature."

Mr. Walker's surprise was less shock and more relief. "I've hopes your generosity extends to presumptuous favors likewise."

"You've come to ask a favor?"

His eyes twinkled. "A right, regular lout, ain't I?"

She leaned back, keeping her posture proper even as she eased into a more comfortable position. "I thought, for a moment, upon hearing I had a visitor, that the new arrival"—she motioned to him—"was someone come to offer patronage to our school."

He grinned. The man had a wickedly handsome smile, there was no denying that. "I ain't got brass enough for patronizing anything but my own flat, the butcher, and the costermonger, and, if one'll have me, a dog-cheap gentleman's club somewhere."

"Will no others have you?" She hoped her comment sounded more amused than investigatory. From the moment Miss Vance and Mr. Headley had mentioned the mysterious Dread Penny Society, she had wondered if Mr. Walker belonged to that "club."

"I concoct penny dreadfuls and was born in the gutters. Gen'lmen ain't exactly clamoring to rub elbows with the likes of me."

She knew that to be an overly pessimistic and simplistic evaluation. "Garrick's was established specifically for artists and writers. I can't imagine you wouldn't be welcomed there."

He smiled once more. Elizabeth ignored the way it flipped her heart around. "I'll make m' application for membership just as soon as I leave here."

She doubted that. "If you have not come to offer my school a generous largesse, what has brought you?"

He sat up straighter. "Have you any familiarity with Mr. King, the penny dreadful author?"

"I know of his work." How she hoped she kept her amusement hidden.

"He's a mystery I cain't sort. No one seems to know who he is despite everyone readin' his stories."

Mercy, this was not a reassuring turn to the conversation. "Does his secrecy concern you?"

He waved a hand, half dismissively, half in amusement.

"Never could resist a mystery. Besides, all us low-life authors"—
his brow quirked upward in a show of laughter—"know each
other. It's an odd thing having one so prominent in our field
who don't belong to that brotherhood."

Brotherhood. Was that his secretive way of referencing
the Dread Penny Society? Might Mr. King be welcomed
into the group, included in their adventures and missions?
Of course, were she to discover their activities were nefarious rather than gregarious, she wouldn't have embraced that
membership. As it was, she hadn't the option.

"Why is it you feel I would have information that you
and your 'brotherhood' have been unable to unearth? Were
you looking for a silver-fork novelist, I might be of more
help."

He bent his elbow against the arm of his chair and leaned
his temple against his fist. "There's the infernal rub, though. I
suspect, Miss Black, I *am* looking for one."

A lump formed in her stomach. "We are still speaking of
Mr. King, are we not?" She filled the question with enough
surprised doubt to convey the impression that she found his
declaration odd at best.

He, however, did not appear the slightest bit put off the
scent. "I've been studying his stories. He don't write the same
as the rest of us. He's got more class, more sophistication."

"You think Mr. King does not know his audience?" She
tried not to be offended by the evaluation, both on her own
account and on behalf of her readers. She put tremendous
effort into meeting the expectations of that particular style
of storytelling, and she thought it insulting to assume that
the working classes could not enjoy a story that included

anything but low phrases and simplified vocabulary. She did not use the same voice as she did in her silver-fork novels, but she did not think it so misguided to occasionally sprinkle a higher word into her narrative.

"He writes blasted well—forgive the phrasing. I weren't insulting his work. I'm only trying to find him. If he is a higher-brow novelist tossing himself into the world of penny dreadfuls, I figure I'd do best to ask another silver-forker."

"I can say I have not heard even the vaguest of whispers about one of our 'brotherhood'—to borrow your word— writing in your area of storytelling." Heaven knew she'd worked hard to prevent those very rumors. "Why is it so important that you find him? It has to be more than wishing he'd join your club."

"My club?" he repeated with a lift of that expressive brow.

She smiled as if to dismiss the choice of words. "An attempt at humored exaggeration."

"I'm a dog at a bone when it comes to mysteries. Cain't leave 'em be." He rose. "If you've not heard anything, I'll ask elsewhere. That Mr. Headley you was with at the salon seemed well-versed in the silver-forks. I'll see if I cain't run him to ground."

The last thing she needed was this man asking too many questions and drawing undue attention to Mr. King. "I can ask about Mr. King," she offered as she stood, keeping her tone casual. "Of course, I haven't the first idea how I would reach you to tell you if I hear of anything useful."

"Darby always knows where to find me."

Elizabeth nodded in acknowledgment. Though she and Mr. Darby were not truly close, she was acquainted with him well enough to send a note should she find a means of misdirecting Mr. Walker's efforts. "I cannot promise to make any earth-shattering discoveries, but I will send word if I discover anything useful."

"I thank you, Miss Elizabeth." He dipped his head. "If ever I can do anything for you . . ."

It was the customary response, one he likely meant to be rhetorical. She, however, knew an opportunity when she saw one.

"I will hold you to that, Mr. Fletcher Walker."

The flitter of surprise in his expression gave way to one of his core-warming smiles. "I'm very much looking forward to it."

And with that, Elizabeth suspected, she had entered into a deal with the devil.

CHAPTER 7

For a man who'd not been able to read for most of his childhood, Fletcher had become surprisingly adept at skimming correspondence. He sat in a rattling hackney, quickly reading the letter in his hands by the dim late-evening light slipping in through the dingy windows.

Proceed with your efforts. King must be identified, dethroned if a threat or a turncoat.

Fletcher had expected this response from the Dread Master, but confirmation was a good thing.

Report as you discover more.

Fletcher carefully refolded the single sheet of red-edged paper—the Dread Master's personal stationery. He also favored brief, almost gruff sentences. Both tendencies helped Fletcher know the correspondence was authentic.

He tore the paper into long, thin strips, then tore those strips into smaller pieces.

"Has the Dread Master offered his nod of approval?" Hollis asked.

"Aye."

Hollis eyed the growing pile of paper bits. "He still requires secrecy?"

Fletcher dropped the pieces of paper into a small silver flask he kept on hand for just this thing. No one would think to check it for torn correspondence. "He has reason enough to hide who he is."

"Even from the Dreadfuls?" Hollis's tone was dry.

Fletcher simply nodded.

"Is it Irving?" Hollis asked.

Fletcher didn't so much as raise an eyebrow.

"Kumar? Donnelly?"

"I ain't saying a word, Hollis."

"But this is *me*." He looked a little hurt. "Don't you think you can trust me?"

"It ain't a matter of trust. This ain't my secret to whisper about. I don't even *think* his name if I can help it. Cain't risk a slip of the tongue."

Hollis seemed to accept it but still didn't look pleased. "Does the Dread Master give any weight to the possibility that King is a mole?"

"He believes it worth looking into."

Hollis nodded. "And Miss Black had no ideas for you?"

Miss Black. His visit with her had been . . . interesting. She hadn't dismissed his search nor his work out of hand, but neither had she been particularly keen on helping. Then again, she had, in the end, offered her assistance. His lips tugged upward at the memory of her informing him she'd hold him to his offer of a favor. She had gumption. One didn't often come across a refined lady, and a beautiful one at that, who also happily went nose-to-nose with a man of the working class. He liked it.

"She had no bits for me, but she swore to tell me if she learns anything."

The hack took the next turn slowly, an indication they were nearing their destination. Time enough for one more brief topic.

"The girls are arriving soon from the country. Doc'll be on hand. We'll need you there, putting on your airs an' all."

"One of these days the DPS will discover I've more than one talent at their disposal."

Fletcher allowed a twist of his mouth. "You don't have to be highfalutin tonight. Just make your case about educating the poor."

"I'd do that either way."

"I know it." He leaned more comfortably back against the squabs. "Doc means to have a couple of ladies from the charitable society with him to meet the girls' coach. A disapproving cove nearby"—he motioned to Hollis—"along with them women, oughtta keep Mrs. George's macks a touch less violent."

Hollis rubbed at his face. "This is a riskier undertaking than usual. The sweep made quite a ruckus over losing his climbing boy, but the pimps of London have been known to kill when denied their prey. I have my doubts they will remain quiet."

Fletcher knew it well enough, but he wouldn't be deterred. The girls likely hadn't the first idea what awaited them at the end of their journey. This world was a cruel old place.

The literary salon proved "a crush," as the fine and fancy

were always saying. Hollis's identity as a penny dreadful author was a tightly held secret, and thus he was invited to these sorts of gatherings now and then. For the first time, Fletcher had come under his own invitation rather than as his friend's guest. He didn't know who'd issued it or why.

With all the grace of one born to the aristocracy, Hollis greeted the others, received and made introductions, and spoke of the most recent literary offerings with both authority and a critically honed eye. Fletcher assumed his best manners as well, though no one would ever have believed he hailed from anything but the streets. He didn't mind. He wasn't trying to pull the wool over anyone's eyes. He was who he was.

"Headley, I believe." Hollis extended his hand to a gentleman Fletcher vaguely recognized.

"Darby," the man answered. His gaze turned to Fletcher. "And you're . . ." He thought a moment. "Walker, I believe."

Fletcher lifted his chin a fraction in acknowledgment. There was something a little too dismissive in the man's tone.

"Headley is a friend of Miss Black's," Hollis explained. "We met him at that salon a couple of weeks ago."

"Ah." Fletcher allowed a nod and a little tweak of his mouth, showing just how little impressed he was with the connection. "Is Miss Black here this evening? I'd enjoy another gab with her."

"She is all that is proper and good." Mr. Headley spoke with an edge perfected by those always scouting out reasons for offense.

Fletcher eyed Hollis before returning his attention to Mr. Headley. "I don't recall saying she weren't."

"Forgive me," Headley said. "I was defaulting to an abundance of caution, not knowing how ladies are generally spoken of amongst—" He suddenly seemed to recognize the dangerous ground upon which he was treading.

Fletcher wasn't going to let the man wriggle free so easily. "Go on, then. I'm full curious how you mean to end that sentence."

Headley pressed his lips closed and took a quick breath. "Again, forgive me. I fear I tend to misspeak. When one lacks the opportunity to rewrite one's words, one is far more likely to use them incorrectly."

A sentiment often heard amongst writers. As far as Fletcher knew, Headley was not an author but was included among the group because of his support for and enjoyment of literature. Was he, like Hollis, secretly an author himself?

"No harm done," Hollis said. "One does hear a great many odd whispers about the penny dreadful authors. You certainly cannot be blamed for wondering about their characters."

That was brilliantly managed, really. Should Headley choose to take up the new topic, they might learn something. If not, no one would likely note it enough to wonder at Hollis's curiosity.

"Abundant whispers." Headley's eyes grew wide with anticipation. Here was a man eager to discuss the topic. Brilliant. "They are all quite contradictory, though. One doesn't quite know what to believe."

Hollis nodded.

"The only consensus I can find," Headley continued, apparently not needing encouragement to flap his gums, "is regarding the existence of the Dread Penny Society. It is real, no one argues that, but the nature of the fraternity is an utter mystery."

Hollis turned to Fletcher with a look of inquiry. Lud, the man had a knack for appearing to know absolutely nothing.

"If there were such a society, and I were a member, would I tell you lot?" Fletcher shook his head with a look of amusement. "Further, if there was such a thing and it were villainous, I'd not be a member, would I?"

Headley narrowed his gaze, a smile twisting his lips. "Are you trying to convince me it doesn't exist?"

"Are you trying to convince me you didn't follow what I just said?"

He ruffled a bit. "No offense intended. I simply find the whole thing very intriguing."

Hollis, true to form, kept his air of vague indifference. "You seem to be among the number who suspects this society of infamy."

"Why are they so secretive unless their works are something of which they ought to be ashamed?" Headley asked. "It does make one wonder."

It made Fletcher wonder that perhaps Headley's wasn't an idle curiosity. There was reason to believe the elusive Mr. King was opposed to the actions of the Dreadfuls. Could there be a connection here?

"Do you think the secrecy truly comes of shame?" Hollis asked. "I haven't been able to decide, myself."

"If one is doing good works, one would not hesitate to make those good works known," Headley insisted.

It was neither Hollis nor Fletcher who responded but

Miss Black. "That holds true only if one's motivation in doing good works is to be known for doing them. Perhaps this mysterious society values the results of their work more than the credit."

He wasn't often at a loss for words, but her unexpected bit of generosity, coupled with the sight of her in a gown of sheer gold over an underlayer of black, left him chucked all of a heap. Not many women did that to him. Indeed, the woman standing beside her didn't.

"You are forever thinking the best of people." Headley spoke to Miss Black the way one spoke to an older child who thought herself grown up.

"That, sir, is not true," she said baldly. Miss Black turned her attention to Hollis and Fletcher. "A pleasure to see you both again. I would very much like to introduce you both to Miss Serenity Vance." She indicated the woman next to her. "Miss Vance, this is Mr. Hollis Darby and Mr. Fletcher Walker."

Miss Vance smiled at Hollis. "Mr. Darby, I know of your family, of course." She turned to Fletcher. "And, Mr. Walker, I know of your writing."

"Of course," Fletcher said, earning a light laugh from the woman.

Miss Black spoke once more. "Mr. Darby, you will not be offended, I hope, if Mr. Walker joins me for a quick turn about the room. He posed a question when last we met for which I now can provide an answer."

She was direct, he would give her that.

"Of course not," Hollis said. "Assuming Miss Vance will

not take offense at being left in my undistinguished company."

"On the contrary," Miss Vance said. "I would find that delightful."

Hollis dipped a quick bow, then offered his arm to Miss Vance. The two of them moved toward the milling crowd.

Elizabeth offered Headley an abbreviated dip before slipping her arm through Fletcher's and walking with him toward the edge of the room.

"You do not do things subtly, Miss Black," Fletcher said with a laugh.

"My father always said I was too bold for my own good." She did not sound bitter about the parental observation.

"I must say, miss, you look a regular beller-croaker tonight."

She eyed him sidelong. "Is that a compliment or a complaint?" Her neck craned as she watched him.

"It ain't a complaint."

A bit of pink stole over her cheeks. The woman was near torturing him. Beautiful. Stunning, really.

"You're a fair sight, I'll grant you that," he said.

"Believe it or not, I did not request your company in order to be lavished with praise. I have some information for you."

"Regarding our friend Mr. King?"

"The very same." She shot him a look of warning. "Now, do not get your hopes up too high. What I have are merely hints, nothing of true significance."

A hint was more than he had now.

"A few whispers are reflecting what you, yourself, have

sorted: that there is noticeable refinement to Mr. King's writing. Your idea that he may hail from slightly elevated origins appears to be held by more people than merely you, though the consensus is not a broad one.".

Irving had been right on that score, it seemed. "Any gossip 'bout his being a writer of highbrow works as well?"

"That I haven't heard," she said. "I suspect if King were a pseudonym for one of my colleagues, the whispers would abound in that direction."

A regular dead cargo that bit of information.

They continued their slow circuit of the room. He knew he *looked* the part of a gentleman worthy of taking a turn around a gathering with a lady as beautiful and refined as Miss Black, but he also knew she was miles above his touch. Yet he was enjoying imagining she wasn't, that for this night, he had, in fact, made something grand of himself.

"What is Mr. Headley's story?" He eyed the man as their steps took them past him. "He gabs about the penny dreadfuls more than one'd expect."

Miss Black laughed. "He is an admirer of the literary set, mostly because he finds some satisfaction in the veneer of celebrity but hasn't the cachet to toss his hat in with the truly important and exalted. He reads, yes, but the man cannot write. Trust me, I have been the recipient of a few of his letters."

She had a dry wit. He liked that.

"There's plenty here who'd likely declare *I* can't write."

Miss Black looked around as if shocked. "Are there a great many illiterate people in attendance?"

"Have *you* read my work?" He'd wager she hadn't, yet she'd defended him as a writer.

"I know that at least a few of my students read your offerings. I thought it best to know what they were about."

She *had* read his work.

"And what was your assessment?" he asked as they turned the corner of the room.

Miss Black had a very pleasant smile. "Does my opinion matter so much?"

"Ain't my pride asking. Just curiosity." Truth be told, it was a fair bit of both.

"You tell a very good tale, Mr. Walker. And, though the more torrid details are perhaps a bit beyond what most of my parents prefer their daughters read, I could find nothing in your writing that was truly dastardly. You strike a very good balance between the two."

"And the writing itself?"

She laughed lightly. "I have already afforded you two compliments in one evening. If you'd like more, you will simply have to come to another soiree or salon and make up sweet to me then."

The idea was more tempting than she likely realized. "I've met m' quota for tonight?"

"Indeed."

"Very well." He offered a winning smile of his own. "I'll simply sniff you out another day and accept your offer."

"It seems, Mr. Fletcher, that we find ourselves deeper and deeper in each other's debt. I owe you a compliment, and you owe me an as-yet-undefined favor."

She wasn't wrong. "Half the fun of such debts is in the paying of 'em."

Miss Black slipped her arm from his, raising an eyebrow almost flirtatiously. "We shall see."

With that, she moved in a swirl of gold toward the other guests, leaving him in a baffled haze. A happily baffled haze. Miss Black was not entirely the stuffy Society lady she seemed to be. Mr. King was the mystery at the top of his list, but this surprising lady was quickly making her way there as well.

THE VAMPIRE'S TOWER
AN URCHINS OF LONDON ADVENTURE

by Fletcher Walker

Chapter II

"Six this week," Jimmy said as he and Morris walked through the London fog. "I ain't seen the Black Maria anywhere near these past weeks. Don't seem to be the Bobbies nipping off with urchins."

Morris didn't think so either. "But if they ain't being snatched by thief-takers, where are they all?"

"Sleeping somewhere other than the Inn?"

Morris shook his head as they turned onto Fleet Street, looking for an apple cart or ginger beer seller who'd pay 'em a few coins for guarding their goods. "We'd see the missing ones out making their coins if they were still around. No-one's seen hide nor hair."

Jimmy scratched at his head, just below his hat brim. "We could look for them, but we'd not have time to earn our rent for tonight."

"I don't want to sleep on the street," Morris said. "'Specially if someone's snatching urchins." He let out a tight breath. "But we gotta look or no one will."

"We've another mystery to solve then, do we?" Jimmy grinned at the promise of a puzzle.

"Seems we do." Morris liked a riddle as much as his friend did. "Have we enough extra for the Innkeeper tonight?"

"We can use some of what we've secreted away," Jimmy said.

It'd be worth it. They might've been only twelve years old and not the oldest of the Inn's urchins, but they looked after the others.

Rather than stop at the costermonger cart and enquire after pay, they kept on.

"All the missing 'ns work this area," Jimmy said. "Whatever's snatching 'em's likely around here."

They'd solved many a mystery on the streets of London. The skeptical in Town would probably be surprised at how many of those answers were otherworldly. They'd found and defeated ghosts, encountered monsters, outsmarted villains. If history held true, they weren't searching out anything humdrum.

"John-John was the last to go missing," Morris said. "He always does his diving near Covent Garden. I'd say we'd do best to sniff around there a bit."

The market was busy, as always. Sellers shouted flattering descriptions of their wares. Most were probably lies. Ends didn't meet on the streets of London without a bit of stretching.

"I see a flower seller I know," Jimmy said. "Perhaps she's seen somethin'."

Morris nodded, looking over the crowd for anyone he

thought might have something to offer. A boy with a familiar, dirt-smudged face slipped around the back of a vegetable cart, nipping a carrot before scurrying off. Morris followed quick on the boy's trail. The little one was fast, but not fast enough.

He snatched hold of the boy's arm. "Morris here, George. Only Morris."

That put an end to the fight just beginning. "Thought you was the police."

"Have the police been snatching up urchins, then?" Morris had been sure that wasn't the answer to their mystery.

George shrugged. "Someone 'as."

"Then you ain't seen nothing." A disappointment, that. "John-John works this corner of things. Jimmy and I thought maybe someone would have an idea what's happened to him."

George snapped off a bite of the carrot, talking as he chewed. "John-John told me he'd come into the cream and wouldn't need to filch here no more. I said he had the best fortune of anyone. Maybe he weren't so fortunate."

Morris could see the worry growing in the boy's eyes. "Maybe he were. Maybe ol' John-John found himself a flush post after all."

George's little brow angled sharply. "Don't sell me a dog, Morris. This ain't my first day on the streets."

He ought to've known better than try to tell a lifelong urchin to imagine the best when the worst made more sense. They learned young that it was better to be clever than rosy-eyed.

"Did he tell you anything about going anywhere or with anyone?"

George shook his head. "Only said he'd be nose-deep in the clover. He were right pleased."

Didn't sound like he'd been stolen. Maybe John-John really had just gone to a better situation.

Jimmy returned, looking as confused at Morris felt. "Becky, what sells the flowers, says John-John left to work for some swell."

Same as George said.

"Odd, though," Jimmy continued. "She said Sally, who disappeared from the Inn last week, told her the same. That she'd a chance for something better and meant to take it. Becky said neither of them seemed afraid."

Morris scratched at the back of his neck. "So maybe we ain't searching out a kidnapper but a do-gooder?"

George spoke again, still working at his carrot. "Sally wouldn't've gone off without Mary. Best mates, ain't they?"

Morris met Jimmy's eye. There was truth in George's view of things. Neither Jimmy nor Morris would trek off to a grand opportunity without the other. Sally and Mary were the same.

None of this made a lick of sense.

The three of them wandered away from the market, none speaking. Where had the missing urchins gone? Were they in danger? Had they all gone to the same place? Was none of it connected and they were just chasing steam?

George whistled low and long. "A grand bit o' wheel there, i'n'it?"

There was no need to ask what he'd seen that'd so

impressed him. The same gold-accented carriage Morris had seen a week earlier rolled slowly down King Street. Fitting that it'd be on a lane named for royalty. It looked the sort of thing a monarch'd ride in.

"Could you imagine having money enough for something like that?" Morris mused aloud. "Hard to even think of when we's spending our days nipping carrots off carts and dropping coins in the claws of the Innkeeper."

"Maybe John-John got 'imself a job polishing the gold on a carriage like that." George motioned to the vehicle with his stub of a carrot. "He could eat for weeks just selling what rubbed off on the cloth."

"All the more reason to look for 'im," Jimmy said. "He might have a few cloths to spare."

George wandered off, looking for coins or whatever work he could manage before returning to the Inn. Jimmy and Morris walked on together.

"Do you really think John-John and Sally went to work somewhere?" Jimmy asked.

Morris shook his head. "Sally would've told Mary. And John-John would've crowed about it to all of us before claiming his fortune."

Jimmy stuffed his hands in his pockets. "Maybe this time, instead of going up against a ghost or a monster, we're facing down a rich man."

"Almost more scary, i'n'it?"

"Not *almost*."

Morris glanced back as they walked, eyeing the gilt carriage once more. It had stopped, and the door was open. He tugged at the sleeve of Jimmy's coat, motioning at the vehicle with his head.

A pair of bare feet, small like a child's, could be seen standing on the paving stones facing the carriage, but the open door hid the rest of the little one.

"Who's that?" Jimmy asked.

"Don't know." Morris stepped closer, studying what little he could see. "Ain't a gentry child, not barefoot like that."

Something was tossed to the ground. Green. Leafy. He recognized it in the next instant: the top of a carrot.

Jimmy sucked in a breath. "George?"

The little feet stepped up into the carriage. Morris's heart dropped to his stomach. George. Disappearing into a rich man's carriage, just like they'd worried had been happening to the urchins of the Inn.

He ran. He ran fast and hard, Jimmy close on his heels.

The carriage began rolling away, but was slowed by the press of vehicles on the busy street. Morris and Jimmy wove around hackneys and coaches, keeping track of the one they sought. If only it didn't get going too quickly.

It picked up pace. Morris made a lunge for the back, managing to snatch hold before the carriage sped out of reach. Jimmy snatched hold right beside him. Clinging for dear life, they rode the carriage further from Covent Garden, further from the streets they knew, and, Morris feared, closer and closer to danger.

.This one was smaller than the rest. The master wouldn't like that, but the children were getting wise and wary. It was becoming more and more difficult to lure them away with the promise of fortunes or food or comfort. He knew better than to frighten them; they'd raise the alarm. His master needed a full supply of fresh, young victims when the time for rejuvenating arrived. He would not disappoint his master. He didn't dare.

CHAPTER 8

The streets of London were a very different place depending on how one was dressed. When Fletcher donned the weeds he'd been born to wear and swaggered down the lanes, he found himself among friends: his fellow gutter-risers, those who'd begun as he did, many who were still there. When he wore the togs of his current state in life, he walked the streets alone. Nods were replaced with head dips. The gazes were distant. He was a stranger. A trespasser.

Fletcher didn't know which he preferred. Some days, like today, the decision was made for him. This was the day the abandoned girls were to arrive in London. His role in this mission required the veneer of a gentleman. The Dread Master organized most of these more complex efforts, and Fletcher had learned long ago to trust the man. Though his approach wasn't always what Fletcher's would've been, his strategies had proven brilliant over the years.

"Black yer boots, sir?" A street urchin, likely no more

than seven or eight years old, leaned against a wall, shining block under one foot, a penny spinning in one hand.

The penny pulled Fletcher's attention more sharply to the lad. A mere second later, he knew him. Henry, who had no surname, was one of Fletcher's informants, his eyes and ears and loyalty secured a year earlier when Fletcher had purchased him a bootblacking license so the local constabulary would stop harassing him and let him earn his meager living. Those with many options in life certainly enjoyed taking choices away from those who had few.

"My shoes could use a good polish." Fletcher kept his tone and posture casual. Gentlemen regularly stopped to have their boots touched up. Doing so wouldn't garner any attention. He set his foot on the boy's blacking stand. "I've a fair bit of spotting and mud on these."

"Been traipsing about?" On the surface, it was an impertinent question. Fletcher knew it for the code it was.

"A little. I mean to do a bit more this morning, weather permitting."

Henry nodded as he brushed dust from Fletcher's shoes. "A fine morning for it."

"Is it?"

"Fine, but it ain't perfect."

Something had gone wrong, then. "Rain or wind, do you suppose?"

"Wind."

So not a disaster, but a hiccup. "Should I summon a hack, then, instead of walking?"

Henry shrugged. "Keep a weather eye out." He shot

Fletcher a grin. "'Weather eye out.' How you like that bit o' wordplay?"

"A fine bit. You could be a writer someday."

Henry shook his head as he returned to his work. "Everyone what knows me would laugh themselves to fits if-fen they heard you say I'd amount to anything. Folks like me don't waste time with dreams."

"They laughed at me too, Henry," he said. "And while they laughed, I worked and I planned. They ain't laughing now."

"All the workin' and plannin' in the world ain't always enough," Henry said.

"I know it."

Fletcher set his gaze on the street around him, eyeing the comings and goings. He kept his interest vague and set his mouth in a line of judgment. He'd be more believable as a well-heeled gentleman with that expression on his face. He watched the spot up where the post coach let off its passengers, and where the poor girls they awaited would shortly be arriving.

Doc Milligan was there already, flanked on either side by ladies of formidable size and mien. Fletcher had met them on a couple of previous occasions, when they'd volunteered to help Milligan treat some of the less fortunate in Town. They were in position, ready to intercept the unfortunate souls.

Down Fleet Street on the opposite side of the waiting doctor, Stone stood, flipping a penny in his hand. He would keep an eye on things from that end. Irving stood near a pasty cart, slowly making his way through a bit to eat, looking for all the world like a man in his dotage, slow in more ways than one. A few other Dreadfuls would be around corners, tucked just out of sight.

He looked back at the boy, this time catching sight of a penny dreadful tucked in his coat pocket. Fletcher recognized the telltale purple cover.

"You reading Mr. King's latest?" he asked.

"Aye." Henry kept diligently shining. "He spins a good tale, Mr. King."

"That he does."

Henry looked up at him. "I read yours too, Mr. Walker. I like Morris an' Jimmy. They're like me and all the other urchins."

"They're meant to be," Fletcher said. "They's like the boy I were. It's stories the likes of you and I can relate to. It's stories we live every day."

"'Cept with monsters and ghosts and such," Henry added.

Fletcher grinned. "Except for that, aye."

An overfilled post coach rumbled down the road. People stepped out of the way, too accustomed to its arrival to be in awe of it. Henry brushed firmly at Fletcher's boot, not appearing to notice anything but his work, though Fletcher would wager he was as aware of it all as he himself was.

Milligan stepped up to the coach, so close that those disembarking had to slip around him. A few thuggish men attempted to shove him out of the way. The good doctor wasn't a large man, but he wasn't moved. The women with him made a noticeable objection to the jostling they received from the men. Fletcher was too far to hear what was said, but it wasn't hard to guess.

Stone inched closer from the other side. Irving watched

the fracas with curiosity. He said something to the pasty seller that pulled his attention to the ruckus. One of the would-be macks shoved one of Milligan's assistants. The pasty seller shouted. More people took note of the confrontation.

A young girl, likely fourteen or fifteen, stepped off the carriage, wide-eyed and clearly afraid. She, he felt certain, was one of the poor girls they were waiting on. Another girl, alike enough to be a sister, looked over her shoulder.

The doctor said something. The girls turned their gaze to him. More jostling. More angry shouts from the others who'd been awaiting this arrival. Ought he to step in? It was such a delicate undertaking.

"Mr. Walker?"

Ah, toss it. He knew the sound of Miss Black's voice. Under any other circumstances, he'd have been happy to see her and chat a spell.

"Miss Black." He spoke as casually as he could manage. He'd not wish to encourage her to linger.

"Are you meaning to drop in on your publisher?" she asked. "I know many of the penny dreadful publishers are found on Fleet Street."

"Are you dropping in on yours?" He eyed the stack of twine-bound papers in her arms.

She smiled with amusement. "On this end of Town?"

No, the silver-fork publishers weren't in this area. She would just be passing through—which would take her directly through the fray churning at the post-coach stop. *Toss it all.*

He turned his attention back to Henry. "Don't miss the dust on the tip there, lad."

"Aye, sir." Henry leaned lower and polished with ever more gusto.

Fletcher turned a little more, his back almost fully to Miss Black. The rudeness was necessary; he needed her to move on. If she tried to get involved in the mission, she might ruin it all.

"I enjoyed our conversation the other evening," she said. "Those salons can be a touch dull. It was a nice change."

He nodded without looking at her. "It was a bit dull."

Out of the corner of his eye, he saw her brow lower in confused surprise. He hadn't meant to imply that her conversation had been dull, but, s' help him Baub, he couldn't correct the misunderstanding. The rescue was underway, and growing messier, and he'd be unable to help if he was busy keeping her from noticing too much.

"A pleasure seeing you again, Miss Black." He offered a quick bow without moving his foot from the block nor turning toward her at all. It was a dismissal; there was no way she could see it as anything but that.

She paled a little. "I—" She shook her head, dismissing whatever it was she meant to say. "Forgive me for disrupting your day, Mr. Walker."

She pulled her pile of papers against her chest, almost like a shield. Chin tipped high, she walked away.

Blast it all. He'd hurt her. It had been necessary, for the Dread Penny Society, for her, for the safety of the girls being shielded by Milligan and his assistants. He'd had to. He couldn't've done differently. But now she thought ill of him, and it bothered him. It bothered him a great deal.

"Henry."

"Aye, sir?"

"Track Miss Black, will you? I suspect she don't know how quick the weather can turn."

He had his equipment packed in a flash. Fletcher tossed him a sovereign, which he tucked safely in his interior jacket pocket. As he walked down the road, keeping just the right distance behind Miss Black, he took to spinning his penny once more. The other Dreadfuls would recognize him and his connection and know they'd need to be circumspect.

Miss Black didn't seem to note the fray nearby. Owing to the pressing crowd, she never came near enough to see much detail. That was a spot of luck. Henry stayed close on her heels.

Milligan, walking behind his assistants, who each had an arm around one of the sisters, slipped away from the angry men who'd come specifically to rush the girls away to lives of misery. Stone moved closer but couldn't interfere without drawing too much attention.

Fletcher swaggered in that direction, calling on all the confidence he claimed. He set his feet on a path that placed him between Milligan and those in pursuit. Fletcher stopped, pulled out his watch, and, with deliberate slowness, checked the time. It was just enough of a barrier to stop the men long enough for Milligan to slip around the corner where Fletcher knew their carriage would be waiting.

One of the brawny blackguards bumped him, swearing loud and long.

Fletcher eyed him with disdain.

"Ye're in m' way."

Fletcher raised a brow and dipped his head in annoyance

before stepping the tiniest bit away, not quite enough for the man to move easily around him. It'd delay him a bit more.

A flower girl, nosegays in her little hands, came around the corner where Milligan had disappeared. She passed Fletcher without acknowledgment, moving to where Irving stood. "Bouquet, mister? A penny each."

"Have you sold many?" Irving asked.

More code, more unstated questions and inquiries.

"Five just now, sir."

Five—Milligan, his two assistants, and the two sisters. Five pennies.

"Sounds like I ought to buy some as well, seeing as they're so popular." Irving purchased a couple of bouquets. He flipped a penny before handing it to her. She flipped it in precisely the same way.

They were done. The girls were safe and away, though it had been a near thing. Miss Black had almost undone it all, had nearly set herself unknowingly in danger.

As he casually sauntered down the street, he couldn't entirely clear his mind of Miss Black's expression as he'd dismissed her so coldly. She wasn't going to be happy with him. He regretted that. They'd had something of a friendship beginning between them. That was likely gone now.

Keeping secrets saved lives, but it also complicated things.

CHAPTER 9

Fletcher Walker was an aggravation of the most frustrating sort. He'd conversed amicably with her at the salon. She wouldn't go so far as to say he'd been flirtatious, but he'd certainly been friendly. Yet he'd acted just now as if she'd overstepped herself with her simple greeting when they'd crossed paths on the street.

There was nothing to be done but write him into the next installment of *The Lady and the Highwayman* and make certain something miserable happened to him. One did not treat an author poorly without consequences.

Furthermore, one did not pull the wool over an author's eyes easily. Did Mr. Walker truly think she would take no note of the bootblack following her through the teeming crowd or that she wouldn't realize it was the same little boy who had been shining his shoes when she'd spoken with him? He hadn't acted as though he thought her dim-witted.

A thought entered her mind that slowed her steps. He had teased her about being in this area of Town in order to supply her publisher with a manuscript, knowing this was the area where the penny dreadfuls were produced. *Had* he been teasing? She had her suspicions about his participation in the mysterious Dread Penny Society. Did he suspect her secret as well?

Surely not. She'd not given any hints. She'd been careful to assume a neutral position, neither praising nor criticizing the penny dreadfuls. And she had purposely pretended to have "discovered" vague information about Mr. King to turn suspicion away from her. Had it not been enough? Had she given away more than she realized?

The street was not nearly so chaotic as it had been earlier when an argument had broken out between a group that had met the posting coach. In the cacophony, she hadn't been able to make out precisely the topic of disagreement, but it had been heated and the crowd diverse: fishmongers, gentlemen, primly dressed women, flower sellers. She'd even recognized one of the onlookers: Irving Abbey, who'd begun his career writing for the *Times* and had, in his later years, turned to penny serials. He'd watched the proceedings with the curiosity a journalist never outgrows.

Elizabeth had also noted with delight just how many in the crowd had copies of the much-decried "low literature" serials tucked in pockets and baskets and coats. She even spotted a familiar purple cover. That never stopped being exciting to stumble across unexpectedly.

The young bootblack hung back now, not following so closely. Indeed, the more distance she put between herself and the ruckus, the farther away he kept. He did not, however, stop his pursuit. She didn't feel threatened, but it was imperative that she accomplish her business without being seen.

How did one shake a young boy following close on one's heels? With a sigh of both amusement and annoyance, she stepped into the one nearby shop she felt certain he'd not enter: a seller of unmentionables. She would remain long enough for her shadow to move on. Her chemise and corset and stockings had always been quite serviceable, a matter of necessity when she was young and her father gambled away all the family's resources. She'd never given much thought to changing that, but perhaps she should. A touch of lace and a completely unnecessary ruffle would be such a joyful extravagance.

Elizabeth tucked her stack of papers against her chest. This story was doing particularly well. She had every expectation of the next installment being likewise as successful, perhaps even more so. Her school had patrons and students enough to be financially stable. Provided her questionable writing endeavors didn't become known and undermine everything, she'd have enough extra funds for a few frills.

She peeked through the shop window and out onto the street. No sign of the bootblack. As a precaution, she slipped in and out of a few more shops, careful to give the impression of casual interest and being utterly certain she didn't leave her manuscript papers anywhere.

At last, more than thirty minutes behind schedule and no longer being followed, she headed toward her original destination. Her identity was too vital a secret to trust even to her publisher, and so she had enlisted the help of the brother of a former pupil, a young man who worked as a clerk in a business near the building where her penny dreadful publisher had its offices. He had a friend who worked in that building who had a friend who kept books for the publisher. It was a rather ridiculously complicated means of doing something as simple as turning in stories, but it had protected her secret.

"I liked your most recent," Timothy said upon receiving her stack of papers.

"Thank you."

He carefully tucked her pages under his arm. "I'll hand these over."

"I do appreciate that you arranged this for me and that you've never given me a moment's worry over your trustworthiness."

He smiled, his crooked teeth making the expression all the more endearing. "You looked after my sister after our parents died. I'd keep every secret you have if it would pay you back for that."

"How is Mary?"

"Happy as a lark."

Elizabeth was glad to hear it. "Please offer her my love next time you see her."

Timothy nodded and slipped inside his building. He could be counted on. She didn't spend a moment worrying over the delivery. She had allowed herself time to undertake errands but, in reality, had little else that had to be seen to. The afternoon was hers.

Upon reaching the shop of her favorite bookseller, she came across a man she knew vaguely but hadn't seen in some time: Quintin Hogg. He ran a ragged school for London's most destitute children.

"Ah, Miss Black," he said upon her greeting him. "How are your efforts at Thurloe?"

"Challenging."

He nodded knowingly. "The education of children is never simple, is it?"

"Though our challenges are not identical," she said, "I would welcome any wisdom you have to offer."

He tucked the book he was holding under his arm. "Come call on me at my school one day when you have a bit of time. I will happily share any insights I have."

"Thank you very much."

Mr. Walker's dismissive treatment had cast a pall over her day, but Mr. Hogg's offer of help brightened everything.

CHAPTER 10

Janey Smith had the look of one who'd seen far too much of a cruel world despite not yet having reached the age of fourteen. The wariness in her eyes belied the hardness of her expression.

"What kind of woman is this Miss Black?" She clearly expected the worst. "Doc Milligan said I weren't to go to a bawdy house or work in the street." She showed not the slightest embarrassment at referencing those places and professions.

"She's a headmistress of a girls' school," Fletcher said.

Janey tossed him a look of disbelief heavily tinged with cynicism. "I ain't one for learnin'. Haven't any use for it anyhow."

There was a lot to argue in that, but he felt it best to fight this battle on one front at a time. "I ain't bringin' you to enroll you, sweetie. I'm hopeful Miss Black is in need of a chambermaid."

The bit of hope that entered her eyes broke his heart. Too many poor children lost the ability to believe in better things to come. That Janey had managed to keep any part of that belief spoke to her strength and determination. If only Miss Black had a place for her, even for only a time.

He couldn't bear the thought of the streets claiming yet another child, especially one barely clinging to the tiniest shred of hope. If Miss Black didn't have room for Janey, he'd keep looking until he found something. Too many people had given up on him when he was a tiny urchin. He wouldn't do the same.

"You don't talk as fine as Mr. Darby." Janey made the observation with a tone of insult, but Fletcher knew better. She was curious and nervous, and, he would wager, alone for the first time. Her older sister had been taken that day to an acquaintance of Irving's who they hoped could employ the girl for a time. They wanted to find the girls a situation where they could be together, but that would take time.

"I ain't as fine and fancy as he is," he said. "I've learned to be more proper, and I have a roof over my head now, but my origins are still there in my words and views and such. That don't ever go away, not entirely."

"The lady at Dr. Milligan's surgery said the country'll always be in my voice. She said it like it were a bad thing."

Fletcher shook his head. "Don't you pay no heed to that. Sounding country ain't nothing to be ashamed of. People'll notice, just as you noticed my street talk, but show 'em you're worth listening to and they'll heed you."

"Will Miss Black?"

He offered a slight shrug as they turned up the walk to the front door of Thurloe Collegiate School. "She's not said anything about my speaking."

Janey nodded, assuming a determined expression. Poor thing tried hard to look and seem as independent as possible. She'd been a little flirtatious when he'd first met her at Milligan's, something he'd seen far too many young girls employ when interacting with men. It was a way of defending themselves, he felt certain. If they acted older, they might not be taken advantage of as much, and flattering a man's ego made him less likely to lash out at her. It condemned the men of the world that girls learned such things, yet too many men didn't see it or didn't care or thought it their right to make this world dangerous for the girls and women in it.

His firm knock was answered by the housekeeper, a no-nonsense woman he'd been quite impressed with during his previous visit. She didn't have the look of defeat too many servants wore, neither did she give the impression of being a tyrant. If Janey were employed under this woman's watch, she'd be treated well and would learn all she needed to find honorable employment.

"Mr. Walker for Miss Black," he said.

They waited in the entryway while the housekeeper left to see if her mistress was available.

"She didn't look at me like I were a slug or something." Janey sounded genuinely surprised.

Fletcher chuckled. "They're good people here. Behave as you ought, and they'll treat you right."

"I know how to behave."

"I don't doubt you do."

Miss Newport descended the stairs from the upper landing. Her gaze fell on them, and she smiled warmly. "Why, Mr. Walker. What brings you here?"

"Would you believe I came to see you?"

"No." Her eyes sparkled with humor. "I do believe you

would say that, though, if it meant getting a bit of flirting done while you wait for the person you actually came to see."

"He ain't one for flirting," Janey declared. "Says it ain't 'propriate."

Fletcher eyed her pointedly. "In our circumstances, sweetie, it ain't."

Some of her bluster died, and color touched her cheeks.

"Janey, this here's Miss Newport, a fine lady what teaches music here at the school. A curtsey'd be your best greeting."

"I know." Janey spoke defiantly but also humbly.

"Miss Newport, this is Janey, a young woman recently arrived from the country."

"Essex," Janey said.

Miss Newport, good soul that she was, smiled kindly at the girl's brashness. "I have never been to Essex," she said, "but I'm certain it is lovely."

Janey twitched her head and shoulders, not quite a shrug but something like it. "It ain't awful. Quieter than London."

"Everywhere's quieter than London," Fletcher said, earning him a smile from them both.

The door to Miss Black's office opened, and the housekeeper stepped out. She met Fletcher's eye and, with a dip of her head said, "Miss Black'll be with you in a moment."

"Thank you."

She slipped away. In the next instant, Alistair Headley stepped from the office. That man was like an itchy rash, arriving unannounced and unwanted, and proving a source of annoyance. Fletcher adjusted his position, keeping himself between Headley and Janey. He didn't think the man was any kind of threat or would ill-use the girl. She'd simply endured enough in her life without adding another misery.

"Walker." Headley spoke his name as if identifying an insect crawling on his sleeve.

"Headman," Fletcher returned.

"Head*ley*."

Fletcher pulled in his brows, tipping his head forward. "What was that?"

"Head*ley*. My name is Headley, not Headman."

"Are you sure?"

Headley's eyes narrowed. His mouth pulled tight. The man, it seemed, had only just realized Fletcher was poking at him. The game might've gone on longer, but Miss Black stepped to the threshold of her office, pulling Fletcher's attention there.

"Mr. Walker." She motioned him inside.

Fletcher turned back to Janey, indicating she should step in ahead of him. Miss Black eyed the girl as she passed, but didn't object.

"Would you be terribly put out if I closed the door?" Fletcher asked. "I've a personal matter to discuss and would appreciate a bit of privacy."

Miss Black looked from him to Janey and then back again before nodding.

He pushed the door until it latched.

"How can I help you, Mr. Walking?" Miss Black asked.

"It's Walker."

She tipped her head and narrowed her eyes. "Are you sure?"

Oh, that bit of wit deserved a grin, and he gave it one without hesitation. "I've come to ask a favor."

"Have you?"

"Told you this weren't gonna work." Janey assumed a petulant posture in the spindle-armed chair she occupied.

Fletcher sat on the edge of Miss Black's desk, facing his frowning charge. "What'd I tell you this morning when we was leaving Doc Milligan's?"

"Quit sayin' 'bung your eye,'" she muttered.

Behind him, Miss Black did a poor job of covering a laugh with a cough.

He looked over his shoulder at her. "I did have to tell her that."

"Let us hope she heeds your excellent counsel."

He arched a brow, letting his doubt show. He turned back to the girl. "I know you ain't been given many reasons to hope in this life, Janey, but I need you to try. Just for a bit."

"What if she won't listen to you?" She motioned to Miss Black.

"I *don't* particularly wish to listen to Mr. Walker," Miss Black said. "And he doesn't always wish to listen to me, especially when he's having his shoes polished."

That was too pointed a remark to misunderstand. He couldn't explain his reasons to her, but leaving her in the dark meant risking her cooperation now when they needed it so badly.

"I will, however," she continued, "listen to *you*, Janey."

"To me?" All the girl's bravado disappeared. "I ain't a fine speaker."

"Neither is Mr. Walker."

Fletcher laughed and crossed to the chair where Janey sat, standing behind it. "Tell her why we've come, sweetie."

Miss Black moved a chair from the side of her desk and placed it beside Janey's, then sat looking at her with kindness and patience in her eyes.

Janey took a shaky breath. "We was bought by Mrs. George," she said.

Miss Black looked at him with both shock and doubt, but Janey wasn't fibbing. He gave a subtle but firm nod.

"When we got to London," Janey continued, "Doc Milligan took us away and made Mrs. George's bullyboys leave us be. He might've paid her after it all, I don't know."

They hadn't given that horrid woman so much as a ha'penny. She'd threatened Milligan, who'd kept her occupied until the authorities arrived. She'd been none too happy. He'd not heeded her in the least.

"Fanny went with one of Doc's friends, and I's come here with Mr. Walker on account of he says you're a good 'un."

Miss Black's expression softened the more she listened to Janey. She might have been put out with him, but she didn't hold that against this girl who was in so much need.

"Fanny's her sister," Fletcher explained. "Mrs. George makes her living running a handful o' bawdy houses and selling girls to macks on the street."

Anger touched the sadness in Miss Black's eyes.

"Dr. Milligan, a friend of mine, got wind of Fanny and Janey's situation and stepped in. He'd not see either of 'em turned out on the street, but he ain't able to house them at his surgery, he bein' a bachelor-variety doctor."

"You've been separated from your sister?" she asked Janey.

At that, the girl did something Fletcher never expected—she burst into tears. "We didn't want to come. We knew what kind of woman Papa had sold us to. He didn't care. He got five pounds each for us. That'd buy him a good bit of gin." She wiped her nose on her sleeve, hiccupping through further tears. "But Fanny and I were together, and that made it not so bad."

"Not so bad." Fletcher knew what it was to settle for that. There were so many children needing help. He'd had great hopes of his stories selling better and better and saving more and more urchins. He wasn't doing so well anymore.

Lud, he needed to find King.

"Mr. Fletcher, would you tug on the bellpull, please?" Miss Black turned to Janey again and handed her a clean handkerchief. "Take a moment. You've endured quite an ordeal."

Janey wiped furiously at her tear-drenched cheeks.

Miss Black stood and joined Fletcher. "Did you truly tell Janey that I was 'a good 'un'?"

"I did. Stranger still, I meant it."

She smiled. "Is there a reason a 'good 'un' doesn't warrant so much as a 'good afternoon' when her path crosses yours outside of political salons and literary soirees?"

Lud, she was decidedly upset about that still. "Last we saw each other, I weren't in a position to offer any 'good afternoons' or 'how do you dos,'" he said.

"Your shoeshine spy certainly would not have begrudged you a brief conversation while he worked."

A shiver of apprehension spread over him. "Shoeshine spy?"

She actually rolled her eyes. "I am not only a 'good 'un,' I'm also a smart one. I see things, and I piece things together." Not a reassuring declaration.

The office door opened, and the housekeeper poked her head inside. "Yes, Miss Black?"

"Would you take Janey to the kitchen and see to it that she has a cup of tea and something to eat?"

"Of course, miss." The housekeeper motioned Janey to the doorway, and the two of them disappeared into the entryway.

"Thank you for that," Fletcher said. "Milligan fed the girls as much as he could, but he primarily treats the poor. He don't have much to spare."

"Have you considered that Dr. Milligan might be your elusive Mr. King?"

The question caught him so off guard he could not, at first, respond. "Milligan?"

Her expression was serious. "Rumors are rife that the Dread Penny Society undertook another kidnapping—or rescue, depending on who you ask—a couple of days ago. The timing coincides with Janey and her sister arriving in London."

"They were *rescued*," he insisted.

"And if your friend, the good doctor, is connected to events possibly connected to the Dread Penny Society, it increases the likelihood that he is writing for the penny dreadfuls."

She had declared herself smart and observant. That was proving far too true for his peace of mind. Setting her on the scent of the elusive King might have been a mistake.

"You're assuming this society actually exists. I ain't convinced it's real."

"Are you attempting to make me believe that you are not, yourself, a member?"

Fletcher tapped his chin. "I suspect your friend Mr. Headcheese harbors that same idea."

Her eyes danced. "Headcheese?"

"Did I get it wrong again?" He shook his head and clicked his tongue. "I cain't never remember that cove's name."

"How long would Janey need to be employed here?" she asked.

"I'm not entirely sure. Milligan's asking around, hoping to sort out a situation where the girls can be together."

"A kindness to them both," she said. "If Janey is willing to work, and I suspect she is, and if she takes your advice on avoiding certain unsavory expressions—"

"—Which *I* hope she will."

"Then I can give her a roof over her head and keep her belly full. I cannot say how long I could keep her employed here, though. I will have to look more closely at the ledgers."

He understood financial difficulties all too well. "I'll appreciate whatever you're able to do."

"I will do whatever I can," she said. "Mrs. George will have no second opportunity if I have any ability to prevent it."

Here was the fierce compassion he had come to Thurloe in search of. "I'd wager Doc Milligan will find something for the girls soon enough. He can be trusted."

"Can *you*?" she asked.

Before he could offer a single syllable in response, she continued. "Janey will be well looked after. Tell the good doctor where she is and have him send word if another situation is found for her." She stepped to the doorway, pausing to look back at him. "And Mr. Walker?"

He watched, waited.

"Offer my greetings to the Dread Penny Society."

THE VAMPIRE'S TOWER
AN URCHINS OF LONDON ADVENTURE

by Fletcher Walker

Chapter III

Just when Morris was certain he couldn't hold on to the back of the carriage a moment longer, it slowed, rolling to a stop at a tall iron gate. He and Jimmy had been in a number of odd fixes during their twelve years of life, so they knew what to do without saying a word.

They hopped off the carriage and, ducking down to stay as low and hidden as possible, followed the vehicle through the gate. They darted quick behind a hedge, waiting for the wheels to grow distant enough for them to safely move.

Morris's first glance at their surroundings shocked him; almost nothing did that anymore.

"It's a blasted castle," Jimmy said. "An honest-to-Baub castle."

They'd wandered past the gates of Buckingham and Windsor, so a castle wasn't a completely unfamiliar thing. But to have ridden the back of a carriage, one containing ragged little George, right to a castle gate? He'd not been expecting that.

"An old one, too." Jimmy's surprise hadn't silenced him. "Knights-and-armor old."

"Aye, but it ain't crumbling. Someone's living here and seeing to the ol' pile."

"Someone who convinced George to roll off with him."

They needed to find George and make certain he was safe. If the master of the castle was the one sweeping urchins off the street, they needed to know why and where they all went, and why none of them were ever heard from again.

Up ahead, the gilded carriage rolled on, not to the front portico but toward the stables. That made more sense; George weren't exactly a fine and fancy visitor. But would George be staying in the stables, or should they sneak over toward the castle and try to find him there?

"Look!" Jimmy, who was never spooked, sounded up-ended.

Morris followed his wide-eyed gaze to the top of a tall, narrow, stone tower. "I don't see nothing."

"It was there. A minute ago."

"What was?"

"Somethin' . . . floated by the windows up top." Jimmy hadn't looked away. "*Floated.* Swear it did."

"What kind of thing?"

Jimmy shook his head. "A person, maybe. I ain't sure."

"A person *walking* past the window?" That seemed more likely.

"Didn't look like walking."

Morris looked back again but saw nothing. There wasn't even any light up there. But Jimmy wasn't one to make things up, and he didn't get shaken easily. He'd seen something.

"We can't leave George here," Jimmy said firmly.

"But we don't know where he's being taken."

Jimmy squared his shoulders. "No. But we know where *that* is." He pointed up at the tower.

"You want to go chasing after a mysterious figure in the tower?"

"It's the threat," Jimmy said. "If George is in danger, that's where it'll be coming from."

"And if the other urchins were brought here and are in trouble, they'll be there as well."

Jimmy looked to him. "We're doing this again, then, are we? Running headlong into trouble, solving mysteries, courting danger?"

Morris allowed a cheeky smile. "It's the only thing we do better than picking pockets."

He spit into his palm. Jimmy did the same. They clasped and shook hands, then moved stealthily toward the tower.

<hr />

The master was wandering the castle, still half asleep, but becoming more and more alert. Time was running short. Once he was fully awake, he would be thirsty. The consequences of not having an adequate supply for his feast would be dire.

There was little time to gather enough children.

So very little time.

CHAPTER 11

Within two days of Janey's arrival at Thurloe, Elizabeth was utterly attached to the girl. Hers was a sweet temperament, an admirable work ethic, a roaringly funny wit, a sometimes-too-colorful vocabulary, and she quickly claimed the undying loyalty of every teacher and student at the school. Her sister was likely very much the same, and if Elizabeth was careful with the school's funds, she might be able to take on both girls. Her penny dreadful income gave Thurloe extra income but also extra risk.

She paused in her herb gathering, her mind spinning in too many directions. Spending time in the school's kitchen garden usually proved soothing, but not today. Mr. Walker was determined to find Mr. King. If he knew the truth, would he be willing to keep her secret? Safeguarding her reputation meant she had no one to discuss the matter with, no one to celebrate or commiserate with. What a welcome release it would be to claim that needed bit of comradery.

She turned at the sound of footsteps on the flagstone

walk. Had he come to call? Her heart, that odd, illogical organ, leaped in anticipation. Mr. Walker hadn't looked in on Janey the last two days, but Elizabeth fully suspected he would. He intrigued her, though she wasn't entirely sure why.

It was not Fletcher Walker who approached but Timothy, her contact of the contact she had at her penny dreadful publisher.

"Good morning," she greeted.

He answered with a quick, abbreviated bow. He was not usually so rushed in his interactions. Indeed, there were times his nonchalant manner tried her patience. "I've a family concern, Miss Black."

Her heart dropped to her boots. "Is something the matter with your sister?"

He shook his head. "With my brother."

Cold creeped through her chest. Timothy didn't have a brother. He was referencing Mr. King via the code they had developed between them. "Has something befallen your brother?"

"Not as yet."

She hooked her arm through the basket handle and began a slow walk along the garden path. Timothy walked alongside her.

"Tell me of your brother's troubles."

"He has an odd employment, as you know."

She did, indeed.

"The man he works for has been getting a world of bother over him lately. Busybodies and such asking questions."

That was not reassuring at all. "Has his employer offered any satisfaction to these curious souls?"

"Mostly that he don't know the answers to their questions."

The complicated method of handing over her manuscripts was an annoyance and a frustration at times, but keeping her publisher unaware of who she actually was had been crucial. She knew people would inquire, and the fewer people privy to Mr. King's identity, the safer her secret.

"And do you happen to know who these inquisitive people are?"

"As near as I've been able to determine, there've been a few, but one bloke more than any others. A persistent bugger, from what I hear."

That described Fletcher Walker rather perfectly. Elizabeth suspected he was behind these recent inquiries. Agreeing to help him find Mr. King and feeding him false whispers had apparently not distracted him from his efforts as she had hoped.

"Have these questions caused your brother's employer any concerns?"

"Not enough to make a fuss. Mostly he's worried about my brother, knowing he likes his privacy."

That would be reassuring if not for the continued concern in Timothy's eyes.

"Is there something else your brother needs to know?"

"The man who gets my brother's papers from the man I give the papers to is feelin' a little spooked. My man told him there weren't nothing wrong or unlawful about any of it, but he's still nervous. Might make it harder for my brother to get his work finished."

That was a difficulty. Removing even one person from

the delivery chain increased the chances of her identity being discovered. Causing the publisher any increased annoyance might lead him to decide even the surprising success of King's stories wasn't worth the hassle.

"I think I know who is making the inquiries," she said. "I will see if I can't distract him."

Timothy bit back a smile, bringing an answering one to her lips.

"I didn't mean it the way you are clearly thinking," she said with a laugh.

"Yes, miss. Is there anything else I can do for you, Miss Black?"

"I thank you, but we're getting on quite well. We have a chambermaid now, and she is proving an enormous help."

He grinned. "I saw her on my way around the school. Gave me a saucy look, she did, tossing a penny around as she worked."

"A penny?" That was an odd affectation.

Timothy shrugged. "You see it around now and then, street children and mongers mostly, but gentlemen sometimes, too."

Pennies. An idea niggled in the back of her mind. *Pennies.* "Did the man who interrogated your brother's employer flip pennies about?"

"Not that I've heard."

She nodded. "If you do hear, let me know."

He eyed her with curiosity. "I'll keep m'ears perked."

"Thank you. And thank you for all the help you've been. I could not possibly have managed any of this without you."

He reddened at that but lost not a drop of his aplomb.

"My pleasure, Miss Black. And don't you fret. I'll do all I can for my brother."

She was reassured, but still not wholly at ease. Her silver-fork novels were acceptable and would not draw anything but approval. They didn't, however, bring her the same satisfaction. Without her penny dreadfuls, she would be lost. They had become a part of her.

She adjusted her basket of herbs over her arm and walked slowly back toward the kitchen door. Two of her youngest students ran past, giggling.

"Good morning, Miss Black," they said, nearly in unison.

"Good morning, girls. How are you today?"

"Lovely." Penelope described most things as "lovely," and she did so with utter sincerity. "Miss Newport says I can learn a new song on the pianoforte. I love playing music. It makes my heart happy."

Beside her, Lillian spun in a circle, arms stretched out.

"And you, I suspect, have your dancing instruction today," Elizabeth said.

Lillian nodded.

"Dancing makes her heart happy," Penelope said.

These girls made *Elizabeth's* heart happy. Seeing them blossom, watching them grow into caring, intelligent, joyful young ladies brought her deep satisfaction. And helping them discover their passions, the pursuits that brought them joy, felt like she was changing lives for the better.

Not far distant, a group of students played hopscotch. Some of the older girls sat on a bench, heads bent over a book. The rest of her girls would be inside having lessons, writing letters home, passing quiet moments.

Years of toil and tears had created this school, this dream come true. Writing penny dreadfuls had proven a fulfillment of a dream she hadn't even known she'd had.

She loved both. The school gave her purpose. Mr. King gave her hope. If juggling her two passions grew too risky, which would she be willing to lose? How could she possibly choose?

CHAPTER 12

Fletcher looked out over the gathering of Dreadfuls in the council chamber, wishing he had the answers to all the problems being discussed.

Who was King? They still didn't know.

Who was undermining Hogg's ragged school? They hadn't the first idea.

Were the burned-out remains of lucifer matches Joe kept finding around the school grounds the work of someone nefarious or simply mischievous, and neglectful, children? He couldn't say.

How were they to continue their rescues and philanthropic efforts if their funds continued to dwindle? Considering his income had taken more of a hit than anyone else's, he really didn't have that answer, either.

"Miss Black stumbled across our rescue of them Smith sisters." Irving was the first to bring up that near disaster. "She'll have recognized Fletch and Hollis, no doubting that. And the rescue was hot gossip within an hour. If we're not more circumspect, the game'll be up quick as a frog off a log."

"Any suspicions she had were focused on me," Fletcher said.

"Why is it you're thinking that?" Brogan asked.

"She thought I was having her followed."

"Were you?"

Fletcher just laughed. Stone nodded knowingly; not much escaped his notice.

"She did take in Janey without too many questions," Fletcher said.

"And Fanny," Hollis added.

Fletcher hadn't heard that.

Doc explained. "She visited me yesterday, havin' tracked me down with impressive speed, considering she and I have never interacted before. She said Janey was rather desperate to be with her sister again. Since she'd been led to understand that both girls were in temporary situations, she wondered if they might wait at Thurloe until more permanent arrangements could be made. She would feed them, see to it they had a new set of clothes, and pay them a small wage. And, more importantly in her view, they would be together."

Hollis rubbed the back of his neck. "That will be a burden to her, no matter her willingness. Her school is in the black, but I suspect only just. Educating the middle classes is far less profitable than the upper class."

"Could we offer to help with the girls' expenses?" Irving asked.

Fletcher pushed out a breath. "That'd be a tall ask, considering our funds ain't what they once were."

Irving shook his head, slowly and with frustration. "That

elusive Mr. King needs persuading to join our society. Adding his resources to ours—well, that'd see us in fine feather."

"We could use a tycoon." Brogan laughed.

Fletcher managed to laugh along, but his amusement was limited. He used to be their "tycoon." Not being a doctor like Milligan, or a master strategist like Stone, or having connections to important people like Hollis, money had been the best he'd had to offer.

"I'm getting closer to sorting the man," Fletcher said, not mentioning the "slightly" that ought to have been included before the word "closer."

"Either we need him among us," Hollis said, "or we need to find a means of reestablishing one of us as the top of the market."

Fletcher hadn't shared with the general membership his suspicion that King might actually be one of them already. The Dread Master had agreed with the need to consider it, and Fletcher was keeping his eye on everyone. He also hadn't mentioned that King likely had a more formal education than most of them. They couldn't afford to have too many people asking questions and drawing attention.

"I'll find him," he said as both a promise and a warning, should such be necessary. "When I do, the lot of us can stage a dethroning if need be."

"Spent loads of time looking at petticoats and corsets and them kind of lady things." Henry, the bootblack, spun his penny in his hand as they talked. "She wandered in an' out of a lot of shops, but she weren't interested in buying nothing."

Odd. "Why do you say that?"

"She was looking for me more than anything." He flashed a gap-toothed smile. "A clever mort, that one. Not many fine folk can sort out that they're being followed."

"Then you didn't see where she were going in the end?"

"She's smart; she ain't a genius." There was nothing quite like the cocky self-assurance of a life-hardened child of the streets. "She talked to a clerk on the street, gave 'im her papers, then went to York Place."

"What did she do on York Place?" Perhaps that was a clue to her search for King.

"Went inside Mr. Hogg's school."

That was decidedly unexpected. "Well, I'm dished."

"She were in there too long for me to stand about waiting. Cain't shine shoes while tailing a bird."

"The women are a distraction, Henry."

The boy's gaze narrowed on him. "That Miss Black's a looker. And clever, too. An' I hear she's a writer like you."

"She is a writer, sure enough," Fletcher said, "but not like me."

"Ain't as popular?"

He shook his head. "Her writing's far more proper."

"The way she were lookin' at you while I shined your boots, I don't think your improper writing bothers her much."

That was intriguing. "And how was it she was looking at me?"

"Before or after you wouldn't talk to her?" Henry pushed

away from the wall he'd been leaning against. He slipped his penny into his pocket, then took up his bootblacker's kit. "If I were you, I'd not disappoint her like that again, guv'nah."

Fletcher chuckled. He was receiving advice about women from a ten-year-old. He tossed him a sixpenny bit. "Drop a word in m'ear if you see that clerk again, the one she gave her papers to. That bit's curious enough to chew on."

Henry tucked the coin in his pocket and tugged at his cap. "Sure enough will, sir."

The mystery niggled at his brain as he wandered down the street.

Why had Miss Black given her papers to a clerk on the street? Why had she gone to Hogg's school?

How, exactly, had she been looking at him?

Perhaps it was his distraction, perhaps it was pure, unadulterated curiosity, but his feet took him to the front door of Thurloe School. He was ushered in and shown to the school's drawing room, where a full dozen women, some younger and some far older than he, watched him enter.

He sorted it quickly. It was likely the teachers' calling day.

"I were hopin' to talk with Miss Black," he said to the room at large, unsure who to address directly.

A woman, likely near Irving's age, answered. "She's comforting one of the students. A little tiff amongst the girls." She tapped the sofa beside her. "Do sit and visit a spell. Miss Black will be but a moment, I'm sure."

The woman's eyes held a heap of mischief. Visiting with her would be a joy. He took the seat she offered.

"I'm Fletcher Walker," he said. "And I suspect you're trouble."

"He has taken your measure, Constance," one of the other teachers said.

Fletcher leaned closer and, lowering his voice, said, "I like trouble."

"And I like you far better than that Mr. Headley who calls on our Miss Black. He wouldn't know trouble if it handed him an embossed calling card."

Fletcher laughed out loud. Smiles lit the faces around the room. Apparently, he and Constance weren't the only ones who found Headley unimpressive.

Another teacher, her dark hair liberally sprinkled with gray, moved to a chair closer to his. "Your name is familiar. Are you the Fletcher Walker who writes the Urchins of London tales?"

"I am." It was, in fact, his most recent offering. "'Ave you read them?"

"I confiscated a copy of *The Vampire's Tower* from a student who was supposed to be doing her mathematics. I, of course, looked over the story so I would know what she was reading. I have a concern."

He braced himself for her inevitable disapproval. Whatever her complaint, he'd likely heard it before. "What's that?"

"Morris and Jimmy are about to enter that castle. Do they realize it is home to a vampire? I am terribly concerned that they haven't the first idea how very much danger they are truly in."

Her "concern" was for his characters. She had more than skimmed the story; she had read it and been drawn in.

"Are the missing urchins there as well?" the teacher pressed. "I'm very worried about them."

He smiled and shrugged. "You will have to read the next installment and discover for yourself."

"You wouldn't make me wait, would you?" She batted her eyelashes with a laugh.

"That is an unbreakable rule of authors: never reveal what's in the next chapter."

Her expression fell. "Then I suppose it would be futile to ask you to inquire of Mr. King what precisely lurks in the forest."

"If I'd the first idea who Mr. King is, I'd ask him that myself." No matter his frustration with the man, he had to admit King could weave a good tale.

"But according to the unbreakable rule of authors, Mr. King wouldn't tell you." The cheeky comment came from Miss Black.

He stood and offered a bow.

"Have you come to look in on Janey?" she asked.

"I ain't harboring the least worry about her bein' mistreated. I mean to thank you for bringing her sister here. She grieved being apart from her." He was grateful, but he was also worried. "Having both girls here ain't a small expense for you."

She waved that off. "We'll manage. Those girls should be together."

Her compassion shone through. He wished he could tell her about the Dreadfuls and the work they were doing. She would applaud it, he felt certain. She would understand his longing to do more. She might have some idea how they could stretch their limited resources. But revealing their activities was too dangerous for any of them to take that risk.

"Did you call for a particular reason?" she asked.

He hadn't the first idea why he'd come by. "Only to make my 'thank you.' And to offer you a good day, I suppose."

It was odd for him to feel so awkwardly uncomfortable. He rubbed at the back of his neck, scratched at his hair. Though her lips remained in a neutral line, a smile brightened her eyes. The twinkle only further upended him. It was not an experience he was at all accustomed to.

He took a step closer to the door. Looking back at the gathering of teachers proved a mistake. Half looked intrigued; the other half appeared amused. At his expense. He turned his attention to Miss Black. The smile in her eyes had shifted to laughter.

He dipped his head and beat a hasty retreat.

He, who had helped rescue countless children all over London, who was acting figurehead of a clandestine philanthropic society, had been fully flustered by a single, subtle smile from a woman he wasn't even sure respected him.

Morris and Jimmy it seemed, weren't the only ones who'd wandered unknowingly into imminent danger.

THE LADY
AND THE
HIGHWAYMAN
by Mr. King

Installment III,
in which our Heroine is delivered a most cold
Rejection and asked a Favor quite unexpected!

Oh, the joy in Lucinda's heart each time she was included when her neighbors called on one another, making their way from one house to the next in the light of day and the safety of the group! She came to know each of them during these calls and valued their association.

Miss Higgins was kindhearted, of a sharp mind, and the dearest friend one could hope for. The man whose oddly high-pitched voice had so captured her attention when first they'd met a fortnight after her arrival in the neighborhood was Mr. Jennings, and his mother, Mrs. Jennings, was the silver-eyed older woman who'd joined them.

Also among their number during the visits was, nearly without fail, the aloof and handsome Sir Frederick. He never smiled, though he did not truly seem unfriendly nor unhappy, and he never laughed. Though he did not, in her estimation, seem to be that odd sort who lacked any sense of the humorous. He also never spoke ill of anyone beyond the highwayman, and even those criticisms weren't overly cruel nor sharp, but simply expressions of uncertainty regarding the would-be thief's character. Sir Frederick was an oddity, a mystery, and more and more, a friend.

Nearly two months after Lucinda's arrival in the area, after the passage of a lonely Christmas, Miss Higgins very kindly included her in an invitation to do a bit of shopping in the largest town of any note in the area. They departed just as soon as the morning light hit the roads, knowing that if they did not dawdle, they could achieve their goals at market and return home before nightfall. Lucinda prepared a list, one added to by her housekeeper and butler-gardener-coachman, then traveled with Miss Higgins to the various shops an hour away.

What a delight to be away from home and from the forest that she had come to eye with such suspicion! Maybe, just maybe, Fate was beginning to smile on her.

She purchased ribbons and embroidery thread. She found adornments enough for redecorating a bonnet, and salt for addressing the issue of slugs in the vegetable beds. While Miss Higgins shopped for gloves, Lucinda moved toward the stationery shop, wanting to buy parchment and ink, though to whom she would send a letter, she did not know. She simply took comfort in the warm familiarity of such things.

Her path took her past a gentleman having his shoes shined near a sparsely laden vegetable cart. She knew him on the instant, his ice-blue eyes and firm-set jaw identifying him as her handsome neighbor, Sir Frederick.

What a pleasant surprise to see him again. They had enjoyed many a conversation and had, in her estimation, developed the beginnings of a friendship between them. He would certainly be equally pleased to see her. Oh, blessed Fate, to be showing her such kindness today!

"Sir Frederick! What a pleasure to cross paths."

He met her gaze with little warmth in his own. "Miss Ledford." His greeting began and ended with that: her name, uttered with neither excitement nor any apparent desire for interaction.

Perhaps she was misunderstanding his tone. She would try again. "Have you come to town to do a spot of shopping?"

His gaze fluttered over her armful of bundles. "Have you?"

Teasing, no doubt. Amusement pulled her lips upward. "I have. My next stop is the stationers for parchment and ink. I haven't any."

Far from pursuing the line of conversation, Sir Frederick looked once more to the young boy polishing his shoes. "Mind you don't miss any spots."

"Looks a beller-croaker to me," the poor polisher said, eyeing his work. "But if you ain't satisfied, I'll scrub at it some more."

Lucinda waited, certain her friend would speak with her once more. Surely. Alas, she was to be disappointed. He never looked to her again. He acted quite as if she was not even present.

Humiliation burned in her cheeks. She refused to meet the eye of any of the passersby. Sir Frederick, who had on the many occasions in which they had been in one another's company not seemed ashamed of her presence, had issued what appeared to be a very pointed cut. Oh, that she were wrong!

"I have enjoyed our conversations these past weeks," she said, attempting one last time to draw his gaze. "Calling on new neighbors can be uncomfortable, even a touch miserable, when one is newly arrived."

"New neighbors can be miserable," he replied.

Oh. She rested her hand against her stomach, which had spun into a knot. Did he consider *her* "miserable"? It sounded as though he was saying precisely that.

"A pleasure seeing you again, Miss Ledford." The bow he offered was brief and small, and unmistakable. He kept his foot on the block used by the tiny shoeshine boy. There was not so much as a glance of farewell in her direction.

She had been dismissed, coldly and swiftly. The rejection had drawn the notice of a lady and gentleman not far removed. The lady commented behind her hand to her companion, both watching Lucinda with a humiliating degree of pity. To be made an object of ridicule when she was so very newly arrived in the area, striving to be accepted, struggling to feel any degree of hope for her future in so strange and terrifying a place was a heavy burden for her heart to bear, and proof that Fate did not, in fact, look on her with any increasing degree of fondness.

"Forgive me for disrupting your day, Sir Frederick," she said quietly before moving as far from him as her suddenly very weary and overwhelmed limbs could take her.

Cruel Fate, it seemed, took delight in her misery.

◦──✦──◦

Two days passed in the silence of Calden Manor. Lucinda had ample time in which to contemplate Sir Frederick's refusal to speak with her save to indicate that her company was "miserable." What was she to do if he convinced the rest of the neighborhood to shun her as well? Could she live here year after year so utterly alone? How could it be endured?

Night had not yet fallen, though dusk threatened on the horizon. Lucinda stood at her bedchamber window, looking out over the thick forest. What was hidden within those trees that so frightened her neighbors? Their worry had etched its way into her heart, making her eye the dark expanse with great misgiving. All the neighborhood lived in terror of the forest. There had to be a reason.

She leaned against the window frame, watching the branches and treetops sway in the wind. Her lungs filled with the air of her room, air nearly as cold as that found outside owing to the lateness of her ordered delivery of coal.

She heard what she was certain was a knock at the front door. Her housekeeper took to bed every night just as Lucinda finished her evening meal, and her butler-gardener-coachman never came in the house. If she had indeed heard a knock, she would have to be the one to answer. She, alone. Undefended. With no one to turn to should the unexpected visitor have nefarious intentions.

Another knock, unmistakable this time.

"You mustn't be a simpleton," she said. "The night is not yet dark. You can most certainly answer the door."

One trembling step at a time, she descended the stairs and crossed the entryway, knocks continuing to sound at broad intervals. No matter that she assured herself she had no reason for alarm, her pulse quickened with every step she took.

She opened the door an inch, peering through the tiny crack between the door and the frame. As the identity of the new arrival became clear, her burgeoning fear gave way to confusion.

"Sir Frederick."

He dipped his head. "Miss Ledford. I am in need of a moment of your time. I have come on a matter of great importance." He motioned to a child, a girl no more than ten years old, whom she'd not noticed before, cowering behind him and watching her with concern.

No matter that he had treated her most rudely when last they met, she could not be cold to a child. She motioned the two of them inside, closing the door behind them.

"What has brought you here, Sir Frederick?" she asked.

"I have come to beg a favor."

That was unexpected. "Have you? Do you not think it presumptuous to ask a favor of someone whom you would not even speak with two days ago?"

"I would not presume to do so were the favor for myself," he said. "I ask, rather, on behalf of the child." He motioned to the small figure beside him. "Tell her why we've come, little one."

The child looked up at her with fear.

Lucinda opened her arms, and the little girl rushed into them. She leaned her slight weight against Lucinda, clinging to her.

"Please, miss," she said, her breath trembling with each word. "Please don't make me return to the forest."

"The forest?" Lucinda looked to Sir Frederick. "This child was in the forest?"

He nodded. "She needs a safe place away from the dangers she has escaped."

"And that safe place is here?" Lucinda could not account for his decision to bring the child to her.

"I am hopeful that it is, indeed." He offered a dip of his head.

This was not the apology nor the explanation she was owed, but it was a help just the same. Whatever his reasons for not speaking to her in town were, he would trust her with the welfare of this little girl.

With another nod, he stepped from the house, disappearing into the quickly approaching night. The tiny child clung to Lucinda.

"Am I to stay here?" she asked.

"Of course, dear," Lucinda said. "And I will endeavor to keep you safe from whatever you've fled from in the forest."

The girl's chin quivered. "The forest has . . . a monster!"

CHAPTER 13

Ah, bung your eye."

The latest installment in King's *The Lady and the Highwayman* was well written, intriguing, enjoyable, and maddeningly familiar. In it, the heroine had been publicly rebuffed by her sometimes-infuriating neighbor on the street of the nearby town while he had been getting his shoes shined. He had then asked her to take in a poor, destitute child. It was Elizabeth and Fletcher's last few interactions but set in a different context.

Only Miss Black was privy to the details of both those interactions. Even "beller-croaker" was used, a turn of phrase she'd taken note of when he'd used it. She had to have told Mr. King about their conversations, which meant either she'd found him some time ago and hadn't told Fletcher or she'd known King's identity all along and had been lying about it from the beginning.

"Bung your eye," he said again.

The hackney he rode in pulled to a stop in front of the York Place mews. He had received word from Joe, Hogg's stablehand, that Daniel, the climbing boy who'd been freed by the Dreadfuls, had something of significance to pass along to Fletcher. Daniel had given Joe the penny Fletcher had provided him with, a sure sign that the matter was one the boy considered important. If it was important to Daniel, it was important to Fletcher.

He tucked his copy of King's penny dreadful into the pocket of his jacket and stepped from the hack. He paid the fare and made his way to the mews. Joe was in a stall, brushing a horse.

He looked up briefly as Fletcher approached. "That Danny is the best little spy I've ever encountered."

"Discovered something, did he?"

Joe kept at his work as he spoke. "Knows a lot about fire."

"A sweep would," Fletcher said. "Does fire play a role in what he wants to tell me?"

"Hear 'im yourself." Joe motioned with his wire brush toward the back of the stable where Daniel was sitting on a stool, untangling a length of rope.

The boy'd cleaned up nice. His clothes were a touch less dirty. Fletcher had been a little older than Daniel the first time he'd lived anywhere reliable enough for tidying himself up. That hadn't been an overly friendly place. These mews would be a far better arrangement for Daniel. That knowledge eased some of Fletcher's worries for the boy.

"I see he's still staying here." Their rescued little ones didn't usually remain with their first guardians for very long.

"He likes the work, and he's helpful," Joe said.

Fletcher smiled. "And you've grown fond of him, I'd wager."

Joe simply nodded. "It's like havin' a little brother around. A cheeky little brother."

"I'll go see what your cheeky sibling has to tell me, shall I?"

"He has a colorful vocabulary," Joe warned.

"So do I." He wandered back to where Daniel sat. "I heard you tossed in your penny."

"Had something to tell you."

Fletcher pulled a penny from his pocket and spun it about. "I'm listening, boy."

"Someone's hanging around the school."

"I've heard Miss Black, who runs a girls' school, has been coming around."

"Ain't a woman."

That was a useful bit of information. "What does this man do that makes you think I'd need to know he's been here?"

"Been inspectin' the place, but not to know if it's safe."

"In what way, then?"

"The man I worked for, Mr. Allen, weren't just a sweep. He used sweepin' to sniff around homes and such for ways in and out and for sorting if they were worth fencing."

Fletcher had, himself, once been employed by a man who'd used honest work for hiding criminal undertakings, and he'd no doubt Daniel had been required to participate in the robberies just as Fletcher had been. He still carried a load of guilt over all the times he'd been made to do a bust and all the pockets he'd picked to survive. Did Daniel carry a heavy conscience as well? It was little wonder so many never escaped that life.

"Do you think someone means to burglarize the school?" he asked.

Daniel shook his head. "Ain't nothing in there worth makin' off with. The napper is lookin' for a way in, but the torches he carries ain't the type for lighting his way. He'd use a lantern if all he wanted was light."

"An arsonist?"

The boy shrugged. "Just thought you ought to know, since Mr. Hogg's school is important to you."

"It is important to me, on account of how it helps street children who live a life like I did."

Daniel eyed him with curiosity. "You did?"

"Aye. Lowest of the low, I was."

"Lower'n me?"

"Lower than the gutter itself. But a school like Hogg's and a good-souled few people like Joe gave me a way out. I cain't promise your future'll be cherries, but you'll not drudge away for the likes of Mr. Allen anymore. I'll swear to you that."

"It weren't the drudging that I hated most. I'd've robbed every house he asked me if he'd stop whippin' me."

Joe looked over, pain and concern in his eyes.

"Whipped you bad, did he?" Fletcher asked.

"Aye." Daniel looked up from his rope and over at Joe. "I told Mr. Fletcher what I seen. Can I have m' penny back now?"

"Soon as I'm done," Joe answered.

"And you'll read more 'bout them vampires?"

Joe glanced at Fletcher, allowing the tiniest bit of amusement to show. "Soon as I'm done."

That seemed to satisfy the boy, and he set back to work, not saying anything further.

Joe stopped Fletcher on his way out. "I've seen blood-stains on the boy's clothes and scars on his back and arms. That Mr. Allen beats him fierce. It was a good thing you got the boy away from the blackguard."

"I'd not leave any child in that sort of danger," Fletcher said. "Too many cain't escape it."

"But Daniel did, and the urchins here at the school have," Joe said. "That's somethin'."

"Sure is." It was something he meant to make happen more and more, if only he could keep his income flowing.

Fletcher stepped outside. The Dreadfuls suspected someone was attempting to undermine Hogg's ragged school, but this went far beyond that.

Was Hogg in danger? Were his students? Fletcher couldn't rest easy knowing that might be the case.

He moved with purposeful step to the front of the school. A knock, a quick explanation to the housekeeper, and he was shown into Hogg's office.

He wasn't alone. Miss Black sat across from his desk. She looked at the door briefly, then her posture stiffened. She turned slowly back, looking at him fully, brows up, eyes wide.

Hogg looked at him as well. "Mr. Walker. This is unexpected."

"My apologies," Fletcher said. "I wouldn't interrupt if it weren't urgent."

"What is it?"

"I've come to offer a warning. Someone's been casing your school."

"A burglar?" Hogg guessed.

"The current theory is an arsonist."

Hogg's shoulders grew rigid. Miss Black sucked in a breath.

"I cain't divulge my source," Fletcher said, "but it's a reliable one. I'd suggest extra caution."

"Can you think of anyone who would wish to destroy your school?" Miss Black asked Hogg.

"Plenty," he said. "There are those blackguards who are upset that our efforts take young children off the streets and out of their reach. There are others who simply hate that we educate children who they feel don't deserve it: the destitute, those with less than pristine backgrounds, immigrants."

"This makes my concern of adopting more effective teaching methods seem rather insignificant," Miss Black said.

"For any school, improved teaching is never an insignificant pursuit."

Fletcher stepped back toward the office door. "I ain't meaning to take up more of your time. Let me know if I can do anything to help."

Miss Black rose. "I should be going as well."

Proper farewells were offered, and Fletcher quickly found himself on the school's front step with Miss Black beside him. Miss Black, who apparently knew Mr. King and was lying to him about it.

"Perhaps we might share a hackney," she said.

A good suggestion. No sooner were they situated inside the hired conveyance than Fletcher jumped on the topic biting at his brain.

"I read Mr. King's latest installment."

"And what is your opinion of it?"

She showed not the least trepidation. Did she think he

wouldn't notice the parallels? Perhaps she didn't realize King had used what she'd told him. "I didn't care for his portrayal of me."

That captured her full attention.

"You told me once that you were smart and sorted things easily. I ain't exactly bacon-brained myself, dearie. For King to have written what he did, you have to know him, and know him well enough to tell him bits of a private conversation you and I had. The jig's up."

She folded her hands quite primly on her lap. "Would you care to hear about another jig that is up—one involving you?"

There were any number of jigs involving him. Which one was she thinking of?

She tugged on the ribbons of her wrist bag and reached inside, pulling out a coin. She held the penny between her finger and thumb, eyeing it with almost theatrical interest. "Janey has one of these she carries with her at all times. She says she received it from you. Her sister has one she received from Mr. Irving. The little sweep who was rescued from his awful employer and who now works at Hogg's stables carries one as well. Your shoeshine spy did too. I have seen Mr. Irving and yourself jaunting about the streets, tossing and spinning pennies. Both of you are penny dreadful authors. Coincidence?" She slipped the penny back in her bag, then looked to him once more. "Or membership token?"

He didn't know whether to be impressed or annoyed. The hack rocked and swayed as it navigated the uneven streets of London.

"So what do we do now?" he asked. They both knew things the other wished they didn't.

"You tell me about the Dread Penny Society, and I will tell you about Mr. King."

"That ain't my bit to share."

"I find myself with similar constraints," she said.

He could appreciate that. "We share what we can, then."

She nodded. "You first, please."

"The Dread Penny Society *does* exist." That much he could admit to.

"So does Mr. King."

Neither was telling the other anything they didn't already know. He'd get nowhere in his search for King if she wouldn't share more.

"I'm a member." She likely didn't realize how shocked she ought to be that he'd told her.

"I know Mr. King very well." Something in her tone told him her revelation was a significant one for her as well.

"The DPS ain't villains like some think."

She nodded. "Mr. King is adamant about privacy for very good reasons, none of which I am at liberty to disclose."

"Will you tell me if that ever changes?"

She agreed. "And will you tell me what the membership requirements are for your secret society?"

It was an unexpected question. "Do you think King'd be interested in joining?" That would solve a great many of their difficulties.

"Perhaps."

Promising. "We ask very little. One must write penny dreadfuls."

"Which King does."

"And be dedicated to relieving the suffering of the vulnerable."

"I believe you will find that to be a significant aspect of King's character."

Interesting. "Bein' trustworthy with the group's secrets is an absolute must."

"King can keep a secret, believe me. Anything else?"

There really wasn't, but he couldn't help but add one more thing. "We require members don't neglect to wear their trousers to meetings."

"Really?"

"Ain't none of us allowed to violate that rule," he said.

"I will relay that important information." She nodded slowly. "And where does the DPS meet?"

"*That* I ain't permitted to tell you, Miss Black."

"We know enough of each other's secrets, I believe, that, at least in private conversation, you may call me Elizabeth."

"Fletcher," he said with a dip of his head.

"If I am understanding correctly, Fletcher, Mr. King can join your Dread Penny Society if he commits himself to the care of the vulnerable, keeps the group's secrets, wears trousers, and can find the group's meeting location."

"That'd be the bulk of it."

"I do have one more question. Why is your organization the 'Dread Penny' Society? Do you find pennies particularly upsetting?"

He shook his head. "It's in part a play on words. *Penny* and *dreadful* flipped about. It's also a callout to a man in America, a slave who argued for his freedom, who made a case for all people's freedom. Dred Scott's his name. He's the sort of bold we aspire to be."

The hack came to a stop outside Thurloe School. Elizabeth moved to slip out.

"Tell Mr. King I look forward to someday meeting him," Fletcher said.

"I will."

"And, Elizabeth?"

"Yes?"

"I look forward to seeing you again, as well."

She smiled and stepped out, but turned back before closing the door. "Thank you for sending me Janey. She is a delight."

"Send Mr. King my way, and I'll consider us even," he said.

"Be careful what you wish for, Fletcher Walker. The result may not be quite what you bargained for."

"Is something wrong with Mr. King?"

She raised a brow, but offered no explanation.

The mystery of Mr. King was growing. The pull he felt to Elizabeth Black, however, was eclipsing even that.

CHAPTER 14

"B e certain to speak to Gunderson about your music program," Mr. Headley said, following Elizabeth around the drawing room as she straightened furniture and knickknacks. "He has strong feelings about the importance of musical instruction."

She was hosting a salon that evening, one focused on the state of education in England. Her other purpose was, as always, to make certain the influential in Town thought well of her and her school. She had done this before. More often, in fact, than Mr. Headley had.

"And Horner is a stickler for the most basic education, so you ought to de-emphasize your science and more complicated mathematic courses. He won't appreciate those classes being offered to female students."

Elizabeth took a calming breath. She knew all of this. And he must have realized she did. Yet he had spent the better part of the last ten minutes explaining to her, in a voice of authority, what he apparently doubted she comprehended. Mr. Headley could have fine manners when he chose, and he could be very thoughtful, but at times he was an absolute thorn.

Still, she knew what was expected of a well-mannered lady. Antagonizing him when she needed all the allies she could muster for the evening's efforts would have been foolish. She simply smiled politely and finished her inspection of the room.

"Midgley is in a position to help financially," Mr. Headley continued, keeping on her heels as she stepped into the entryway. "You must do all you can to convince him of the value of your efforts."

When she turned to face him, he very nearly collided with her. "Why does the success of my school matter so much to *you*?" It had not before occurred to her that he must have had some reason to be so determined to see her school—and *her*—succeed. They were not family. He was not truly courting her, at least not with any urgency.

"For one thing, I, too, have invested in this school." He spoke with a small upturn of his lips, adding a teasing quality to his very mercenary explanation. "For another, I appreciate what you are doing here. These young girls receive a good and proper education. They leave your school better prepared for life and less likely to fall on times of poverty and misery. Any feeling person must appreciate that."

While his first answer was clearly a jesting one, his second emerged with inarguable sincerity.

"These girls deserve the chance to rise above their difficult circumstances," she said. None were destitute by any means, but none had been born to the degree of wealth girls at other schools claimed. Neither were they candidates for ragged schools or trade apprenticeships. Thurloe Collegiate School filled that gap.

"The right word dropped in the right ear tonight will help with that."

She stifled a sigh. She could always count on Mr. Headley's condescension to ruin a moment.

She didn't truly blame him; if one went by the view and opinion of the general public, women were designed to be condescended to. They were meant to keep quiet and be soft and not cross any lines no matter how small. Revealing she wrote sordid tales of intrigue and romantic derring-do was a rather enormous line. Standing up for herself to a man at or above her station would be considered one as well.

Fortunately, Ana appeared, saving Elizabeth the difficulty of determining how to appropriately respond to Mr. Headley when what she wished most to do was tell him to take himself off.

"I am so very nervous," Ana said, fussing with the small ruffles at the cuff of her pale-blue dress. "I haven't the first idea how to interact with important people."

Elizabeth remembered well feeling the same way when she first began undertaking the herculean effort of securing the earliest patrons for the school she meant to open. "You needn't think of this as playing a part, Ana. You love this school and the girls in it. You are personable and enjoy conversing. There is only one gentleman I will suggest you not discuss your music classes with; Mr. Headley or I will point him out to you. Otherwise, simply be your good, kind-hearted self."

She squared her shoulders, an almost comical sight

considering her slight build. "If you have that much faith in me, then I shall have a bit of faith in myself."

If only Mr. Headley considered her so competent.

"Be certain you greet your guests personally," he said.

Elizabeth, her back to him, looked to Ana and rolled her eyes. Ana bit back a smile, all the while maintaining her flawless aura of grace. She would be a welcome addition to the evening's undertaking, not merely because she would make a good impression on the guests, but because Elizabeth so thoroughly enjoyed her company.

The guests began arriving within minutes of the expected time, and Mr. Headley whispered advice to her regarding each new arrival. Good heavens, did the man think she couldn't retain the slightest bit of information in her, apparently, minuscule mind? She was juggling two separate successful literary endeavors, including one that required detailed strategy and subterfuge. She was headmistress of her own school despite not having reached the age of thirty. She balanced ledgers, coordinated schedules, met with tradesmen, oversaw her staff. Could he not afford her the tiniest bit of confidence?

By the time the last of the arrivals had been greeted and motioned into the drawing room, Elizabeth knew she would have to maneuver away from Mr. Headley most of the night or she would be hard-pressed not to physically shake him. Such unladylike behavior would end the evening's endeavor before it even began.

She was nearly finished with a chapter of her penny dreadful in which Lucinda was facing an upsetting situation. Her heroine was handling that challenge with more dignity than Elizabeth was facing hers. The thought gave her pause.

Was she casting Mr. Headley in the role of the dangerous entity in the forest? A laugh bubbled inside. How unexpected. She had occasionally thought of Mr. Walker in the role of the frustrating Sir Frederick. How many other people in her life were making an appearance in this story?

"Miss Black, come add your voice to our debate." Mr. Horner motioned her over.

She slipped quickly in that direction, hoping Mr. Headley would be distracted enough not to follow. "What is the topic of your discussion?"

"Some in Parliament are pushing the passage of a bill requiring the education of all children from all classes and monetary circumstances," Mr. Horner said. "We were discussing the positives and negatives of such a proposal."

"As an educator myself, I most certainly have strong views on this matter," she said.

"We knew you would."

Mr. and Mrs. Horner, the widower Mr. Gunderson, Mr. Midgley, the aged Miss Barrow, and Mr. Rowland all watched her, waiting for her continue. This was a complicated shoal to navigate. She needed to show herself knowledgeable and firm, while not offending those with differing positions, but also not appearing weak in the eyes of those whose views matched her own. Sometimes conversations required the most ridiculous of dances.

"As there is also talk of further extending voting rights, we would do well to consider the benefit of an educated populace when that populace is granted a voice in the running of our nation." She could see that controversial topic didn't sit well with everyone in the group and quickly added, "I am not taking a position on the topic of broader suffrage, only including education as a positive element should the vote be granted to more people."

That appeased them. Oh, what she wouldn't give to actually be Mr. King, a man dependent on no one's approval who could enjoy a degree of freedom a woman with a school to keep solvent would never know.

"Literacy allows for the reading of the Bible and other improving texts," she added, "which we can all agree would be of benefit to everyone and, which, perhaps, would help address the crime we experience here in Town."

"But literacy also means such individuals are spending their time and their money—likely stolen coins—on low literature," Mr. Midgley objected. "It is not, after all, the upper classes or even the educated middle class who read those shocking penny dreadfuls."

That received nods of agreement. Little did they know how many upper-class people read those sordid tales. And that at least one well-educated individual *wrote* them. She kept her thoughts to herself. She hadn't the freedom of being fully forthright.

"A more formal education might turn their literary tastes higher, though," Mrs. Horner said. "That is another positive of educating the less-fortunate."

"And what would they benefit from reading of far-off places they can never visit or of lofty positions they can never attain? Why acquire such newfound literacy if it merely fills their minds with empty hopes?" Mr. Midgley asked. "What we will create is a generation of discouraged and disappointed people. They will feel cheated of something that was never promised to them, and the entire kingdom will be made to suffer for it."

"Suffer, how?" Elizabeth hoped her question sounded more curious than indignant, though she felt a tremendous amount of the latter.

"Workers who are discontented with their lot in life are unlikely to be good workers," he said. "The poor, who, through education, believe themselves entitled to wealth and comfort, will never recognize that they, themselves, are the cause of their low station."

"And those who are not?" Elizabeth posed the question without thinking. If she was not careful, she was going to be the cause of her own low station.

"Are not *what*?" he returned, clearly surprised that she had not simply agreed with him. "Are not poor? Are not educated?"

"Are not actively creating their difficulties? Are we to deny them the betterment of their minds because of their birth?"

He had no immediate answer.

Mr. Horner entered the discussion. "I am certain Miss Black is not proposing education be offered beyond that which is helpful and appropriate. The poor have no need of Latin, for example."

Most of those gathered tonight likely also thought girls had no need of higher mathematics or education in the sciences, yet both were taught—and well received—at Thurloe. Would gaining or keeping the approval of these patrons mean she would be required to change that? She wouldn't, but it might very well cost her their support.

"As our students here at Thurloe do not hail from that

portion of society, I feel I am less of an authority on those matters." It was the truth, though that didn't mean she didn't have an opinion. "Our girls' families are from the middle class, far from poverty but lacking the cachet and wealth to either choose a more exclusive educational establishment or have their education seen to at home through a governess, a dancing master, and a musical teacher, and so forth. We are providing the same level of education they would be receiving under slightly different circumstances and not contributing to any disenchantment or confusion."

Mr. Gunderson looked askance at her mention of dancing and music instruction, but as such was quite acceptable in a young lady's education at home, which was what she had referenced, he didn't appear to truly object. Perhaps she had tiptoed her way around that difficulty.

"Offering these very useful educations to young ladies who will, then, prove themselves quite able and respectable members of society is a worthwhile pursuit, I believe." She offered a soft smile, one meant to take any self-serving edge off her words. "All of the young ladies who have completed their studies here are raising fine families, teaching in other respectable institutions, or otherwise proving themselves an asset to the kingdom."

She received a few nods of approval, even a quiet "Bravo" from Mr. Rowland.

"One does not object to the education of those who ought to be receiving it," Mr. Midgley said. "But indulging the indolent and criminal-minded in their demand for more resources, when their contribution will not be increased by the investment, is nothing short of robbery. One must wonder what the ragged schools are about."

Elizabeth did not trust herself to respond without setting fire to every bridge she was attempting to build. If only life did not require her to toady to men like Midgley.

She dipped a brief curtsey and stepped away under the guise of greeting other guests. While she offered mindless "good evenings" and "so glad you are here" to others nearby, she took deep breaths and calmed her overwhelmed mind. *Indulging the indolent and criminal-minded?* Was it any wonder those born into the worst of conditions struggled to escape when this was the assumption people made about them?

"You look troubled," Mr. Headley said as he stepped up beside her near the tall windows.

"Nothing unexpected, unfortunately. Mr. Midgley expressed some rather disparaging opinions about the education of the poor."

"Did he dismiss your students as too poor?"

She shook her head. "I do not think this will negatively impact the perception of Thurloe, but it is still discouraging."

"You cannot fight all the world's battles," he said not unkindly. "Focus on the purpose of this evening for now. It is important enough to warrant your full attention."

Though he was not wrong, she found herself unappreciative of the advice. She knew perfectly well that the evening's undertaking was important, yet something in his response rather annoyed her.

She gave her usual smile and nod. Heaven knew she had perfected that polite but empty response over the years.

"Besides," Mr. Headley continued, "those running the

ragged schools will be quite accustomed to opinions such as Mr. Midgely expressed. They will have undertaken their efforts despite the naysayers. Unkind words are unlikely to close their schools."

Mr. Headley kept speaking, though Elizabeth no longer heeded him.

Attitudes like Mr. Midgley's were precisely the sort likely to motivate someone to undermine Mr. Hogg's efforts. Hogg's school took in the lowest of children, the poorest, those Mr. Midgely would dismiss out of hand. Was it possible he would do more than merely "dismiss" them? Would a man of his standing be upset enough, and violent enough, to take more drastic measures?

She hoped not but couldn't feel entirely certain. Her suspicions were strong enough to warrant discussing them with someone who would take them seriously.

"Pardon me," she said to Mr. Headley, then slipped from the room, making her way to the kitchen.

Janey was there, just as she had hoped.

"I need to send a quick message to Mr. Walker. Are you able to get word to him?" Elizabeth knew Fletcher had given Janey a penny and that it was connected to the mysterious Dread Penny Society.

"I surely can, Miss Black."

"Would you send word that I need to speak with him?"

"Now, Miss Black?"

"Please."

Janey left forthwith. As she slipped out, Elizabeth saw her take a penny from her apron pocket and fold it in her tight fist.

If she were Mr. King instead of Miss Black, would she have access to these seemingly magical pennies? Surely *he* would have been permitted to join the Dread Penny Society and wouldn't be relegated to spending an evening offering up empty smiles and nods and being careful never to give the impression of anything other than perfect propriety.

She played that role well the remainder of the evening. Compliments were frequent enough to tell her she'd successfully convinced the attendees she was all that was prim and proper. She didn't mind the charade. It allowed her to spend an inordinate amount of time daydreaming of adventures and mysteries . . . and penny spinning.

CHAPTER 15

All the guests had left, and the school was quiet. Elizabeth sat in her office, lantern lit, attempting to work on her next silver-fork novel. If too much time passed between releases of her respectable work, people might begin to wonder. Her thoughts, though, continually returned to Lucinda, her standoffish gentleman neighbor, and her mysterious highwayman.

She had come to thoroughly enjoy her "shocking" literary pursuits despite the way it complicated her life.

"Well, Mr. King, it seems you have thrust me into an unwanted crisis of identity. I don't know whether to curse you or thank you."

A soft rap sounded. She listened more closely and heard it again. A knock at the front door. This late?

She stepped from her office, pulling her knit wrap more closely around her shoulders, and moved slowly, cautiously, toward the door. Lucinda had managed to conquer her fear when an unexpected arrival had interrupted her nighttime tranquility. Elizabeth could certainly summon her courage as well.

If the person on the other side had nefarious intentions, she would need to be prepared to defend herself and her school, but she hadn't the first clue how to accomplish that.

She stepped to the long, narrow window beside the door, pulled back the curtain, and peaked outside. Dimly lit by the gas streetlights, Fletcher Walker stood on the front step, as confident in this odd moment as ever. He spotted her in the window and, to her amusement, winked.

She opened the door, then leaned against the doorpost, tipping her head at a jaunty angle. "This is highly inappropriate, Mr. Walker. It is well past the time for callers."

He held up a penny before flipping it to her. "Janey'll be wanting her penny back."

"Do penny messages always bring you so swiftly?"

"Yes," he said quite seriously. "Though, any note from you would have had my feet moving at a fine clip toward Thurloe."

"Because I am so frightening?"

He smiled. "No."

"Then why?" She knew she wasn't keeping her enjoyment of their banter hidden, but she wasn't bothered by her transparency.

"I think that'd be obvious."

The man could certainly be flirtatious when he chose to be. "Because my air of authority is so strong it can be felt several miles away?"

"Several counties, in fact."

She motioned him in. "You do realize if word of your visit at this late hour spreads, my reputation will never recover."

"Never fear, darlin'. I am shockingly good at keeping secrets." He slipped past her.

"I'm quite talented in that respect, myself."

He looked back at her, eyes dancing. "What dastardly secrets are you keeping, Miss Black?"

"Not dastardly, per se, but definitely of interest." She motioned him into her office.

"Of interest to me, by chance?" he asked.

Oh, he didn't know the half of it. She simply shrugged and moved past him, sitting in a chair by her empty fireplace. He eyed it.

"It's a touch cold tonight to not be having at least a small fire."

"This fireplace smokes," she said. "Several do throughout the school. We're bundling until I can get them swept."

"If Janey's summons was for me to sweep the chimneys, you'll be sorely disappointed. I've done a lot of things in my time, but sweeping ain't one of 'em."

"Then I suppose you'll have to be going," she said with a smile.

He answered with one of his own. "I'll take m'chances." He sat. "Janey made your summons sound urgent. Has something happened?"

"I had a soiree here at the school tonight."

He pressed a hand to his heart. "And you didn't invite me. I'm wounded, I am."

She knew a jesting tone when she heard one. "I was cultivating support and approval for my school. Are you truly disappointed to have not been included on my list of—"

"Victims?" he supplied.

"Potential advocates in society," she corrected.

"*My* approval would likely turn society off of your work here," he said. "Wise of you not to have me on your list."

"But I know you care a great deal about the welfare of children, so your approval of my efforts here means something to *me*." It was more than she'd intended to admit, yet, there it was.

"You're changing children's lives for the better, Elizabeth. That's a fine thing."

"The Dread Penny Society would condone my efforts?"

"We've helped a number of schools. We've enough of us dedicated to education and children's welfare to make 'em a focus."

"You said at the York Place ragged school that, when pondering who might want to hinder or stop the mission of Mr. Hogg's school, one had to consider those who oppose educating the poor."

He nodded. "That the children are poor is most naysayers' objection."

"Someone who was here this evening said something very much along those lines and fervently enough to be more than an idle observation."

He sat up straighter. "Made threats, did he?"

She held up a hand to forestall that train of thought. "Not directly. I cannot say with any authority whether or not he might be prone to violence, but his words struck too close to those you and Hogg expressed concern over that I could not be easy about it."

Fletcher rose and, scratching absentmindedly at his jawline, paced away. "I'd assumed our would-be arsonist'd be a lower- or working-class bloke. Not that the uppers cain't be just as despicable. They've other methods, though: laws and keeping back funds. Arson seems unnecessary."

"Do you think he can be eliminated as a suspect, then?" She wasn't certain one way or the other, not having been a detective before.

"We've not enough to go on." He leaned against the mantelshelf, turning to face her. "You've a better acquaintance with this loudmouth than I do. Where would we go to spy on this lout?"

We. That was an intriguing word choice. She stood and stepped over to him. "Are you suggesting we form a partnership?"

That barely-there flirtatious smile of his made a reappearance. "I think we could make a fine team, Elizabeth."

She couldn't tell if it was a bit of flattery or a genuine compliment. This might be her one opportunity to be a pseudomember of the famed Dread Penny Society, though. She could hardly turn that down.

With confidence, she said, "He is likely to be where most fashionable people will be tomorrow evening: the opening of a new opera."

Fletcher nodded. "I've a mate with access to a box he'd allow us the use of."

"That sounds ideal," she said. "May I ask who this unsuspecting benefactor is?"

"Hollis Darby."

That made a great deal of sense. "How do you intend to keep our true purpose a secret from him?"

"I'll tell him I'm hoping to impress you with a fine evening of fashionable society."

"He'll think you're courting me." Surely he didn't want to give his friend that impression.

"I can survive them sort of whispers."

Was that a tone of challenge she heard in his voice? "I can make the effort believable, if you can."

He leaned closer, his voice lowered. "Then I will see you tomorrow evening, Elizabeth."

His nearness, the warmth in his eyes, the lowness of his tone—all conspired to set her pulse thrumming in her throat. "Tomorrow evening."

Swiftly, silently, and without a backward glance, he slipped out.

Good heavens. What had she agreed to?

THE VAMPIRE'S TOWER
AN URCHINS OF LONDON ADVENTURE

by Fletcher Walker

Chapter IV

Sneaking unseen into an unfamiliar place would be far easier in the dark of night. But the sun wouldn't drop out of the sky for hours, and they needed to check on George and any others who were there, now. And they needed to find out what had slid past the tower window.

Morris waved Jimmy alongside the treacherous tower, both boys eyeing the grounds for anyone wandering about. They didn't dare get caught sneaking around, no matter if there was danger here or not. Most people took a dim view of trespassing.

Footsteps rustled nearby. Morris and Jimmy ducked down behind a thick shrubbery. They held their breath. No one ever passed.

"There's got to be a window or somethin'," Jimmy whispered, slipping farther around the tower. Morris followed, acting as lookout.

Around they went. The tower was larger than it had seemed from across the yard.

"Anyone coming?" Jimmy asked.

"No. Any windows low enough?"

"No." Jimmy abruptly stopped. "But there's a door."

That pulled Morris's attention. Jimmy wasn't looking straight ahead or even up a little. His eyes were angled down.

"A cellar?" Morris guessed. He couldn't think of anything else a door in the ground would lead to.

"Or a crypt." Jimmy really had been spooked by whatever he'd seen in the tower window to jump to that possibility.

"A crypt'd be under a church, though." Morris reached for the iron-ring handle. "I'd wager this is our way in."

Jimmy shoved out a breath. "Mind you, if this proves to be another monster, I run faster than you do."

He eyed Jimmy. "You owe me for that redcap, you know."

A bit of amusement tugged at his friend's mouth. "We escaped the murderin' goblin, didn't we?"

"*You* escaped. I fought the blasted thing." It had been one of their more terrifying adventures.

Jimmy rolled his eyes. "I came back and helped, di'n't I?"

"If there's a redcap down here," Morris said, pointing into the dimness beyond the door, "I'm closing this and locking you in with it."

Jimmy sobered quickly. "It weren't a redcap. I don't know what it was, but it weren't that."

Morris swallowed, telling himself to hold it together. They'd urchins to search out and rescue. It wasn't anything they hadn't done before.

"Are we goin' to be able to see in there?" Jimmy asked.

"I've no idea."

Turned out, they could, but only just. And being able

to see when there were no windows and no lanterns and no candles wasn't reassuring.

"Where's the light coming from?" Morris whispered, carefully tiptoeing across the empty expanse, which was nothing but pillars and a stone floor, though they couldn't see the entire space all at once. The tower really was larger than it seemed.

A sound stopped them up short. A howling sort of cry.

"Wind?" Jimmy asked, voice so low it was almost silent.

"That weren't the wind wailin'."

"I didn't think so." Jimmy was an odd sort, always rallying when the danger grew. None of the worry that had shook his voice when he'd first seen the shadowy figure in the windows above remained. With firmness, he said, "Let's sniff out the stairs, see if we can't Jenny the situation."

They wove around more columns, more turns. The cellar was musty, dank, and bitterly cold. Still no lanterns or torches or candles, but somehow still plenty enough light for seeing their way. Again the cries were heard overhead. Without needing to consult, Morris and Jimmy moved faster, searching every turn for steps.

They came upon an alcove carved directly in the thick stone outer wall. Morris sucked in a sharp breath. On an iron platform at the base of the alcove sat a dusty, beaten-up, probably centuries-old coffin. The walls around it glowed, but for no reason he could see.

"Blimey," Morris muttered, a shiver sliding down his spine. "This *is* a crypt."

"Told you I ain't addle-headed."

"And I ain't so soaped that I mean to stay here, staring

at a glowing coffin." Morris stepped backward, putting more distance between himself and the alcove.

"But how do we get out?" Jimmy looked around. "Never did find the stairs."

"We could back slang it." Morris poked his thumb in the direction of the door they'd used to climb into the crypt.

"Won't fudge, mate. We came to undertake a rescue. We don't walk away."

He wasn't wrong about that. They'd never once refused to help someone in danger, no matter the terror of the situation, and they wouldn't start now. "We keep looking for the way up, then. And we keep a weather eye on that dead bloke. I don't trust him one lick."

They moved quick but quiet, following the outer wall, eyeing each twist and turn around the pillars. Was it meant to be a maze, or were they simply getting turned about?

"Something ain't right about this." Morris felt certain they'd returned to a section of the crypt they'd been in before. But it all looked so alike. Same stone. Same pillars. Same odd, unearthly glow.

Before Jimmy could answer, the creak of a rusty hinge echoed throughout the crypt. A door? Or—Morris's heart leaped to his throat—the coffin?

"Cheese it," Morris said, moving swiftly away from the direction he thought he remembered the alcove being, Jimmy close on his heels.

Nothing but solid walls. Was there no way up? No way out?

"We back slang it, after all," Jimmy said. "Find another way up the tower."

"What if the door we came through is the hinges we heard?"

Jimmy didn't even slow down. "Better than the coffin."

But they didn't find the door.

They found stairs. Narrow, winding, stone steps leading up and out of the crypt. They rushed, ran.

There were no more hinges creaking.

Now, there were footsteps.

❦

The master was awake.

CHAPTER 16

You swells sure know how to complicate simple things." Fletcher eyed his reflection, clad in Hollis's dress coat.

"You think attending the opera is a simple thing?"

"Always is down in the gallery." He still felt more at ease in the section of the audience where the servants and apprentices and poor folk watched.

Hollis shook his head. "If you think this is complicated, you should see how my brother prepares for a trip to the theater. It is like watching a performance before the performance."

The Darby family were termed "old money," except society didn't realize most of that money was gone. Hollis's grandfather had begun draining the family coffers back during the brief reign of the Prince Regent. His father had taken up the task shortly after Victoria ascended the throne. Hollis's older brother had inherited a fortune so small it was hardly worth the effort to spend irresponsibly.

"Maybe it's for the best King is draining away at my income," Fletcher said. "Being well-to-do is a lot of bother."

"You've played uncomfortable roles on behalf of the Dreadfuls before. Why does it rankle so much more this time?"

He flicked a hand, frustration getting the better of him.

"Perhaps because Miss Black will be there?" Hollis asked a little too innocently.

The fact that his nervousness increased at the guess told Fletcher his friend wasn't entirely wrong. Still, admitting as much wasn't on his short list of things he wanted to do. "Miss Black knows my origins."

"Does she?" Hollis clearly doubted it. "I doubt even the Dread Master knows all the details of your early life."

"The Dread Master values privacy."

"He's certainly convinced you to." Hollis set his hat atop his head. "I can't convince you to tell me who he is, and I know more of your secrets than anyone."

"As I said, this one ain't mine to tell."

"His identity impacts everyone in the society, including me. That makes it not entirely *his* secret."

This was an old argument between them, one Fletcher knew how to deflect. "And the state of your family's coffers impacts more than just you, but you'll not hear me whispering about it to anyone."

Hollis looked the tiniest bit repentant. His brother went to great lengths to hide the situation, in part to save his own pride but also to help assure that his son and daughter would not be rejected outright when they were grown.

"You're telling me I can't complain about you keeping others' secrets when you're also keeping mine?"

Fletcher nodded.

"Will you ever tell me who the Dread Master is?" Hollis asked. "Maybe on my deathbed?"

"Not even then." Fletcher tossed him a grin.

"Cruel, Fletch. You're cruel."

"What's cruel is these shoes. They pinch like a pensioner's pocketbook."

Hollis laughed. "What is an evening at the opera without a little suffering?"

"You ain't sweetening my opinion of this mad endeavor. Keep flapping your gums and I'm likely to let Miss Black take herself to the opera."

Hollis walked with him to the front door of Fletcher's town house. He didn't live in the grandest area of Town, but his address was nothing to be ashamed of.

"You'll have the company of a beautiful and clever woman," Hollis said. "If that's not enough to give you some enjoyment, then I'm not certain I know who you are anymore."

"She *is* beautiful," he admitted almost without thinking. "And, I suspect, clever enough to make me feel like a simpleton."

The carriage Doc Milligan had agreed to provide for the night sat outside. It was serviceable and clean, though little else could be said in its favor. If he didn't already look utterly out of place in Hollis's togs, then spilling out of that scraggly equipage to collect Elizabeth would do the trick. No doubt,

Mr. King's next installment would feature an inept buffoon arriving at the heroine's doorstep in laughable disgrace.

When she answered her door, however, she didn't seem the least struck by his appearance. She simply smiled, noted that he was right on time, and stepped outside to join him in the carriage, the sight of which didn't even slow her step.

"I have heard from Miss Newport, who heard from a friend who is friends with Mr. Midgley's sister—Mr. Midgley is the man we are spying on, you will remember—that he will be in the same box as Mr. Moon, current chairman of the London and North Western Railway." Elizabeth hadn't waited even a moment after the carriage door closed to speak. "I believe that box is not far from the Darby box. Near enough we should be able to watch him without difficulty."

"Watching can be helpful," Fletcher said. "We'll be too far for listening, though."

"Perhaps we shall have to make a call at their box."

Fletcher leaned back against the carriage squabs, eyeing Elizabeth with doubt. "They'd not bat an eye iffen *you* dropped in, but me taking a peek, well, they'd just as like toss me down to the gallery where I belong."

The gas streetlamps cast light through the carriage windows, gently illuminating her face. "I think you underestimate yourself, Fletcher Walker."

"I think you *over*estimate me, Elizabeth Black."

She threaded her gloved fingers, watching him with keen interest. "What if I told you Mr. King read your most recent offering and has expressed concern that you will soon surpass his sales and put an end to his reign of success?"

He hated to admit how much good that did his oft-battered pride. And yet . . . . "I'd say Mr. King is either too generous or too insecure. His writing's something new and unique. There's a reason he's at the top of the heap."

Her interest grew more pointed. "If his success relies on the newness of his approach, is there any longevity in that?"

"You care a lot about Mr. King's success."

"I do." She made the admission without the least hesitation. Just how close were she and King?

He leaned forward, elbows on his legs. "Have you no care for *my* success?" He allowed a bit of flirtation.

She cocked an eyebrow and, with a hint of coquetry herself, said, "Oh, I care very much about your success this evening."

"Do you, now?"

"This is my first venture into the world of clandestine spy work. If you fail, I will as well." She leaned forward, mimicking his posture. "And I care very much about *my* success."

He lowered his voice to a more intimate whisper. "How very ambitious of you."

She matched his volume and tone. "Do you find ambition in a lady intimidating?"

"On the contrary. I find it irresistible."

"How very un-British of you."

He laughed. "The Brits worth knowing agree with me."

"A shame I am unacquainted with anyone 'worth knowing.'"

Fletcher never enjoyed anyone's company as much as those who brought a smile to his face. She was firmly on that list.

Though he'd grumbled a great deal to Hollis about how

he had to dress when among the fine and proper, Fletcher realized within moments of arriving inside the Royal Opera House that his friend had been bang on the mark. If not for the togs of refinement, Fletcher would've been as out of place as Prince Albert in a fish market. Instead, he walked with Elizabeth on his arm feeling entirely at home. Or very nearly, at least. He was playing a part, after all; he didn't truly belong in this glittering world of finery. And he knew Elizabeth knew it. He would do well to remember that, no matter the enjoyment he had in their conversations.

She greeted a few people, dipped curtsies, smiled. She knew more people than he did, but he was surprised at how many familiar faces he spotted amongst the theatergoers, and not merely those in the pit and gallery.

McCallister Rhys offered a bow as Elizabeth and Fletcher approached their box. Dreadfuls didn't often acknowledge their acquaintance outside of meetings at headquarters unless their connection was already well established and known. What was behind the unusual break from protocol? Rhys didn't say anything. Perhaps he had been greeting Elizabeth.

"Who was that?" Her question put paid to that theory.

"A man named Rhys. He also writes penny dreadfuls. I'm surprised to see him here. He ain't Society."

She leaned in closer and whispered, "Are the two mutually exclusive?"

"They ain't exactly birds of a feather."

"Many would say we aren't either."

How true that was. "Seems you're to be a risk-taker tonight."

She set her free hand on his arm, sighing lightly. "Do not blame me if I prove terrible at it."

"Oh, I intend to blame you, Miss Black."

They stepped into their box, and he led her to the chairs at the front. The formalities were all seen to. She was seated. He was seated. She pulled out her fan and began plying it with grace and elegance. He told himself not to fidget or glance longingly at the gallery. If he pretended he belonged in this world, others wouldn't wonder what he was doing among them.

Elizabeth set her hand atop his, an innocent gesture, one employed in an almost incidental manner, but the casualness of it ill-prepared him for the impact of the simple touch. His pulse pounded in his ears and chest. His thoughts momentarily emptied.

"Mr. Moon's box is just there." She motioned beyond him with her head. "And Mr. Midgley is in the box even now."

Fletcher adjusted his position enough to glance in that direction without being too obvious about it. He recognized Mr. Moon as well as another gentleman in the box. He did not, however, know which of the other half-dozen men was their target.

Elizabeth, apparently, guessed at his ignorance. "He is the shorter of the gentlemen who are standing—the one with the sour face and overly thick muttonchop whiskers."

The curtain rose. Elizabeth's attention shifted to the stage. Her hand, to his surprise, remained on his. She may well have merely been embracing her role in their charade, but he hadn't any complaints.

One thing he knew about operas: few were in English.

This one, from the sound of it, was in Italian. He knew little of that language beyond "Yes," "No," and the colorful expressions used by the Italian musicians who busked on the streets near Covent Garden. Elizabeth, however, became entirely engrossed in the music.

"I ain't got the first idea what they're singing about," he whispered, "but it's nice."

"I will let you in on a secret, Fletcher. I don't understand Italian, either."

"Seems to me I should've come with Hollis. He could've translated."

"Perhaps," she said. "But would he have held your hand?"

Fletcher shrugged. "He might've tried, but I'd not've enjoyed it half as much."

"You're enjoying it?" She sounded a little doubtful.

He raised their entwined hands to his lips. "I'm enjoying it immensely."

Fletcher kissed her fingers one at a time, lingering over each one. His pulse picked up with each kiss, his heart pounding ever harder.

"It's a shame some of the rules Society has," he said.

"What do you mean?" Her voice was airy, almost noiseless.

He unbent her fingers and, palm to palm, turned her hand in his. "I'm not overly fond of gloves."

"We're attempting to blend in." Her voice grew ever more unsteady. "Clasping bare hands would draw attention."

He leaned the teeniest bit closer, dropping his voice to an intimate whisper. "Perhaps another time, dear."

"Perhaps," she whispered.

He threaded their fingers once more and returned his

attention to the stage. They sat that way through the remainder of the first act. As the performance reached its intermission, Elizabeth slipped her hand free of his.

"Should we call on Mr. Moon's box and see if we can get any helpful information?" She, apparently, hadn't been distracted from their purpose, more was the pity.

Fletcher looked over at the box. "He's ain't there."

"He's not?"

No one else had left that box. "How often do gentry coves take themselves off before the opera's over?"

"More often than you might think. They make an appearance, shake the right hands, then go spend the evening at their club."

"I suspect he might have."

They watched awhile longer, but Midgley never returned, neither did anyone from the box appear to be expecting him.

"Seems we've lost our quarry," Fletcher said. "Not the greatest spies, you and I."

She didn't mirror his humor, but said, in all seriousness, "I suppose there's no reason to remain, then."

No reason? Was sitting together swapping banter and holding hands not at least some reason? He'd thought she'd been enjoying herself enough to stay. Fool that he was, he'd even let himself imagine she'd been pleased to be with him.

Fletcher called upon all of his acting skills and walked with Elizabeth out of the opera house without giving the least indication he was disappointed. He'd learned long ago to hold himself together in times of difficulty. When he'd been rejected from the poor schools in London for being too poor. When he'd finally been admitted to a ragged school like

Hogg's only to struggle to learn and to have the other students laugh at him every time he declared his intention to make a success of himself. When he'd endured one beating after another from masters and landladies and been tossed out on his tiny ear for objecting. He knew how to hide his pain. No one would guess it was there now—not even her.

They sent word to the line of carriages that they were ready to depart. Elizabeth did not seem in the mood to talk, so they waited in silence. Milligan's carriage arrived. Elizabeth was handed up, but the driver motioned for Fletcher to wait a moment.

"Thought you'd want to know Mr. Midgley's coachman said he'd be taking his master to the Serpentine tomorrow during the fashionable hour."

That was helpful information, indeed.

Fletcher thanked him, tossing the man a gold coin, before climbing inside the carriage.

"Turns out, Elizabeth, this evening weren't a complete waste."

She was clearly intrigued.

"Care to undertake an outing tomorrow?"

She smiled. "Absolutely."

Perhaps it hadn't been such a disaster after all.

CHAPTER 17

Elizabeth had been to Kensington Gardens before. She rather loved it. The flowering shrubs. The beautiful, towering trees. The meandering paths winding through the deep green grass. There was hardly a more peaceful place in all of London. Being there with Fletcher proved both *more* enjoyable and less.

She delighted in his company. He was witty and kind, never spoke down to her, and treated her as someone worthy of his time, which not all men were willing to do. Yet he also upended her. Her usually ordered thoughts jumbled and fogged. Being with him was a most pleasantly uncomfortable experience.

She spun her open parasol against her shoulder, enjoying the breeze and the vista. "I do wish Kensington Gardens sat closer to Thurloe. I would come here every day."

"I thought fashionable people made the outing to Hyde Park quite regularly."

Hyde Park and Kensington Gardens adjoined one another, separated by the meandering Serpentine. "Fashionable people with a great deal of time on their hands come here often. I have left Thurloe more the past few days than in the previous months combined."

He offered her a sparkling smile. "You're welcome."

"You're taking credit, are you?"

"Of course I am. Men don't often get credit for things."

"Pish." She laughed. "Men receive credit for *everything*."

He sighed theatrically. "We are rather despicable, ain't we?"

"A few of you aren't terrible."

"Am I included in that few?"

She offered no response. He laughed. Oh, how she enjoyed his company.

They wound toward the Serpentine, coming across a man who recognized Fletcher on the spot. He was not dressed to the first stare of fashion, but neither did he appear destitute. "Fletch, it's yourself, is it?" An Irishman, apparently. "Fancy you're being here."

Fletcher gripped his friend's hand vigorously in greeting. "Good seeing you, Brogan." He looked to Elizabeth. "Miss Black, this here's Brogan Donnelly, a friend of mine."

She knew that name well. "A fellow author of penny dreadfuls, I believe."

The Irishman nodded. "Are you familiar, then, with the lowest rung of literature?"

"Yes, and I am also familiar with the penny dreadfuls."

Mr. Brogan appeared impressed. "Witty and beautiful." He gave Fletcher a look of approval. "Don't tell me a ragamuffin like you is courting this rare gem?"

"I'm doing my best." He slipped her arm through his. Did he not mean to tell him that they were on a mission to obtain information for the Dread Penny Society? Was Brogan not a member? That seemed unlikely.

Still, if that was the better approach, Elizabeth would follow Fletcher's lead. She set her free hand atop his arm, assuming the posture of the countless courting couples in the gardens. Fletcher's eyes met hers, and the look he gave her would have convinced even the greatest cynic that he held her in tender regard. She didn't know what to make of that. Was he a very gifted actor, or did he feel more for her than he'd let on? She didn't know which was truer of herself.

"What is it you see in this ol' bag o' bones?" Mr. Donnelly asked. "He's not horrifying to look at, I suppose, but you're a fair bit above his touch."

"You ain't lying," Fletcher said.

"I don't think of us that way," she said. "We're both writers. We both care about the welfare of children. We're both deeply intrigued by mysteries."

Fletcher grinned. Mr. Donnelly did as well.

"Then I wish you all the good fortune you can muster." The Irishman offered a bow and moved along.

"I hadn't thought of that difficulty," Elizabeth said.

"That people will realize we're mismatched?"

She shook her head. "That people will *think* we're mismatched."

He tucked her closer. "We are, dear. No matter that I'm employin' my best manners, we ain't on the same ladder rung."

She tipped her chin upward. "It seems to me you have your eyes on the wrong ladder."

"Perhaps you're right."

"Perhaps I am."

She and Fletcher walked on as well, her arm still threaded through his, her hand still resting on his arm. Elizabeth hadn't realized until that moment how lonely she often was. She enjoyed the company of her fellow teachers, treasured Ana's friendship in particular, and appreciated her opportunities to spend time with other silver-fork novelists and literary societies. But so much of her life was spent alone, in her office, working on matters related to her school or pursuing the deeply satisfying passion she didn't dare admit to.

"Have you ever taken a boat out on the Serpentine?" Fletcher asked.

"I haven't. I have watched the boaters, though. It seems like a lovely way to spend an afternoon." And more exciting than the sedate walks along the gardens to which she usually limited herself.

"It most certainly is, Miss Elizabeth." He slipped his arm away from hers but held her hand, tugging her toward the edge of the water where the boats were being watched over by men eager to accept the fee for hire.

"We are going to go boating?" She couldn't quite hide her excitement. "You don't think that will be viewed as inappropriate, do you?"

"I ain't the one to ask, dove." They reached the Serpentine. "How much for the boat for a time?" he asked a man standing beside a particularly promising rowboat.

He was quoted a not unreasonable price. The offer was accepted.

"You know how to stay afloat, sir?" the boatman asked.

"This ain't my first time on the water." He turned to

Elizabeth, a challenge twinkling in his eyes. "Have you decided if you'd be putting paid to your reputation if you take a tiny boat ride with me?"

She couldn't be entirely certain it would meet with approval from the greatest of sticklers, but she didn't think an outing that was as public as a carriage ride in the park could truly be declared scandalous. And, oh, how she would love to have an adventure.

"We will further convince people you are courting me," she told him.

He held out his hand to her once more. He must not have objected.

She set her hand in his. The simple touch—through both of their gloves—sent waves of warm awareness over her. How was it this man, who stood in a position to uncover a secret that would destroy the stable life of independence she had carefully created for herself, made her feel alive in a way no one else ever had? Perhaps it was because, as Mr. Donnelly had pointed out, Fletcher wasn't as bound by the expectations of the upper class. It made him both an adventure and a risk.

They were soon situated. A push from the boatman sent them out onto the water. Fletcher took up the oars, pulling them through the smooth water. They lazily meandered out onto the lake. A light breeze cooled the air, and birdsong echoed from the trees surrounding the lake. It was peaceful and serene. A slow smile tugged at her lips. The moment was perfect.

"Keep that expression on your face, Elizabeth, and I'll think my wooing is working."

"Is that not the goal?" she asked.

"That, my dear, is always the goal." He didn't look at her as he continued to row, but his tone was a touch too innocent—and amused—for his comment to be anything but good-spirited banter.

"And our spying expedition?" she pressed.

"An added bonus." He winked at her, pulling the oars as he guided the boat along the lake, parallel to the shore.

"I've never been a spy, though I suspect I would be quite good at it."

He laughed. "I haven't any doubt in you."

"None at all?" She couldn't hold back her smile.

"You sorted that Janey could get word to me and pieced together that Midgley might be part of the trouble at Hogg's school."

He left his list at that, but she suspected there was more.

"And?" she asked.

"And you were bang on about this being the right spot for today's spying."

Was she?

He motioned with his head toward the bank. Midgley stood on the path near the Serpentine, and he was not alone.

"Is that Mr. Headley speaking to him?"

"It ain't the Prime Minister."

The two men were deep in conversation, the topic appearing to be a heavy one.

"Are they chums, then?" Fletcher asked.

"They are acquainted, but I don't believe theirs is a close connection."

"Are you certain about that?"

She wasn't. Not any longer.

"How's Headley feel about educating the poor?" Fletcher asked.

She looked away from the unexpected meeting occurring on the shore, her thoughts spinning. "When I told him of Mr. Midgley's comments, he seemed unconcerned."

Fletcher continued rowing but slower, the boat hardly moving. "On account of him thinking Midgley wasn't in earnest?"

That wasn't it, exactly. "It seemed more that he thought my worry was misplaced or unjustified."

That brought a rise to Fletcher's eyebrow. "Throwing you off the scent, perhaps."

Perhaps. "But he wouldn't have any reason to suspect I knew of the trouble at Hogg's school."

Fletcher's gaze returned to the men, his eyes narrowing. "It's suspicious."

"What do we do now?" She had far less experience with this kind of thing than he did.

"Watch," he said. "Both of 'em."

"You can do that?"

He assumed an entertainingly haughty expression. "I've a few useful talents, Elizabeth."

"Writing, for example," she said. "Your most recent installment was quite well done."

"I'd return the compliment, but you ain't published anything in more than a year."

He tracked her writing? That was both flattering and worrisome.

"Running my school has taken nearly all my time," she said. "That has left me little opportunity for other pursuits."

"You've been attempting to save Hogg's school as well."

"What can I say? I like to keep busy."

"And you like to sort out mysteries."

The difficulty being, so did he. The more they worked together, the harder it would be to keep her secrets from him. As much as she was enjoying playing spy, she had to be careful else these moments of adventure might cost her every bit of security she had fought for.

CHAPTER 18

Fletcher was falling in love. There was little point denying it any longer. He'd always been something of a flirt, but it was different with Elizabeth. He didn't banter with her merely for fun. He longed for that sparkle in her eyes and the saucy looks she tossed him. The challenge she presented and the rush of excitement as they sorted puzzles together left him feeling more alive and content than nearly anything else.

It was utterly frustrating.

He loved her, but a great deal stood between them. Her school and the very proper appearance it demanded. Her knowledge of King and the secrets she insisted on keeping. His tight-lipped protection of the DPS. The fact that Brogan was right about the social chasm between them. It was a terrible lot to get past.

He made his way amongst the flower sellers out along the Strand, assuming the appearance of casual interest as he approached a particularly ragged young seller.

"How much for a handful?" he asked.

"Tuppence for a posy," Gemma said. "*Penny* for m' thoughts."

"I'd be interested in both."

As he exchanged the required coins for her admittedly wilted blooms, he listened intently.

"The two coves you asked over have been seen about. Gray-haired one mostly grumbles to 'is own kind about us who ain't got the money he has."

That sounded very much like Midgley. "And the young, yellow-haired one?"

"Odd sort, him." The girl's soot-smeared brow pulled in thought. "Chats with folks what even us low lot keep clear of."

"Like who?"

"'Ave you heard of Four-Finger Mike?"

The name wasn't familiar, but he could easily guess the type.

"When he ain't fencing lifted goods, he's collecting on gambling debts."

Fletcher let that hang on his mind a minute. Did Headley have gambling debts? That seemed the most likely explanation. While he couldn't think of a connection between that and Hogg's school, it did paint a picture of a man who might take on something as nefarious as arson.

"Keep an eye on that one," he said. "But keep a distance."

"Will do, sir."

It was an odd thing, having come from a place far lower than this humble flower seller, to be called "sir" by her. Sometimes he forgot just how much life had changed for him.

"How's this spot treating you, sweetie?" he asked. He

worried about her, as he did all the street children he tried to save from the misery they'd been born into.

A look of relief crossed her features. "Much better. I don't know how you managed it, but I thank you for it. 'Tis a fine thing, feeling safe."

"You'll tell me if ever you feel unsafe?"

"Aye."

"You swear to it?" Too many of these children tried to face the impossible alone.

"Everyone knows you look after us gutter types. We trust you." Her brow twisted in thought. "Why is it you're fighting for this school? That ain't a bone you usually gnaw."

"Mr. Hogg helps 'us gutter types.' I'd like him to be able to keep on at that."

She clearly suspected there was more to it. One couldn't keep secrets from the street sellers. They were too clever by half. And they saw *everything*.

"The matter is important to someone who is important to me," he said.

"What's 'er name?"

Too, too clever.

"Never you mind, sweetie." He tossed her another penny. "Send word if you need anything or hear anything."

She nodded and tucked the coin away.

He wandered on, hearing from a few more of his ears on the street. Headley was identified by more than one of them as being connected to Four-Finger Mike as well as with another crooked character they referred to simply as the Mastiff.

By all appearances, the refined Alistair Headley was up to

his eyebrows in shady dealings. Would the realization upset Elizabeth? Would it surprise her?

He was just stepping onto Fleet Street when he spotted the very woman he couldn't seem to get off his mind.

The last time he'd seen her in this area, she'd been supposedly delivering manuscript pages, despite no silver-fork publishers having their offices nearby. She was carrying pages again. Odd, that.

"Want me to trail 'er?" The familiar voice of his favorite bootblack broke into his pondering. Apparently, he wasn't the only one who'd taken note of Elizabeth.

"Weather's treating me well today. I believe I'll go for a stroll." He nodded to the boy, who stood against the wall, glancing over the top of Stone's latest penny dreadful.

"I wish you luck," Henry said. "Slippery as a day-old eel pie, that one."

Though most ladies would take exception to being described as "slippery," Fletcher knew the observation was meant as a compliment. Not many people could outmaneuver the street children of London. Even fewer could outmaneuver Fletcher.

He held out his handful of posies to Henry. "Hold on to these. Unless you find a sweet lass to give them to."

"Aye, sir."

Fletcher slipped around a fruit cart, keeping a close eye on Elizabeth. She wove through the crowd, moving as one who had a destination in mind. He followed.

Just up the street was the building housing King's publisher. Could she be meeting the mysterious author? Perhaps she read for him and was returning his manuscript. More likely still, she was his go-between with the publisher. Fletcher had previously inquired there and had been told even the publisher didn't know King's true identity.

How deeply involved was she with this mystery?

He, at a safe distance, followed her down streets and around corners. She moved quickly and agilely. He struggled to keep pace with her.

Up Fleet.

Right at Bouverie.

Back down Tudor Street.

She turned on to Temple Lane, which spilled back onto Bouverie. Behind her, Fletcher got caught in a tangle of carts. Fortunately, he knew where she'd gone. He'd simply be a little farther behind than he had been.

He finally wove around the clamoring crowd and followed the path she'd taken. But she was nowhere in sight. He peered around buildings and in window fronts. He retraced his steps.

Nothing.

Blimey. How had she managed it? His footsteps brought him back to Fleet Street, none the wiser as to Elizabeth's motives or errands. She was clever and surprising. Was it any wonder he found her so irresistibly intriguing?

A vendor shouted to the crowd, "Eel pies!" bringing a smile to Fletcher's face. *Slippery as a day-old eel pie.* She was, indeed.

Maybe he'd drop in at the Dread Penny headquarters, see if anyone was there and in the mood for a bout of boxing or a game of billiards. Not many steps later he came upon Henry, spinning his penny and grinning wickedly.

Fletcher stopped, inviting him by the lift of an eyebrow to explain.

"A regular gale kicked up while you was gone." Henry hooked a thumb to his left. "Got here a minute ago, wanting to know why you was following 'er."

There, tucked a bit out of the way, stood Elizabeth, little Gemma's humble bouquet in her hand. Henry, the guttersnipe, had given the flowers to Elizabeth.

"How did you answer Miss Black's question?" he asked Henry.

"With the truth."

"And what would that be?"

"That she's a mystery, and you never could resist a mystery."

Well, that was as true as the day was long.

Elizabeth stepped closer to him.

"How is it you slipped past me?" he asked. "No one's ever done that."

She stopped mere inches from him. "I would tell you, but then it wouldn't be a mystery."

It was all she said before moving saucily past him. He grinned, his pulse pounding in his neck. She did that to him more and more often.

"I like her," Henry said.

"So do I."

"There's one thing I can't sort out, though."

"What's that?" Fletcher asked.

"What did she do with her papers?"

He hadn't realized. Somewhere in it all, she'd handed them off, and he hadn't seen a thing.

Miss Elizabeth Black was more than a mere mystery. She was a wonder. A wonder he didn't intend to let get away again.

He hurried after her, careful not to let her get too far ahead of him. This time, he caught up to her.

"I've heard you compared to an eel pie, Miss Black. I find myself inclined to agree." His sudden observation didn't surprise her at all. Apparently, his approach hadn't escaped her notice.

"*I* find myself inclined to be offended." The upward tilt of one corner of her mouth brought an answering smile to his.

"It were a compliment," he assured her.

To his surprise—*pleasant* surprise—she threaded her arm through his, her other hand still holding the flowers.

"Do you mean to tell me how you gave me the slip so easily?" he asked.

"Of course not."

"What about how you managed to deliver them papers you was carrying without me so much as glimpsing the exchange?"

"What do you take me for, a spring lamb?"

"Would you identify Mr. King, by chance?"

"Definitely not."

"Even if I begged?" he asked.

"Especially if you begged."

Blimey, he was enjoying this. "I'll eventually sort out that mystery, you realize."

"The same way your earlier pursuit eventually led you to successfully spy on me undetected?" Her arm wrapped more cozily around his, tucking her up even closer.

"That were impressive, I'll admit," he said.

"How unfortunate the Dread Penny Society isn't eager for new members."

He would look forward to their meetings even more if she were part of them. "The society might very well be on the hunt for new recruits."

"Yes, and you told me the requirements: first, be a writer." She motioned to herself with her flowers.

"A writer of *penny dreadfuls*," he clarified.

"I'm certain that could be overlooked." She waved it off. "Requirement two: a willingness to work on behalf of the less fortunate. I believe our combined efforts to save Mr. Hogg's school prove that point."

He couldn't argue with that.

"And—"

Whatever she meant to say next was interrupted by the sudden arrival of Joe from the York Place mews. His shallow breathing and pale face spoke of near-panic.

"Danny's gone."

"Did he not tell you where he was going?" Fletcher asked.

"He weren't planning on going anywhere. And that chimbler he'd worked for has been seen near the place."

"You think the boy was taken?" Fletcher was quickly coming to that conclusion himself.

"That no-good weren't happy about Danny getting away."

"Beyond unhappy—I've heard he was livid," Elizabeth said. "Perhaps he was angry enough to take the boy back."

Joe pulled out a penny, holding it up directly in front of Fletcher. "Find him."

He'd seldom seen Joe anything but cool and collected.

The snap of his eyes and heat in his voice promised retribution for the thief in sweep's clothing.

"We will," Fletcher vowed. "You know how to get word to the others."

Joe was gone on the instant.

"Am I to be precluded, then?" Elizabeth asked. "I don't belong to the society, but I can still help."

He had no intention of refusing her help. "Tell Janey and Fanny to keep an ear to the ground. Send word if they hear anything. You know how?"

"Janey's penny," she said.

He nodded. "I have to go."

He wished he could stay, spend more time with her. But a young boy's safety was at stake. There was no time for hesitation, not even for the woman of his very dreams.

THE VAMPIRE'S TOWER

AN URCHINS OF LONDON ADVENTURE

by Fletcher Walker

Chapter V

Below them on the steps, heavy footfalls. Above, the crying they'd heard in the crypt, growing louder and clearer. It was children; Morris knew it was. He hadn't the foggiest how they'd get back out, but Jimmy'd been right: they never abandoned the people they'd vowed to help, no matter the danger.

Up and up, around and around. The footsteps below grew faster, louder. There wasn't much time.

The spiral stairwell led, not to a door, but to a landing. A stone floor spread far. Light spilled from a distant window, falling on a group of children huddled beneath it.

"Morris!" Little George pulled from the group and ran to him.

Jimmy grabbed hold of the boy and carried him toward the others. Morris kept beside them, searching for familiar faces. Sally was there. John-John stood guard in front of a group of smaller children who'd also made their homes at the Inn. There were others there Morris didn't know, but they had the look of urchins.

"How'd you find us?" Sally asked. "We've been here ages, and no one's found us."

"No time for tales," Jimmy said. "Someone's on our heels."

Their already pale faces turned ashen, eyes darting immediately to the stairwell.

"He's comin'," Sally whispered.

John-John pulled the tiny ones closer. "Might be he's still sleepwalkin'."

"You know who it is?" Morris turned to face the stairwell, placing himself in front of the children. A poor shield, to be sure, but it was all he had to offer.

"He's a vampire," Sally whispered. "The man who brought us here said so."

George clung tighter to Jimmy, though his fear-filled eyes were on Morris.

"The vampire's come up here before?" Morris asked.

They nodded.

"And he didn't hurt anyone?"

Heads shook.

They likely had mere moments before the monster would appear at the top of the stairs.

"Did you learn anything about him?" Jimmy asked.

John-John answered. "He stays away from the window. It's why we keep close to it."

A figure appeared at the stairs. Morris had never seen anything like it. This monster had the shape of a human, but it was bent and curled. Its head hung forward, eyes glaring at them from beneath its misshapen forehead. The shadows made it difficult to be certain, but its skin was green. A grayed shade of green.

Behind Morris, the children cried out, panic in their voices. He looked to Jimmy. "It ain't a redcap."

"And I ain't runnin'."

The creature floated toward them. Actually floated.

Someone screamed behind them.

"Keep close to the window," Morris said. It might not be enough, but it was what they could do.

"Any weapons to speak of?" Jimmy asked John-John.

"The man that brought us here made sure we didn't have any," John-John's voice shook. "If the vampire's awake, we're done for."

"How will we know if he's awake?" Morris asked, heart racing as the monster drew closer.

"He'll eat us," Sally said.

Blimey.

The creature was close now, near enough for the icy air drafting off it to send shivers over them all.

They backed up, pressed into a tight ball of urchins, tucked under the window, brightened by the spill of light.

The vampire abruptly stopped, hovering before them, still glaring. Its lips curled backward, revealing sharp, dagger-like teeth. *He'll eat us.* Sally hadn't been telling a clanker.

Jimmy set George on the floor next to Sally. "John-John. Sally. Keep the children as near the window as you can. We'll try to bait it."

"We will?" Morris hadn't been part of the planning.

"I owe you for that redcap," Jimmy said, not looking

away from the vampire. "We'll do this'n a proper, the two of us."

Morris nodded. "If we lure it away," he said to the group behind them, "you lot run for the stairs. It'll take you to the crypt, where this fellow was. Empty now. Search for the door that lets you out."

Jimmy stepped a bit to the side. Morris followed. Two bites to eat would be more tempting than one.

But the vampire didn't look away from the huddled mass of urchins.

Jimmy and Morris moved a bit farther. Then farther. They stepped clear of the group, away from the window and into the dimness beyond.

The vampire's head snapped toward them. Without warning, it flew toward them.

"Run!" Morris shouted.

He and Jimmy took off at lightning speed, moving away from the stairs. They'd led monsters on chases before. This was nothing they didn't know how to do. But this monster was fast. Their running and weaving and moving about didn't work like it should.

Its claws swiped at Jimmy, tearing at his coat. Morris whistled, pulling the creature's attention. It moved toward him. This time Jimmy whistled, and the vampire turned again. It never made a single noise. Not any noise.

A horrible realization occurred to Morris. The vampire made no noise. It floated off the ground.

Why, then, had they heard footsteps?

CHAPTER 19

Fletcher stood shoulder to shoulder with Hollis, Stone, and Brogan in the back corner of a pub near Bow Street, all facing a man they'd worked with often. Parkington was employed by the Metropolitan Police, and he'd been invaluable during any number of their rescue efforts, offering information, warnings, advice. If he ever pursued his oft-repeated goal of writing crime-focused penny dreadfuls himself, the man would likely be all but forced into membership among the Dreadfuls.

"Allen has a record of petty thefts," Parkington said, "and we suspect he's been involved in other crimes. He has some connection to Mrs. George, which don't speak well for him."

"Are we nicked in the head, though," Brogan asked, "thinkin' he might be the one who made off with the lad?"

Parkington shook his head. "I'd wager a stack of fivers on it, if I had that much money to rub together. Mrs. George isn't his only questionable associate. He and Four-Finger Mike work together often. If Four-Finger's breathing down his neck, wanting more loot to fence, he'd likely retrieve his climbing boy so he can get back to it."

Four-Finger Mike. The same man Gemma and the others had tied to Headley.

"How do we get the boy back?" Fletcher asked.

"You have to find Allen, which even the Metropolitan Police hasn't consistently managed to do. Flexible as a snake, that one. Finds his way out of most anything. Impossible to get our hands on."

Fletcher folded his arms across his chest. "We ain't the police. We've fewer rules."

Hollis was by far the most genteel of them all, yet he didn't so much as flinch at the heavy hint that they might employ questionable means of achieving their ends.

"The law is still a stumbling block, though," Parkington warned. "The boy is legally bound to his master as apprentice. The law lets Allen claim him on a level nearing ownership."

Stone broke his characteristic silence. "That ain't right, no matter what the law says."

Each of the Dreadfuls had a cause of particular personal importance. For Stone, it was freedom, not on the level of a country or a society, but on a personal and individual level. Had he not already been dedicated to assisting in the rescue of Daniel, Parkington's explanation of the law's demands would've secured his support.

"I'm only saying, as a member of the police force, there are very few circumstances under which I can legally take the boy from Allen."

"We know with certainty he makes a habit of beating the boy," Fletcher said.

"The boy's his apprentice," Parkington said. He held up his hand to halt the immediate objection both Fletcher and

Stone began tossing back. "I ain't sayin' it's right; I'm only saying it's permitted. My hands are tied. Getting myself tossed off my job would mean I couldn't help anyone else. I'm telling you *I* can't intervene."

"But you won't stop *us* from intervening," Hollis finished for him.

Parkington gave a single, silent nod.

"Give us some direction," Fletcher said. "Where do we begin looking for 'im?"

"Look for Four-Finger Mike," Parkington said. "He's slipperier than Allen. Not as sly, but better protected. His network keeps him hidden, lies for him."

"Would they lie for *Allen*?" Fletcher asked.

"Can't say."

"I've heard Four-Finger is connected to someone named the Mastiff," Fletcher said.

Parkington both paled and looked resolute. "You leave that dog to lie. There's no one in all of London as dangerous. Go after the pups. They'll lead you to the boy. But keep clear of the Mastiff."

"But if he's connected to all this—" Hollis began but was interrupted.

"Stick with Allen and Four-Finger. Heed me on this."

"If the Mastiff is the mastermind," Fletcher said, "shouldn't we be taking this down from the top?"

"It's a bigger ask than you realize," Parkington said. "Let the dog lie."

Stone plopped his hat on his head, looking at each of them in turn. "Are we gonna stand around arguin', or are we gonna to find the boy?" He walked directly out.

Stone was not one to suffer fools, nor did he lack in confidence. It served him well much of the time, but England was hardly immune to the disease of prejudice. His stature and confidence, unfortunately, made far too many people look askance at him when those same people would have admired those very traits in a man who looked like they did.

"Keep me abreast," Parkington requested.

"And you us," Hollis returned.

Fletcher, Hollis, and Brogan followed Stone's path.

"Does anyone know how we find this Four-Finger Mike?" Hollis asked.

"Go about asking everyone how many fingers they have?" Brogan suggested. "Anyone answers 'Four,' that'll be your man."

"I've someone who might know how to find 'im," Fletcher said.

"His band of thieves won't rat him out to you," Hollis warned.

"She ain't one of his thieves."

"Ah." Brogan nodded knowingly. "One of your urchins."

"She sells flowers down by the Strand," he said as they caught up to Stone. "She'll not be there 'til the morning, though."

"Leaving that boy in captivity overnight ain't acceptable," Stone said.

"I know." Fletcher hated the idea as well. "But little Gemma ain't the only person I know what's likely to point us toward the blackguard, and the Strand during the day ain't the only place I know of to find her."

Stone couldn't hold still, couldn't seem to stop his tense

bouncing. The man was on edge, and well he might be. A boy was in danger, held against his will. It was no small thing.

"I'm a little useless in this search," Hollis said. "I have no connections to utilize who would have any idea who we were talking about, let alone know where to find him."

"Actually," Fletcher said, "there's someone on your rung of society who does know him."

That pulled all their attention. Fletcher's lead was not an ironclad one, but it was promising.

He turned to Stone. "Follow whatever paths you find that seem promising. I'll fill in Hollis and follow up with the flower girl in the morning. Between the lot of us, we'll find the boy. I know we will."

Brogan slapped a hand on Stone's shoulder. "I've the Irish ability to adventure all night long on little but a hastily thrown-back pint. I'll search the streets with you."

"Headquarters at ten tomorrow morning?" Stone suggested, though it sounded more like a demand.

"Ten." Fletcher nodded.

Hollis looked to him. "And you'll make certain the Dread Master is aware of the situation?"

Hollis spoke of the mysterious head of the Dreadfuls without resentment. Perhaps he had begun to see some value in Fletcher's arrangement with their leader.

"I will," he answered.

Brogan and Stone went one direction; Hollis and Fletcher went the other.

"Who is the person you said knows this Fingerless Mike fellow?" Hollis asked.

"Alistair Headley's been spotted with the man." Fletcher

kept an eye on the street as they walked, noting those he knew, those he didn't, those who seemed out of place.

"Headley?" Hollis was clearly surprised.

"Elizabeth and I have been tracking someone we suspect is connected to the problems at Hogg's school." Lud, how was it *that* urgent bit of business had been so quickly and thoroughly pushed from his mind? "Headley's tied to that man, so I've a few people looking after him."

Hollis eyed him sidelong, blinking a few times. "There's a great deal in those two sentences. I'm not certain where to begin."

"Nothing in it's too odd. I set m' friends on people's trails often enough."

Hollis shook his head. "You *and Elizabeth* have been investigating? How did she get involved? When did you start calling her Elizabeth? And you suspect Alistair Headley? Honestly, I have *a lot* of questions."

Understandable. "She were at Hogg's school when I popped by to tell him of our concerns. Then, at a literary salon, she heard someone souring over education for the poor and how it oughtn't be allowed. Looking in on that bloke led us to Headley. Looking in on Headley pointed me at Four-Finger Mike. Four-Finger Mike, if there's any justice in the world, will lead us to Allen and, through him, Daniel."

"And when did you begin calling her Elizabeth?"

Fletcher allowed a half smile. "When she told me I could."

Hollis responded in kind. "A commendable approach."

"She's surprising, in the best way. Ain't above her company. Sharp. Sense of humor. And she don't seem bothered that I'm nothing much more than a street urchin in nicer clothes."

"And she's a lady born to ease but required to toil. You've moved up in the world. She's moved down. That humbles a person." Hollis knew that firsthand.

"Elizabeth is a survivor," Fletcher acknowledged.

"Which is likely why you get on with her so well. You're one, too."

"All us Dreadfuls are survivors in our own way."

They'd reached the corner where Hollis would turn one way to make his way toward his flat and Fletcher would go another.

"Ten o'clock at headquarters?" Hollis phrased it as a question, though he certainly knew he wasn't wrong.

Fletcher nodded. Hollis moved on.

Alone with his thoughts, Fletcher stood rooted to the spot. He'd kept his worry and panic at bay while they'd searched for Daniel and Mr. Allen. But he knew what happened when he was left helpless, unable to *do* anything to solve a problem involving one of his precious street children. He returned in his mind to the life he'd lived among them, to his own nightmare of a childhood and the desperation he'd felt. It weighed him down, tore at his heart and mind. That darkness would close in on him soon enough. Was it suffocating Daniel, too?

Where are you, little one? I can't help you if I cain't find you.

He walked on, acutely aware of every person he passed, every sound that reached his ears. Yet, somehow, he was surprised when he found himself on the front stoop of Thurloe Collegiate School. His feet had brought him there with his mind none the wiser.

It was too late for calling on a woman, but going home

meant facing his ghosts. He'd done that far too often of late. His Urchins of London tales turned down paths so like his own childhood—without the supernatural beings, of course—that it was like reliving those long-ago years every time he put pen to paper. His childhood was fresh in his thoughts most of the time, and writing about it had, to his surprise, proven helpful, but it was still a heavy lot to bear.

A full quarter hour passed as he stood there, not wanting to leave but unable to convince himself to knock.

Then the door opened. There was no reason for anyone to even know he was there. How could he explain himself? He certainly couldn't ask the housekeeper to send word to Elizabeth, not this late. The whispers would be all over London before the housekeeper even reached the first-floor landing.

But it wasn't the housekeeper. Elizabeth, still dressed for the day despite the late hour, stood in the doorway.

"Did you mean to come inside, Fletcher, or are you particularly fond of doorsteps?"

He pulled his hat off and held it against his chest, assuming the mien of a humble petitioner. "Could I sit by your fire, miss? A bite to eat? Spot o' tea?"

She motioned him inside.

"Are you certain?" he asked. "It ain't a proper hour for callers. I know you worry about such things."

"Don't you think whispers are more likely if you're seen standing on my front step at all hours?"

He couldn't argue with that. Only as he stepped inside did he realize she wasn't wearing any shoes. He'd caught her more ill-prepared for a visitor than she was letting on.

She ushered him into her small office set directly off the

entryway. He'd met with her in there before. This time the curtains were drawn, and the school was entirely quiet. It was a far more intimate arrangement, yet he didn't feel awkward or uncomfortable.

"Any success locating that poor little boy?" Elizabeth asked. "I've worried over him ever since the stablehand told you of his disappearance."

He allowed some of the tension to slip from his lungs.

"We're trying to locate him. The man we suspect took him is proving a wily fellow." He dropped his hat on her desk, careful not to disturb the stack of papers there. "And we've learned he associates with a heap of seedy characters. Not very reassuring."

Elizabeth clasped her hands together, raising them to her lips. Her brow pulled low. "What is to be done?"

"A few of the others are searching tonight, hoping for a spot of luck." He rubbed at his weary eyes. "I know someone what might have information, but I'll not be able to speak with her 'til morning."

"Meaning, to be useful, you now have to endure a night spent waiting." She crossed closer to him. "I suspect, Fletcher Walker, you are a man unaccustomed to being idle."

"I ain't got much to offer anyone. It's blamed frustratin' when even that's snatched away."

She tipped her head to the side, eyeing him with curiosity. "Do you really think that?"

"Think what?"

"That you have little to offer."

He laughed humorlessly, half leaning, half sitting on the

edge of the desk. "If you saw what the other Dreadfuls contribute, you'd full agree with me."

She assumed an expression best described as "disapproving schoolmarm." He actually laughed to see it.

"You should know, Mr. Walker, we here at Thurloe Collegiate School take a very dim view of falsehoods." Though she made the declaration with a tone of laughter, there was an earnestness beneath it. "I have seen you toss yourself, unwaveringly and with determination, into your efforts to help Mr. Hogg. I've watched you interact with the children you have rescued. You do so with kindness and unmistakably genuine concern."

"All us Dreadfuls pour ourselves into this work. Ain't nothing special about that."

She set her hands on her hips. "Are you questioning my authority on this matter?"

He reached out and tenderly brushed his thumb along her chin. "You're being kind, but I know my worth."

"I don't think you do."

He let his hand slip along her jaw, his thumb caressing her cheek. "I'm simply an overgrown urchin. We ain't got a lick o' worth. Never will."

"Well, I am a schoolmistress who stays up late at night writing questionably received works of literary mediocrity. I can see where you would be extremely jealous."

He laughed out loud.

She did as well, but far more quietly. "I see you are no longer concerned about my reputation if people realize you're here."

He dropped his fingers from her face and took her hand, raising it to his lips. "You're a bad influence on me, dove."

Her eyes glistened. "Good."

"Does this mean you intend to be a troublemaker more often?" He caressed her hand between his.

Something in her expression changed. Softened. Tucked itself behind a tiny, unexpected surge of bashfulness. Yet she made no motion to pull away, nor did she object to his compliment or the touch of his hand. There was hope in that, but also confusion.

Their current spots in the hierarchy of things were decidedly uneven, no matter Hollis's insistence that Elizabeth had come down a notch or two in life. Being viewed as proper and appropriate and "good enough" formed a crucial part of the foundation of her school and held a great deal of weight amongst the people she depended on to keep her school afloat. He suspected it meant a lot to her personally, as well.

He cared too much about her to risk that.

"Thank you for letting me grumble to you, dove." He placed a light kiss on her fingertips before slipping his hand away once more. "I'll let you return to your mediocre literary efforts." He winked to make certain she knew he was teasing.

"And I'll let you return to yours," she tossed back.

Oh, she was a temptation, that was for sure and certain. Her wit and sharpness. Her beauty and grace. Her willingness to see him when so many of her standing would simply look right through him.

She was a temptation. But he was a risk.

A good bit of distance was best.

THE LADY
AND THE
HIGHWAYMAN

by Mr. King

Installment IV,
in which our Heroine flees to the fearsome Forest and,
to her shock, encounters the mysterious Highwayman!

Lucinda's little houseguest, she discovered, was called
Nanette. She, like Lucinda, had recently been made an orphan. The poor child, alone and without a home, had wandered into the forest looking for food and shelter. What she
had found, according to her own vague but insistent re-
counting, was a horrendous, terrifying monster!

Nanette grew too distraught after only one or two questions for Lucinda to discern the exact nature of the creature
she insisted resided amongst the trees. The details Lucinda
had gleaned spoke of howls and moans, which might have
been the wind, and flashing eyes in the darkness, which
might have been moonlight reflecting off dew-wet leaves.
The heavy, threatening footsteps Nanette had heard proved
more difficult to explain away.

Nanette quickly found a place in Lucinda's heart. She
was a dear girl, tenderhearted and eager to make Calden

Manor home. Lucinda was unspeakably grateful for the child's company and felt she might be able to do some good in the girl's life.

The matter of Sir Frederick remained unresolved. That he'd cared enough about poor Nanette to rescue her from the forest spoke well of him. That he'd trusted Lucinda enough to bring the girl to Calden Manor called into question the snub he'd offered when she'd crossed his path during her ill-fated afternoon of shopping. She hadn't mentioned the encounter to Miss Higgins, who had, blessedly, not been nearby during the fateful rejection; Lucinda's heart could not bear to see pity or laughter in the eyes of her one and only friend.

Her loneliness, her confusion, and her desperate wish to see Nanette safe and happy filled her thoughts as she and the girl sat around the table in the sitting room late of an evening. Lucinda worked on an intricately detailed fire screen, while Nanette concentrated on a sampler of needlepoint.

"I do hope Sir Frederick will call on us." Nanette sighed. "He is ever so handsome and ever so kind."

Despite her thoughts, Lucinda found she wished for the same. "I too enjoy his company." In her thoughts she added, "Most of the time." He had, after all, shown himself quite capable of being hurtfully dismissive. "And I would like to thank him for bringing you here."

Nanette smiled shyly, sweetly. "He told me you would be kind to me and that I would be safe here."

"That was a kind thing for him to say." Kind as well as surprising.

"I believe he is very fond of you." Nanette's gaze returned to her needlework, though her smile remained.

"What leads you to that conclusion?" Lucinda's heart pounded in her chest as she asked the question. Did she truly wish for the answer? Was she fully prepared to hear it?

"He smiles when he talks about you," the girl said. "Nothing else makes him smile. I think he tries not to, but when he speaks of you, he can't stop."

Lucinda herself had never seen the baronet smile. Not once. Could it be true that she, the lady he had refused to even acknowledge mere days earlier, inspired that rarely seen expression in him? How utterly unexpected!

"His smile makes my heart flutter about," Nanette said. "As if I am a little nervous, but also very happy."

That was a feeling Lucinda knew well. Handsome men had that effect on many an unsuspecting woman, and Sir Frederick was decidedly handsome. She could only imagine his smile would render him even more so.

Her thoughts, jumbled yet pleasant, were interrupted as an unexpected but instantly recognizable scent reached her nose. That of smoke. She glanced in the direction of the fireplace, but, as always, it sat empty and cold. The manor was nearly devoid of coal or firewood. She had taken to keeping blankets nearby and wearing her coat during the particularly intense cold of morning.

Were this any other night, she would have assumed the housekeeper had simply lit a fire in the kitchen. But both of the manor's servants were away that evening, calling upon family and friends. Lucinda and Nanette were alone.

"Do you smell smoke, Miss Ledford?" Nanette asked, her

wide eyes looking about as if expecting to see flames at any moment.

That the girl had detected the same aroma convinced Lucinda she was not imagining the worrisome smell. The oddity warranted investigation.

She rose and crossed to the window. The forest, growing dimmer by the minute due to the setting sun, showed no signs of flame. She pressed her open hand against the window, leaning so near the glass that her face almost touched the cold pane. Nothing along the side of the house appeared to be alight. Curious.

"It smells stronger." Nanette even coughed a little.

Lucinda, herself, could taste a bit of ash in the air and felt the tickle it produced in her throat. She looped one finger around the chain of her necklace, attempting to decide what was to be done. Was the fire they smelled a threat? A fire, and she alone with the girl, with no one to be of assistance!

With a calm she did not entirely feel, she faced her darling charge. "Pull on your coat, dearest. We will make a turn about the house and see if we can't solve this mystery."

They'd made but a half-circuit before the dire truth of their situation became devastatingly clear. A fire, indeed! A wing of the house glowed with the telltale amber of interior flame.

"Oh, Miss Ledford! What are we to do?"

"We must find help, Nanette. We simply must." But where? Her nearest neighbors were some distance away, and she hadn't her coachman to hitch up the horses. Neither could they simply stand idly by and watch the house devoured by fire. There was no choice but to make the journey on foot.

She took the child's hand in hers and turned swiftly toward the road—the road that led directly beside the forest. No matter that she had told Nanette time and again there was nothing to fear in those foreboding trees, no matter that she had told *herself* the same, fear tiptoed over her as they drew nearer.

"Oh, miss!" Nanette's quiet cry quivered, her tear-filled eyes watching the dim forest.

"We will do our utmost to avoid stepping within," Lucinda vowed.

From deep within the woods came a howl, the very sound she had always believed to be the wind whipping its way through the many branches. Hearing it outside of the protective walls of her home, she no longer felt so certain.

"It is the monster, miss," Nanette urgently whispered.

No. She could not believe that. She would not. Another howl sent a shiver over her, filling her with an undeniable dread, the likes of which she had never felt before. Her steps slowed even as her pulse quickened.

Ahead, the road bent, turning directly into the forest. Had it always? She did not remember the path taking her into the woods, no matter that she'd traveled this road many times. Perhaps it was simply that her surroundings were more forbidding in the near-darkness of late dusk. Perhaps it was the influence of too many of her neighbors insisting the forest was dangerous.

"We cannot go into the forest, Miss Ledford," Nanette pleaded. "We must go back."

But looking back, Lucinda was met by the glow of the fire that was surely consuming her home. They could not return there, neither could they hope to save the manor without help.

"We must press forward, dear. We must."

Keeping the girl close to her side, she followed the curve of the road directly into the forest. Seldom had her senses been as alert as they were in that moment. Every sound, every movement pulled her attention. Her eyes could make out so little. Night was nearly upon them!

"I don't want to go into the forest," Nanette whispered.

"We must find someone to help extinguish the fire, and we need to find shelter for ourselves." Even knowing the utter truth of that, Lucinda questioned their current course. She questioned it all the more when the sound of footsteps reached her.

Footsteps. Behind them.

She tugged Nanette's hand, moving more swiftly, praying with all the fervent hope in her heart that they would reach safety and shelter soon.

The footsteps drew closer, louder, faster. Merciful heavens! She and Nanette rushed headlong into the woods, staying on the road as they plunged into darkness. This road would take them to her nearest neighbor, to help, to safety. If only they could manage!

Ahead in the darkness, spots of reflected light suddenly appeared, all in pairs, all at the height of a man. She froze, her breaths tight and painful. They were eyes, she hadn't the first doubt. Were these creatures of the forest? Or people?

Footfalls sounded heavy on the ground behind them,

so near that whatever pursued them must have been nearly upon them. Creatures behind. Creatures ahead. What was she to do? What escape was there?

Nanette screamed. Lucinda pulled her close, offering what little protection she could. She held her breath, waiting for the creatures around them to attack.

"It ain't safe in the forest, miss." A man's voice. Not a creature at all.

Without exposing Nanette in the slightest, Lucinda looked up and directly at the now-familiar highwayman. Her lingering fear, coupled with her utter surprise, silenced her. She could do naught but stare.

"Are you hurt?" He spoke from under his wide-brimmed hat, just as he had all those weeks ago.

She managed to shake her head. They'd been frightened but not injured.

He seemed to look beyond her. In a carrying voice, he called, "Any sight of the beast?"

"No, cap'n," came the answer from the direction of the glowing, shimmering eyes.

"Not a single hair," another voice added.

Did all those eyes belong to the highwayman's people? She shook off the question, rising shakily to her full height once more. She'd come in search of help. Perhaps this man of questionable character would redeem himself and offer the assistance she needed.

"Please, sir," she said. "We need your help."

"I would say you do," he answered. "Being alone in these woods isn't wise."

"There's a fire at our home, and not a soul at hand to

help. I fear the house is lost now, but if there's even the smallest chance—"

"Come along, men," he shouted. "To Calden Manor!"

"You know where I live?" She could not say precisely why that mattered.

Barely enough light shone to illuminate his dimpled grin. She'd forgotten how breathtaking it was. Sir Frederick's smile had set little Nanette aflutter. If Lucinda wasn't terribly careful, the highwayman's smile would have the same impact on her.

At least a half dozen men rushed past her, back in the direction of her home. The highwayman remained with her and Nanette. He, it seemed, was offering his escort and his protection.

"The men'll do what they can for your home, miss," he said.

"I thank you, and them. I would not have guessed when first I encountered you that you would be so immediately helpful."

"And why's that?"

With Nanette tucked against her side as they walked, she lowered her voice to prevent her words from carrying to the child's ears. The poor girl was frightened enough without realizing they were dependent upon the mercy of a criminal. "You were attempting to rob me, sir. Or do you not recall?"

"I assure you, I recall every detail of our time together."

Flattery. "Then you must understand why I am wary."

"If you can face the forest, you can certainly face me. I may be odd, the subject of rumor, a questionable fellow, even. But I am not dangerous."

"Nanette tells me there is a monster in the forest."

"There is," he said quite seriously.

"And can you be certain that monster is not you?" Though she posed the question with some humor, she asked it in earnest.

"Nanette is not the only one to have seen the horrendous beast." The highwayman gave them both a gentle but persistent nudge. "And she's one of the fortunate, to have seen it and escaped. I'd not place money on her being so fortunate again."

No matter that she remained unconvinced of the reality of a monster in the forest, she could not argue the importance of not remaining among the trees. Her home was ablaze. If it were lost, she hadn't any shelter for herself or Nanette.

"Might we send word to at least one of the neighboring estates?" Lucinda asked as she and her dear girl followed the highwayman in the direction of Calden Manor. "The more people we have, the more likely we are to extinguish the fire before the entire house is lost."

"Word's been sent to Hilltop House," the highwayman said. "One of m' men ran that way."

Hilltop House? "Sir Frederick does not have a high opinion of you or your men. Do you suppose he will heed your plea for assistance?"

"For you, Miss Ledford, I suspect he will."

She was not convinced. "Perhaps one of the other neighbors would be more reliable."

"His house is nearest," the highwayman said. "And he's reliable. He'll not neglect you."

His words proved prophetic, at least in some respect. Servants arrived to help save Lucinda's home. Sir Frederick, however, did not come. Nanette eventually stopped asking after him. It was not Lucinda's words that comforted her, though. It was the highwayman's. He said something to her, something Lucinda did not overhear, whilst the remaining flames died down. The little girl took comfort and, from that moment on, would not leave the man's side.

Odd that one who plied his trade in such unsavory pursuits could prove himself so noble. He and his men risked arrest interacting with the Hilltop House servants, yet they did not desert Lucinda in her time of need. Through it all, the highwayman kept his hat tugged low. Had he reason to conceal his face? Was he disfigured? Someone recognizable who dare not invite discovery?

Lucinda and Nanette had taken refuge in the stables, far enough from the house for safety. Blankets had been sent over from Hilltop House to guard against the bitter winter cold. They sat in the hay, wrapped in several layers. Nanette fell asleep, having worn herself to a thread, first with worries over Sir Frederick's absence, then with waxing poetic over the highwayman's kindness to her. In the silence left behind by the girl's slumber, Lucinda could hear the raised voices of those men working to extinguish the flames. The panic she'd heard earlier had dissipated. Was that a good omen, or had they simply given up?

A shadow crossed the open door of the stable. The hat was unmistakable.

"Your house ain't entirely lost, miss," he said. "But none

of us thinks you'd be wise to stay until some repairs've been made. There's a touch too much ventilation just now."

She sighed, pulling Nanette closer. The girl was once again without a home. "Oh, what am I to do? I have nowhere to go."

The highwayman leaned against the doorframe, striking a casual and easy pose. For a man who seemed to have no home at all, he never appeared to be anything but *at home*, no matter where he was. What must that be like? How she wished she knew.

"Sir Frederick has sent word that the both of you are to come to Hilltop House. Rooms've been prepared for you. You're expected."

She could hardly believe it. "Sir Frederick does not particularly like me."

The highwayman slipped farther inside the stables. "I understand the one he speaks ill of is *me*. Rumor has it, he offers nothing but praise for you. Were I you, I'd accept his offer."

Nanette had said much the same thing. Yet Lucinda's mind would not clear of the painful memory of Sir Frederick's public rejection. At least *this* man treated her with kindness. Even the night he'd held up her coach, he'd been courteous.

She carefully laid Nanette down, tucking the blankets about her more cozily. She then crossed to the highwayman, holding fast to the blankets wrapped about her own shoulders.

"Thank you for all you did tonight, and for your kindness to the poor little girl."

He tugged at his wide brim. "My pleasure, Miss Ledford."

"Why is it you have chosen such an ill-advised profession? The more I come to know you, the more I see it does not suit you."

How well she remembered his laugh, no matter that she'd not heard it in some weeks. It echoed with low, rumbling familiarly. "Desperate times, my dear Miss Ledford, require desperate actions of us all."

"Are you wanting for money on which to live?" She knew the moment she asked that could not be the case. "No. When you held up my coach, you did not take anything."

"You didn't have what I was looking for," he said.

He stood so very near, the warmth of him chasing away the chill of the night.

"What was it you were looking for?"

"Hope."

CHAPTER 20

Elizabeth decided to forswear late-night visitors. Not because she hadn't enjoyed the feel of Fletcher's fingers caressing her cheek or the warmth of his hand enveloping hers—she certainly had—but because the muttonhead had done all of that, yet hadn't come by or sent so much as a single word in the two days since.

Men were, at times, utterly frustrating.

To think she'd sat at her desk, watching him through the window, eager at the thought of his company, worried over the heaviness in his expression, confident enough in his trustworthiness to not tuck her latest installment by Mr. King away before letting him in. She'd believed in him, and he had essentially disappeared.

Her publisher, delighted by the unparalleled success of her current serial, had begged for her to write faster so they could begin the next story as soon as possible. She'd used every spare minute, and a good amount of the time usually reserved for sleep, attempting to finish her tale.

She'd carefully wrapped her papers in water-wicking

leather as a guard against the constant drizzle of the morning and had delivered her pages to Timothy to be handed over to his go-between with her publisher. She needed to stop by Covent Garden to obtain a few things, then head back to Thurloe to see to her duties there. She would need to return to her writing that night, just as soon as the girls finished their evening lessons and activities. There was no rest for the overworked woman behind the famously successful man.

Making her way back down King Street, she came upon Hollis Darby just stepping out of a home and out onto the bustling street. He spotted her only minutes after she spotted him.

"Miss Black." He bowed with every indication of pleasure. "What a delight."

"You are choosing a poor time to step out into the weather," she said. "The drizzle is picking up pace."

"Is that not just like a late English summer?" He tsked good-naturedly as he opened his umbrella. "How is your school faring? You expressed some concern when we crossed paths a few weeks ago."

No one would ever fault Mr. Darby's manners. He was refined and genteel, considerate and civil. Though a woman in her position would do well to court the attentions of such a gentleman, she found she much preferred Fletcher's rougher edges. Of course, those rough edges were currently keeping their distance from her.

"We are doing well." It was nothing less than the truth. The unexpected success of *The Lady and the Highwayman* had cleared her head of concerns over funds. "Several influential people have spoken highly of us lately, which has garnered interest from a few new families with daughters of schooling age."

"I am so pleased to hear it," he said.

They walked along the street, her arm through his as was customary between a gentleman and a lady. She spied more than a few penny dreadfuls in the hands and pockets of people around them. The amount of purple was very encouraging. She also spied a number of copies of the latest Urchins of London installment.

"I have not seen Mr. Walker in a few days," she said. "Last I spoke with him, he was worried over the fate of a young boy whom he feared was in a dangerous situation."

Mr. Darby didn't look the least surprised at her knowledge of the situation. "There is every reason to believe the boy's circumstances are still quite precarious. The man he is with, a thief who spends his time between criminal undertakings sweeping chimneys, is known to be a vicious and dangerous man."

Mr. Darby knew, then. But why? As far as she knew, he didn't write penny dreadfuls and, thus, would not be a member of the Dread Penny Society. Or was he, like herself, writing the torrid serials in secret under a nom de plume? The possibility was both intriguing and reassuring. Still, she didn't mean to press, knowing how closely guarded that particular secret could be.

"And the poor boy still hasn't been found?"

Mr. Darby shook his head. "Sadly, no."

"How is Mr. Walker holding up? He must be beside himself with worry."

"He is being Fletcher."

She couldn't help a smile at that cryptic response. "I'm not certain what you mean."

"When faced with the task of saving a child, Fletcher grows more determined the more impossible it seems. He is currently like a man possessed."

That very much fit the Fletcher she had come to know. "He cares about them."

"He *was* them," Mr. Darby said.

"Though I can hear much of his origins in his voice still, I confess I seldom think of him in those terms. Perhaps because he's grown. Perhaps because he does not appear to be starving or desperate or any of the other struggles that plague so many street children."

"He knows how fortunate he is to have clawed his way out of the too-often-inescapable pit of poverty and ignorance. He also knows that plenty of others worked as hard at it as he did but didn't have his good fortune."

"He is a good man." She spoke as much to herself as to him.

"If we could find the sweep, Fletcher would be a less grumpy man, which a number of us would appreciate."

"I don't know that I would be of much help," she said, "but if I hear of anything, I will be sure to let either you or he know."

He offered his gratitude, then asked, "Would you like to share a hackney? I am certain you would appreciate being out of the rain as much as I would."

Sharing a hackney would also save them money, something they could both appreciate. Their conversation was enjoyable and unremarkable, a pleasant way to pass the time until she was deposited at Thurloe School. Mr. Darby utterly refused to allow her to contribute to the cost of hiring the hack.

"Should you receive an invitation to take supper with us sometime here at the school, I hope you will accept," she said. "Especially considering I am not fighting you on the matter of our 'shared' hackney."

He blushed a little—actually blushed. "Will Miss Newport be present for this hypothetical supper?"

That was a decidedly interesting question. "I cannot imagine she wouldn't be."

He simply nodded, color deepening. Elizabeth rather liked that a man of the world like Mr. Darby blushed as unabashedly as he did. She liked even more that he seemed to be fond of Ana, though when or how they'd met, she didn't know.

She stepped through the front door in time to see Fanny, Janey's sister, stepping from the parlor, carrying the ash bucket and fireplace brush. Her apron was covered with more soot than normal for a routine fireplace cleaning.

Janey met her eye and immediately grew concerned. "I were careful with the ashes, Miss Black. I really were. But that fire smokes something awful, and even a little swipe sends soot down the chimney."

The chimneys had been a headache for months. She'd been meaning to have them swept but had been overwhelmingly busy. Things were looking better now.

"I understand," she assured the girl. "In fact, I'm planning to have all the chimneys swept. That will help make your work less messy."

"I'd be ever so happy 'bout that, miss."

She nodded and kindly dismissed the girl to go about the rest of her work. *Hire a sweep,* she silently added to her list of tasks. No sooner had the words echoed in her thoughts than she realized the unexpected position that placed her in.

Hire a sweep.

Fletcher and the other "Dreadfuls," as he'd once called them, were attempting to find a sweep. And she needed one.

Here was her chance to help.

CHAPTER 21

Elizabeth suspected she would soon be declared the most finicky hirer of chimney sweeps in all of London. She'd sent Mrs. Hale out to spread word amongst the working people in the area that the school was in need of having all its chimneys swept. Setting that particular cheese in her hypothetical trap had brought a great many applicants to Thurloe. But none of them had brought along the young boy she'd once seen in the stables near Mr. Hogg's school—the one now missing and believed to have been abducted by his former master.

The strategy had seemed so inspired. She'd wanted to help the Dreadfuls in whatever way she was able. What if she wasn't really able? What if boring, unadventurous, toe-the-line Elizabeth was the only person she would ever be?

The housekeeper poked her head inside Elizabeth's office for the eighth time. "Another sweep, miss."

She nodded and crossed to the corridor leading to the kitchen, where she had met with each of the previous applicants. Her heart resided firmly in her shoes. Having her hopes crushed seven times in a row had taken its toll.

She did need to have the chimneys swept. Perhaps she should simply hire this latest applicant and admit her plan had been ill-conceived.

Mrs. Hale motioned in the most recent applicant. Elizabeth looked to the door as a surprisingly clean sweep stepped inside. The rotund man's brows sat in a scowl, though his mouth pulled in an appropriately deferential smile.

His climbing boy entered behind him. Elizabeth knew the little one on sight: the child Fletcher was searching for. His face bore bruises. His lip was split. He stood with shoulders hunched, not looking at anyone. Elizabeth pushed down her anger at the obvious beatings the boy had endured and addressed the sweep.

"You are here to inquire after the sweeping job?" she asked.

"Yes'm." He stood with hat in hand. The humble mien didn't fit him.

She asked his price, then made a lower counteroffer. They bartered back and forth a few times. She kept a subtle eye on the quaking boy. How was she to sneak him away?

Having finally settled on a price, Mr. Allen, as she'd discovered he was called, pushed the boy into the parlor with more force than was necessary.

"Pick up your feet, Daniel," Mr. Allen snapped.

Elizabeth watched through the open doorway. Mr. Allen kept a close eye on his apprentice. Getting the boy away would be difficult, impossible once he was made to climb up the chimney. She would have very little time to rescue him, and doing so would be dangerous.

From the corner of her eye, Elizabeth caught a glimpse of Janey slipping from one room to another on the first-floor landing. She took the stairs quickly, catching Janey in an empty classroom.

"I need your help with something," Elizabeth said. "It is extremely important and must be kept secret and, in the interest of being fully honest, it entails a certain amount of risk."

Far from worried, Janey looked excited.

"There's a sweep here cleaning the chimneys. His climbing boy is the one who was abducted from the stables at a school—"

"The boy Mr. Walker's been scouting for?" Janey's eyes pulled wide.

"The very one," she said. "I intend to slip him out of the parlor while his master isn't looking. You must be ready to run with him, straight to Mr. Walker, if you can manage it. If not, then at least somewhere safe until you can get word to him. Can you do that?"

"Gladly, Miss Black."

Beneath her relief, Elizabeth's heart pounded. This was necessary. Needed. And dangerous. Not only would Mr. Allen be angry and, quite possibly dangerous, if he discovered her efforts, her questionable activities would not do her reputation one bit of good. But she had no intention of not doing all she could to save the boy. His life was of far greater importance.

"Wait at the door at the very back of the kitchen corridor. You can slip out unseen that way."

Janey didn't hesitate. They moved quickly down to the main floor. Janey turned at the base of the stairs, heading directly for the spot where Elizabeth meant to send little Daniel if she could only manage to secret him away.

She moved to the parlor. Mr. Allen was spreading thick cloths around the floor in front of the fireplace and barking orders at Daniel to carefully cover the nearby furniture. Elizabeth called on years of cloaking herself in authority and stepped inside the room.

"I am expecting visitors in an hour's time." She spoke firmly but not unkindly. "Do you believe you can be finished with this room by then?"

He reclaimed his submissive air. "Yes'm. I'll make certain of it."

She nodded. "After this one, I would like you to see to the chimneys in the classrooms on the first floor. The students should be finished with their lessons by then."

He gave a quick dip of his head. Darting his eyes toward Daniel, he grumbled, "Don't dawdle, boy."

Daniel jumped at the sound of his master's voice. Every rigid line of his posture spoke of terror.

She had to find a way to get Mr. Allen to turn his back so she could get the boy away from him.

"The furniture in this room is of particular worth to me," she said. "May I ask that you cover a bit more of it? I know that even the most skilled and careful of sweeps can be undermined by a desperately sooty chimney."

Though the sweep allowed a flash of annoyance, he

masked it quickly. "I'll see to it, but you did want this done quickly."

"Cannot the boy, here, cover the furniture while you prepare your brushes or whatever it is you need to do in preparation?" She made the suggestion offhand as she moved almost indifferently toward the door.

"You heard the mistress," Mr. Allen said to Daniel. "Cover more of the furniture."

Elizabeth reached the doorway and spotted Ana. She waved Ana over. In a whisper, she said, "Will you step in the parlor on some pretense and make no notice of what I'm doing?"

To Ana's credit, though she was clearly confused, she agreed.

As Ana moved past her, Elizabeth spoke in a voice just loud enough to be overheard by the sweep. "Miss Newport, will you come speak with me when you have a moment? I will be in my office."

"Of course, Miss Black." She moved to the basket of mending kept under the far window as if searching for a bit of sewing.

Elizabeth slipped out of the doorway but paused just out of sight. Here was the opportunity, if only she could manage to seize it. She spun about and peeked through the open door, attempting to catch Daniel's eye without drawing his master's notice. While the man laid out his brushes, the boy obediently covered furniture.

Finally, Daniel glanced in her direction. With a finger pressed to her lips, she motioned him toward her. He hesitated. She waved with greater urgency.

He looked at his master and then, mouth drawn and eyes wide, moved in her direction. She caught Ana's eye and motioned with her head toward Mr. Allen. "Distract him," she mouthed. She needed to repeat it once more before the message was received.

Ana stepped nearer the fireplace. "This fire smokes something awful. Are you able to address that while you're here?"

"Depends on what's causing the smoking."

Ana had placed herself where Mr. Allen could look at her as they spoke but without either distracting him from his work or requiring him to turn his head in Elizabeth's direction. As the man explained to Ana what sweeping might or might not do to improve the fireplace's function, Elizabeth took a silent, deep breath, and leaped feet first.

She took Daniel's hand as he reached her and tugged him gently into the entryway and out of view. "Mr. Walker has been searching for you, dear," she whispered.

His eyes lit at her mention of Fletcher.

"Miss Newport will hold Mr. Allen's attention. I have another of Mr. Walker's children here at the school—she'll show you her penny if that'll set your mind at ease. She'll take you to him, and he'll keep you safe."

Tears formed in the corners of his eyes but didn't fall. He had grown very still, clearly torn between hope and fear.

"You must go quickly," she said, pulling him toward the corridor where Janey waited. "We will do all we can to keep Mr. Allen occupied for as long as possible."

His little shoulders squared. He nodded.

Janey was waiting by the kitchen door. She had a long

black cloak in her hand, her own gray coat already on. When Daniel reached her side, she set the cloak around him.

"Hood up, ducky. Then no one seein' you will recognize you if that monster of a man gives 'em a description."

He looked back at Elizabeth. Though he didn't speak, she knew the question she saw in his eyes. "Janey won't let anything happen to you. Miss Newport and I will keep Mr. Allen distracted. Mr. Walker will make certain you are safe. Be brave, sweetheart. This is your chance to be free."

Janey gave him a little nudge. He found his courage. They were gone swiftly and without a backward glance.

Elizabeth hurried to her office, slipping in without, she hoped, drawing any notice from those still in the parlor. She quickly took her seat at the desk and attempted to calm her breathing and pulse. *Cool and collected*, she told herself. Once Mr. Allen realized his climbing boy was missing, she needed to give every impression of being both surprised and ignorant of the matter.

She pulled out her ledgers and half-heartedly began checking them, all the while listening for sounds of anger in the parlor.

She didn't have to wait long.

A raised male voice reverberated a few times, growing louder and more distinct with each shout. After a time, she recognized Daniel's name.

He knew.

Elizabeth uttered a silent prayer even as she desperately pushed down her rising panic. This simply had to work.

Ana appeared in the doorway a moment later. She held up well, but Elizabeth could see her concern. "Miss Black, the sweep's little climbing boy is not to be found. Have you seen him?"

"He's not in the parlor?" She filled her voice with surprise, as one would when pondering an unexpected question. She hoped it was convincing.

"No, ma'am."

From just out of sight, but clearly very nearby, Mr. Allen said. "Let me talk to 'er."

"The sweep wishes to ask you directly." Ana's pointed glance told her she would send the man packing if Elizabeth wished. Ana was sweet-natured and often soft-spoken, but she possessed a spine of pure steel when needed.

"Please allow him in," Elizabeth said. She rose as Mr. Allen entered. "Miss Newport tells me your climbing boy is not in the parlor. Would you like me to ask the housekeeper or our chambermaid to make a search of the school? I would guess he is simply preparing a different room to be swept. I did, after all, tell you I wished for great care in protecting the furniture."

"He ain't that hardworking." Mr. Allen's tendency to skip over consonants when he spoke made his words difficult to decipher at times. She managed, though. "I think he's run off."

"I certainly hope not." Elizabeth moved to the bellpull and gave it a firm tug. "Servants miss nothing." She hoped hers was an amusedly knowing look. "I'll ask them."

Mrs. Hale appeared a few moments later. "Yes, miss?"

"Have you happened to see the little climbing boy who came with this man to sweep the chimneys? He seems to have wandered off." She kept her tone casual while still making certain she seemed interested in reuniting him with his captive.

"No, miss. He ain't been to the kitchens, and I didn't see him wandering about the back garden neither. I was out there not too long ago."

Elizabeth hummed in thought. "Is Fanny about?" She looked at Mr. Allen. "Fanny is one of our chambermaids."

"She's on the second floor, Miss Black, seeing to the windows."

Elizabeth nodded. "We could ask her, but I suspect the boy didn't go that far. And Janey"—she looked to the sweep once more—"she is the other chambermaid—hasn't yet returned from market. I sent her to fetch a few things."

"I want the boy back," the sweep growled.

Elizabeth took a moment to breathe, though she kept her expression empathetic. His anger, she hoped, stemmed from frustration and not suspicion. "Mrs. Hale, will you ask Fanny to check the rooms above for the little boy? And then will you check the rooms below stairs?"

"Of course, Miss Black." She dipped a curtsey and slipped from the room.

"The boy is likely simply lost in the school," Elizabeth assured Mr. Allen. "The corridors are a little rambling. I'm certain Mrs. Hale or Fanny will find him shortly."

He huffed from the room. Elizabeth followed after him, afraid he meant to storm through the school himself. She had no desire to subject her students to this man. To her relief, he returned to the parlor. She stopped in the entryway and took a few calming breaths.

"May I know what is happening?" Ana asked her in a low voice.

"The little climbing boy was abducted by this man a few days ago. Those looking for him have been unable to locate him."

Ana pressed a hand over her heart. "Oh, mercy."

"Janey is taking him to someone who will keep him safe."

Ana closed her eyes, relief on her face. It was so very like her to be filled with compassion for someone she didn't know.

"We have to continue to play the role of innocents in all this, though. If that man should suspect, I worry what he might do to us or the school." She set her chin. "I won't allow him to hurt anyone here, but neither could I allow him to continue hurting that boy."

Ana looked momentarily shocked. "When did you grow so bold?"

"I suspect I've always been bold underneath it all. I've simply never allowed myself to let that part of me escape its shackles."

Her eyes twinkled. "There seem to be a great many escapes today."

"Long overdue ones." Elizabeth motioned up the stairs. "Keep watch over the students but be subtle about it. There is no need to alarm them."

"I will."

Elizabeth returned to her office and resumed the motions of work. She needed to work on her next Mr. King offering, but she hadn't the focus for it. Across the entryway was a man she knew to be dangerous, one she had justifiably wronged. She would have to be very, very careful.

The housekeeper came to report that neither she nor Fanny had seen neither hide nor hair of "the little climbing boy." Elizabeth had known that would be the result of their search, but she did her best to give the appearance of disappointment and growing worry.

She returned to the parlor, keeping the mien of worry firmly in place. "We have searched the school and have found no sign of your apprentice."

The lines of Mr. Allen's face deepened. "He's run off, then. Run off, and me wasting my time letting women look about."

"Would you like me to send the maid to Bow Street?"

He immediately refused, insistent and tense. Of course, he wouldn't want the Metropolitan Police involved. He was a known criminal. It was the reason she suggested it. He would leave quickly if he knew she meant to send for the police.

"I need to go find the boy."

"Your concern is commendable." How she hoped she kept the dryness entirely out of her voice.

He grumbled something as he snatched up his brushes. "I'll find him." That bit was said clearly enough for her to understand, as was his angry tone.

Please, please, Janey. Get Daniel to Fletcher safely.

Mr. Allen stormed toward the parlor door.

"What about your furniture cloths?" Elizabeth asked.

"I'll come back for 'em."

He most certainly would not. "I'll have the housekeeper fold them and place them on the back step. You can pick them up there when you are next nearby."

He watched her a moment through narrowed eyes. Had

she pressed her luck beyond bearing? His glare hadn't softened by the time he stormed from the house—out the front door, something tradesmen did not do—and she felt absolutely certain he said, as he left, "I'll find 'im. And I'll find out how he slipped away."

CHAPTER 22

Fletcher bound the pages of the latest installment of his penny dreadful. He would be delivering it to his publisher the next day. It had been difficult to do his work with so much weighing on his mind. Elizabeth. Daniel. Hogg's school. Elizabeth. Mr. King. Elizabeth. Mostly Elizabeth.

A lot stood between them, but a great deal pulled them together as well. Could she overlook the fact that he would reflect poorly on her when she needed to impress the wealthy and influential in society so they would support her school? What if she never told him who Mr. King was? Or what connection she had to him?

He wasn't overly bothered any longer that King outsold him. He, himself, was enjoying King's story and understood its success. But the parallels between his and Elizabeth's interactions and the events of *The Lady and the Highwayman* continued. She had to be telling King about their time together, which meant they must be very close. But how close? And in what way?

He kicked into the fireplace a bit of ash that had settled

on the stone front. His rooms in Charing Cross were generally quiet during the day. Sometimes too quiet. A suspicion had entered his mind in the last couple of days that he couldn't shake. He'd been falling for Elizabeth. Was Mr. King in love with her, too? Did she return that regard? Did he, Fletcher, have claim to any of her heart?

He looked over his shoulder at the sound of approaching footsteps. Only his valet-cum-butler-cum-cook was there. Fletcher knew who he would see.

"Herbert," he acknowledged.

In response, Herbert tossed him a penny.

Fletcher caught it easily in the air. He flipped it over and saw the tiny *J* etched onto the back. *Janey.*

"Send her in without delay."

Had something happened at Thurloe? Was something the matter with Elizabeth?

He moved toward the door just as Janey arrived. Before he could say a word, a little shadow appeared beside her.

"Daniel." He dropped onto his knees in front of the boy. Bruises all over his face. A split lip. The boy'd been beaten. "Any injuries I cain't see, boy?"

He didn't answer but clung to Janey's arm, clearly terrified.

Fletcher looked to Janey. "Where'd you find him?"

"Miss Black found 'im. Sorted out a trap, set it, and slipped him away from that horrid man."

He turned to Daniel once more. "She rescued you?"

The boy nodded, the movement tiny and uncertain. He oughtn't be pressed further. Janey would tell Fletcher the details.

"Was the sweep angry?" he asked her.

"Miss Black got the lad away without him realizing. We were out the house and on our way here without him having noted."

The man surely knew by now. Did he suspect Elizabeth's role? She might be in danger.

He gave Janey back her penny. "Take Daniel to the kitchen. Herbert'll fetch you both a spot to eat." He looked to Daniel again. "Joe's been tearing the city apart looking for you. I'm sending word to him that you've been found."

His chin quivered, but he kept himself quiet and composed.

"Stay here with Janey and Herbert. They'll keep you safe."

"Where're you going, sir?" Janey asked.

"To make certain Miss Black hasn't landed herself in trouble."

Janey smiled. "I think you like her."

"I think I do." He pulled his hat from the rack in the entryway, plopping it on his head. "Thank you for seeing the boy safely here."

"You and your friends saved m' sister and me from Mrs. George. Miss Black saved Daniel from Mr. Allen. That's how we survive, us poor folk. We help each other."

Did Elizabeth realize that by helping Daniel and Joe and, in so doing, miffing the likes of Mrs. George and Mr. Allen, she was putting herself and her school in danger?

All seemed well at Thurloe as Fletcher clandestinely approached. He slipped around the side of the large building that housed the school. No windows appeared to have been jimmied or broken. He saw no signs of violence or shady characters loitering about the place. He ought to have felt relieved. But he knew Allen's type too well to be put at ease. That Allen was connected to the Mastiff, a shadowy figure even Parkington seemed terrified of, only added to the worry.

Fanny stood in the back garden, beating the dust from a rug.

"Is Miss Black here?" he asked.

"She is and all." Fanny leaned her beater against the clothesline pole and nodded toward the school. "I'll show you in. Mrs. Hale's up to her eyeballs in work. Had a bit of a kerfuffle earlier."

She hadn't asked after her sister. Did she not know Janey had been headed for his flat?

She showed him to Elizabeth's office, but turned back before he'd even stepped inside. He entered the room alone.

Elizabeth stood at the window, her back to the room. Tension filled her posture.

"Janey and Daniel arrived whole."

She spun when he spoke. Her surprise gave way to utter relief. That look must have been echoed in his own face.

"Allen ain't a safe man, dove. Tangling with him was a quite a risk."

She smiled a bit, though her pallor remained. "I have become a risk-taker."

"If you get yourself killed, I'll be very put out."

Her smile grew. Heavens, he loved that smile. He crossed the rest of the way to her. She held her hand out to him. He slipped his fingers around hers and pulled her to him. Surely

King couldn't be too much of a rival if she was allowing this familiarity.

"When Janey came inside the flat, I feared the worst, thinking something might've happened to you."

With a saucy tilt to her head, she said, "And if it had, you would have been very put out."

He wrapped his arms around her. "It's a very odd thing, worrying about someone but knowing you don't need to."

"Is that your way of saying you find me competent?"

Fletcher leaned in close and whispered, "I find you far more than that."

"Tempting, perhaps?"

"Immensely." He brushed his lips over her cheek, not a kiss or a caress but a mere touch. He wanted her to have time enough to let him know if she objected.

Her fingertips whispered along his jaw. "Fletcher?" Her uncertain tone caught him up short. Had he pushed things too far? Was he comparing unfavorably to King?

He leaned back enough to look in her deep-gray eyes. Her expression matched her voice. "What's weighing on you, dove?"

"Where have you been?" she asked quietly. "Days and days have passed without even a word from you. You seemed . . . but then you didn't—" She shook her head. "I don't understand why you grew so scarce."

"I thought it best." How was it that every time he tried to make the right decision where she was concerned, he only managed to hurt her? "I'm an urchin, Elizabeth. Certainly, on the outside, I'm better fed now, better togged and housed, but inside, I'm a child of the gutters."

He began to step away, but she slipped her hand to the back of his neck, keeping him there with that simple, tender, very personal touch.

"Did you think I would be ashamed of you?"

"I was more worried you *wouldn't* be."

"I don't understand."

His justified concerns were quickly easing the temptation he felt to kiss her deeply and well. He dropped his arms, then took her hand in his. "I know enough of this world to realize that keeping your school afloat depends a great deal on what the fine and proper think of you. I know perfectly well what they think of *me*." He kissed her hand. "I'm reminding myself of that again."

"You're staying away in order to help me and my school?" she pressed.

He stepped back toward the door. "I'll not destroy your dreams, dove."

King, being a penny dreadful author as well, and quite possibly as low a fellow as he, no matter that he wrote using finer words, was likely as ill-suited a match as he was. King might be willing to risk everything Elizabeth had worked for. Fletcher wasn't.

He offered a bow and a farewell. It was the right thing, but blast it all, it wasn't easy.

THE LADY
AND THE
HIGHWAYMAN

by Mr. King

Installment V,
in which our Heroine and her Young Charge take refuge
with Sir Frederick and discover a horrifying Secret!

Hilltop House was the very picture of an estate where a
gentleman like Sir Frederick would live. The grounds were
immaculate, yet somehow still inviting. The home itself was
regal, stalwart, and elegant, yet Lucinda did not find the estate intimidating.

She and Nanette did not see the baronet upon their arrival the night of the fire. His housekeeper relayed his instructions that they should seek their beds and rest, as he
was certain they were thoroughly exhausted. He also expressed his wish that they consider themselves at home at
Hilltop House for as long as was necessary, insisting he was
honored to have them to stay.

Lucinda was, indeed, exhausted, weary to her very
bones. She was also deeply confused. The highwayman, an
apparent thief and a man living outside the law, had touched
her with his kindness, something she'd not been expecting.

Sir Frederick, who had mere days earlier rejected her so publicly, had also offered hospitality with no apparent hesitation.
How did one reconcile such contradictory behavior?

The next morning, Lucinda woke, dressed, and slipped
from her borrowed bedchamber to the public rooms below.
She approached the sitting room, but hesitated outside the
door. Inside the room, Nanette sat with Sir Frederick on a
cozy window seat, the morning sun illuminating them both.
The girl still wore a shirt of Sir Frederick's that had acted as
an oversized nightdress from the previous evening.

Just as she was about to enter, she heard Nanette say her
name, and Lucinda lingered, listening.

"Miss Ledford was very brave," Nanette said to Sir
Frederick. "She walked straight into the forest, even though
I told her about the monster. I would not be so brave."

Sir Frederick chucked her under the chin. "I suspect, my
little Nanette, you are quite, quite brave."

"You go into the forest, too," Nanette said. "We are all
brave, aren't we?"

"Yes, we are."

Nanette smiled up at him, her look both pleased and a
bit besotted. He hadn't the highwayman's breath-snatching
smile nor heart-fluttering laugh, but Sir Frederick was kind
and handsome, thoughtful and good.

"Miss Ledford says that you think poorly of her."
Nanette's declaration, offered with the frank innocence only
a child could manage, sent waves of heat over Lucinda's face.
"I tried to tell her that you smile when you talk about her,
but I do not think she believed me."

"Not many people believe that I ever smile," Sir Frederick

replied. "I cannot fault her for feeling that way." He made no mention of Nanette's assertion that his fondness for Lucinda had met with disbelief as well.

"Do you like her?" the girl asked.

"Of course I do," he said. "You have seen for yourself that she is good and kind."

Nanette slipped closer to him and leaned her head against his gray-striped waistcoat. "She hugs me tightly when I am afraid. I like that."

Sir Frederick set his arms around the sweet girl. "I knew she would. That is why I brought you to her. I knew you would be safe and cared for."

"Would I not have been safe and cared for here with you?"

He actually laughed, not loudly and not long, but a short, deep, rumbling laugh.

Heavens, he might have challenged the highwayman in that moment for the warmth his laughter roused within her.

"You would have been cherished here, darling," Sir Frederick said.

"Then why did you not keep me?"

Sir Frederick's embrace appeared to tighten around the girl. "Because I could not keep you as safe as I wished to. And I want you to be safe."

"I was not safe in the forest before you found me."

"I know, dear. I know."

The two sat a moment. Lucinda could not help but be touched by the scene. It reminded her quite forcibly of the way the little child had clung to the highwayman the night before. How could these two very disparate men, men who openly disliked each other, be so very similar? Heavens, but Lucinda was confused.

She stepped back into the corridor for the briefest of moments, not wishing to be caught out eavesdropping or lost in thought. With her open palm pressed to her heart, she forced back her rising emotions. Focusing her mind once more, she walked through the doorway, this time making her presence known.

"Good morning," she said.

They turned toward her. Nanette smiled broadly, sliding from the window seat to rush to her. Sir Frederick rose with his usual formal grace and offered a bow but no smile. It was little wonder everyone, Lucinda included, doubted he ever smiled.

Nanette threw her arms around Lucinda's legs. "You are awake."

"As you see." She brushed her fingers over the girl's hair, unable to hide her amusement at Nanette's haphazard appearance.

"You're wearing your necklace," Nanette said.

"And you are wearing your bedclothes." Lucinda shook her head with a smile. "Let's have you run back up to the nursery and ask the nursemaid to comb your hair and see you dressed for the day."

A nod of agreement precipitated the girl's skipping departure.

Alone with the confounding Sir Frederick, Lucinda asked the question she could no longer ignore. "Why did you refuse to converse with me when we spoke in town? You seemed reluctant to even acknowledge you knew me."

"I regretted that then. I regret it now. But, I assure you, it could not be avoided." He spoke with such earnestness that she could not doubt him.

"Why could it not be avoided?" She was being far bolder than she'd once been. Had coming to this area of the kingdom changed her so wholly? Or had she simply discovered a part of herself she'd not before known?

He approached her with a mien of humility she'd not have thought to see in him. "I cannot tell you all. There are secrets in this corner of the world that cannot be shared. In that moment when I saw you, it was imperative, for your safety as much as anything else, that you not linger long. My behavior was intended to see you on your way quickly—not to injure you."

"Was there danger?" She had certainly not sensed any on that quiet street corner.

"There is always danger, Miss Ledford."

She swallowed against the sudden lump in her throat. "Nanette has spoken of a monster in the forest, as has the highwayman."

Sir Frederick rested a gentle hand on her arm. "Our highwayman is not the only one searching for a means of ridding our forest of the threat that hides in its shadows. So long as the horrid creature remains nearby, none of us are safe. Especially the children."

Lucinda pressed her fingertips to her lips, holding back the words of worry that lingered there. "Why are the children particularly at risk?"

"Has no one told you anything of our monster?"

She shook her head.

He held out his hand to her. She accepted it, soothed by the feel of his strong hand around hers. They walked from the sitting room, down the corridor, and into the vast expanse of the portrait hall. On all sides of them, images of gentlemen who resembled Sir Frederick and ladies who also shared a few of his features filled the walls.

They stopped beneath the visage of a kind-eyed man in the fashions of a half-century past. "My grandfather," Sir Frederick said. "The monster first arrived in his time. Few saw it, and fewer still understood it." He motioned to another gentleman a bit farther down the line of frames. "My father encountered the beast more than once. He, you understand, sought it out."

"Good heavens, why?" She could not imagine going in search of a monster.

"To understand it, to separate myth from truth."

"What did he discover?"

Sir Frederick's gaze did not leave his late father's face. "That the monster was, in fact, real, and we had reason to fear it. The beast craves our fears, you see. Takes strength from our terror. Children are less likely to attempt to explain it away as mere imagination or hallucination and, thus, are more likely to be terrified at the very thought of the monster lurking in the dark."

"Does the beast hurt the children? Beyond frightening them, I mean."

"Oh, yes. We have lost a great many these past decades. Far too many." A sadness touched his words as he spoke of children he once knew, children he had not been able to save.

She held fast to his arm. "But not Nanette."

He released a pent-up breath, the sound filled with relief. "Not Nanette. I found her in time. She was fortunate, indeed. I would wager she would not be so lucky a second time."

"The highwayman you so despise said precisely that only last night."

He set his hand atop hers where it rested on his arm. "I do not despise him; I simply cannot approve of his methods. We are, however, pursuing the same goal. That makes us, no matter the oddity of it, united."

"You both seek to destroy the monster."

He nodded.

"The first time I encountered the highwayman, he searched my carriage but took nothing. He said I did not have what he was looking for. Do you know what that is? It must be connected to your cause somehow."

Sir Frederick kept her arm through his as they slowly walked the length of the hall. "Legend tells us that the beast of the forest can be stopped only by a talisman that possesses a strength greater than the fear the monster inspires. Many have conjectured what that talisman might be. We know only that it is powerful and that it will *arrive* in our area when it will be needed most."

"That is why he searches carriages when they pass through. He is looking for some sort of amulet."

"Yes." Much of the disapproval he used when speaking of the highwayman was absent from the simple declaration.

"Why do *you* not search for it?"

His eyes turned to her with tenderness in their depths. "He seeks a cure for the disease which plagues us, while I seek to rescue those already endangered by it. We each have our roles to fill."

"Then you truly do not despise him."

"As I said, I cannot approve of his methods, but I understand them."

"And you truly do not begrudge Nanette and me a place under your roof whilst ours is repaired?"

His voice dropped to something barely above a whisper. "I truly do not."

"Sir Frederick! Sir Frederick!" The housekeeper arrived in a flurry of skirts. "Terrible, it is! Terrible!"

"What has happened?" Sir Frederick asked.

"The little girl."

Lucinda's heart fell to her feet. "Nanette?"

A quick, frantic nod. "She told the nursemaid she was afraid, that she could hear the monster breathing from all the way in the forest, that it was loud and rattling inside her bones."

Sir Frederick tensed beside Lucinda.

The housekeeper continued, voice trembling. "The nursemaid turned to fetch a blanket, thinking the child was merely shaking with cold. When she turned back—" Her words cut off in a high-pitched warble.

"When she turned back—*what*?" Sir Frederick pressed, taking a single step closer to the quaking woman.

"The girl was gone. Simply vanished!"

Lucinda gasped. Nanette was gone!

"The monster," Sir Frederick breathed almost silently.

"We must get her back," Lucinda insisted. "Whatever we must do, we simply have to get her back!"

He turned to face her more fully. "We will, I swear to you. I will not stop until she is safe once more."

"What can I do to help?" Lucinda asked.

He shook his head. "It is too dangerous. You must protect yourself."

"I cannot rest knowing my dear girl is in danger."

"I will do all I can," he vowed. "And I will send for you if there is anything at all you can do."

He was gone a moment later. The determined set of his shoulders gave Lucinda a much-needed bit of hope. Yet, within moments of his departure, that hope proved insufficient.

The Lucinda who had arrived at Calden Manor weeks earlier would have waited and worried and been quite helpless. The Lucinda she was now was not content with such a thing.

Nanette was in danger. Sir Frederick, brave and noble though he was, had rushed to her rescue without the least help or support, a foolish approach indeed when one considered he had a ready and able helper already in the forest.

Lucinda rushed to her room, pulled on her thick cloak, and, though she quaked inside, marched from Hilltop House directly toward the spot in the forest where she had twice before encountered the notorious highwayman.

CHAPTER 23

Whenever Fletcher had a planned meeting with Stone at Dread Penny headquarters, he could count on two things: that he, Fletcher, would do most of the talking, and that Stone would arrive there before he did. This time, however, he crossed paths with Stone on the walk toward King Street.

"You're running late, man," Fletcher said.

"I ain't been doing any running." Stone's humor was so subtle most people missed it.

They walked on.

"How's the boy?" Stone didn't need to say *which* boy.

"Back with Joe. Watched over by a bulldog of a woman who'll not let anyone lay a finger on him."

Stone nodded.

"We're fortunate Miss Black sorted a way to get Allen near enough," Fletcher said. "We'd never've found the little one otherwise. Still stings that he got off, though. He'll only hurt more children."

Stone didn't answer. His gaze had shifted away, watching

something or someone a bit ahead of them. Fletcher looked in that direction as well.

Elizabeth.

He hadn't the first idea how she'd respond to seeing him. Their last encounter had ended with him reminding her she'd do best to keep a distance.

Her expression when she spotted him was unreadable. "Mr. Walker." Her eyes darted to Stone, then back to him, expectation in her gaze.

He knew his part. "Miss Black, this is Stone, a friend of mine and fellow author. Stone, this is Miss Black, headmistress of Thurloe Collegiate School and an author as well."

Stone dipped his head, but said nothing. He was even more aloof when meeting new people, no doubt from having encountered a few too many who considered his race reason for mistreating him. Would Elizabeth be among that number? Fletcher didn't imagine so. She'd not hesitated to help Daniel in his time of need.

"Are you the author who wrote *Spirit of the Sails*?"

His eyebrows shot upward. He nodded once.

"I enjoyed it," she said. "I know so little about ocean voyages. It was fascinating."

His mouth curved the tiniest bit in gratitude. Elizabeth likely hadn't even noticed.

She turned to Fletcher once more. "This is a fortunate turn of events. I have information for you." Her eyes darted to Stone again, uncertain. "Unless this is a bad time."

"*Personal* information?" Fletcher asked.

She shook her head. "Pieces in the puzzle we've been attempting to solve."

Ah. "Then speak all you want. Stone, here, knows the topic."

She didn't look at all surprised. Stone was, after all, a penny dreadful author. "Janey was chattering while dusting my office this morning—the girl enjoys talking—and she said something I found important."

Fletcher motioned her up onto the front steps of headquarters, not intending to actually step inside. Let her think he simply wished to free them from the push and pull of the street. Stone eyed the crowd and the nearby windows, not showing the least connection to the building behind him.

"Janey said that Daniel told her that Mr. Allen kept him in a pokey set of rooms far enough from my school that they'd had to walk quite a distance to arrive there. He also said he could hear a great many animals from where they were—animals and a 'broken trumpet.'"

Those were odd clues, but also very specific.

"If we can sort through that, we might find Allen," Fletcher said.

Stone was wearing his all-too-familiar "thinking face."

Elizabeth nodded. "The bit about animals made me think that, perhaps, the rooms are near the Temporary Home for Lost and Starving Dogs, but that is all the way in Islington. Too far, I think, for them to have walked all the way to Thurloe as quickly as they must have to arrive when they did."

"Near a mews?" Fletcher guessed. "That don't narrow our search."

"The boy said 'a lot of animal noises' but not specifically 'horses,'" Elizabeth said. "He lived in the mews while he was at Hogg's school. He knows the difference."

She wasn't wrong. But where would he have been with so many animals?

Stone suddenly jumped to attention. "London Zoo."

The zoo. Of course. Near enough to walk, though it'd take time, and plenty of animal noises.

"What about the broken trumpet?" Elizabeth asked.

"The elephant," Stone said, stepping down on the walk and hailing a hackney.

Elizabeth's eyes pulled wide with amazed realization. "Of course. The elephant."

Fletcher motioned to Stone with his head. "The man's a bit of a genius."

"I suspect you're correct."

Having summoned a conveyance, Stone waved them over. They all climbed in.

"Sackville Street, Piccadilly," Stone told the driver.

"We're dropping in on Brogan?" Fletcher hadn't realized that was the plan.

Stone leaned against the carriage window frame, watching the street roll past. "We're headed for a slum."

Ah.

Elizabeth lowered her voice, speaking to Fletcher. "Sackville and Piccadilly isn't precisely a slum."

"Brogan don't live in a slum, but he knows 'em well. If anyone can find a needle in that particular haystack, *he* can."

She nodded.

The carriage swayed and jarred over the cobblestones. They all sat in silence. It was normal for Stone, not as much between Elizabeth and Fletcher. Was she uncomfortable? She didn't seem to be, though he'd not blame her if she were.

After a long moment of quiet, she spoke. "I cannot think of a section around Regent Park that isn't too well-to-do to meet our criteria. We must be in search of a small enclave of poverty."

She'd been sorting the mystery still. He should've known. Hers was a keen mind. It was little wonder she was drawn to King's stories. There was a complexity to them many people likely missed. Maybe that was the draw she felt to King himself. Fletcher couldn't compete with that.

Piccadilly was busy as always. Turning off the road onto Sackville brought a needed bit of calm. The carriage pulled to a stop. Stone shifted on the bench, reaching for the door. He met Fletcher's eye. Fletcher nodded. He knew the unspoken message: Stone meant to fetch their soon-to-be coconspirator.

"Are both of these two men part of the Dread Penny Society?" Elizabeth asked the moment they were alone.

From across the carriage, Fletcher folded his arms, shook his head, and let his lips turn up in amusement. "I don't spill secrets so easily as that."

"I will assume that to be a 'yes.'"

"Assume all you want, dove. That don't make it true."

She quirked an eyebrow. "It doesn't make it false either."

"I like this bold side of you," he said. "You are riding around London with an uncouth group of men in pursuit of a band of criminals after having stolen a child away from his kidnapper. You're an adventurer at heart, I'd say."

Her chin tipped up a notch. "Do you mean to spill that secret to all and sundry?"

"Give me a scrap of credit. I ain't so untrustworthy as all that."

He slipped across the carriage to sit beside her. "Has everything been calm at the school? I've worried that Allen might've sorted out your role in Daniel's escape."

"Not a single sign of difficulty." She slipped her hand into his, so naturally, so easily. He ought to pull away—a connection between them would hurt her school—but he couldn't force himself to let go. "I may very well have managed the thing."

"I'll come stay at the school, sleep on a chair in the entryway if need be."

Her arm threaded around his. "I don't think that will be necessary."

"It's a shame you write the wrong sort of stories, my dear. You'd make an excellent addition to the Dreadfuls."

He felt her laugh beside him. "My novels aren't my only disqualification."

"And we're blackguards enough to accept your help while not allowing you in our little club."

"Or even telling me who else belongs to your 'little club,'" she added.

He tucked her up beside him a bit more cozily. This was dangerous ground, but he couldn't resist. The chasm between them felt smaller in that moment. "I've already told you more than I should've."

"You trust me, do you?"

"If you can keep Mr. King's secret as well as you do, I haven't the least worry over you keeping mine."

She moved enough to look up at him. "About Mr. King . . ."

Was she actually going to tell him more of the puzzling

man? He sat up straighter, afraid if he so much as breathed, she'd change her mind.

"He—"

The carriage door opened.

"Blue blazes," he muttered.

Elizabeth put a little distance between them, presenting a more proper picture as Stone and Brogan peered inside.

"Any inklings where we ought to be heading?" Fletcher asked, attempting to look calmer than he felt. He'd nearly learned the secret of King from a woman who'd decided to trust him, even knowing his history. And these two mutton-heads had ruined the moment.

"There's a section of Maida Hill that's a fair hardened area of Town, houses a handful of criminals. Near Regent Park, it is," Brogan said.

"Maida Hill has some of the finest homes in the area," Elizabeth countered.

"That it does, but it also has a good number of pockets that those in the fine homes would be horrified to know rest so nearby. 'Tis on the other side of the park from the zoo, so I'm not fully convinced the lad would've heard the animals from so far away."

"Still, worth looking into," Fletcher said.

"St. Mark's is on the same side as the zoo," Brogan continued, "but there're far fewer struggling people there. A man like Allen would be hard-pressed to go unnoticed."

"Hard-pressed, but he wouldn't find it impossible?" Elizabeth asked.

"There're a few tucked-away spots and bits that are harsher

than others." Brogan *had* been the right person to bring in for this mission.

"Those seem like good places to begin," Elizabeth said. "It's more than we knew an hour ago."

Stone leaned against the side of the carriage, letting Brogan take the lead.

"'Twon't do to wander the slums dressed anything like Quality. We'll be sniffed out as imposters straight off," Brogan said.

"Our work clothes, then?" Fletcher asked. They made a point of dressing whatever part they were assuming.

Brogan hooked his thumb over his shoulder, indicating his flat. "I've enough for us to get on with. Shouldn't take but a minute to change."

"Are you saying you have women's lower-class clothing in your flat?" Elizabeth asked. "Or are you suggesting I dress as a man? Because the first would be surprising, and the second would, I fear, be ineffective at not drawing attention."

Brogan grinned. Stone even allowed the tiniest hint of amusement.

"While I'd be curious to see you dressed so oddly," Fletcher said, "I'll have to agree it wouldn't serve our purposes."

"Then what is the plan?" she asked.

"Brogan's sister lives here as well," Fletcher said. "I think the two of you will get along well."

He knew in an instant it was the wrong answer.

Her posture stiffened. Her lips tightened. "You mean for me to stay here while the three of you pursue this mystery?"

"'This mystery' involves a degree of danger you have never before encountered," Fletcher said.

"I am not afraid of danger."

"It's my understanding, Miss Elizabeth," Brogan said, "that it's you who slipped the lad away from his captor."

She nodded.

"And the safety of your school and wee girls depends on Allen not realizing you played him a nasty turn." Brogan spoke firmly but kindly. "I don't know that even trading your fine togs for those of the working class would fully hide who you are."

"I understand," she said. "But I intend to see this to its conclusion."

"Elizabeth," Fletcher began, but she cut him off.

"You owe me a favor, Fletcher Walker. You agreed to that weeks ago. I am claiming it now."

That was unexpected. "The favor is participating in this pursuit?"

"Oh, I will be participating either way. The favor is that you stop being so stubborn about it."

Brogan looked to him, barely holding back a laugh. "What's it to be, Fletch?"

"I think she'll thrash us up one side and down the other if we try to do this without her."

"Save me the trouble." Elizabeth pressed an earnest hand to her heart. "Thrashing people is so exhausting."

Brogan laughed. "M' sister has some clothes you could try. We'll see if we can't make you less recognizable."

Fletcher climbed out of the carriage, then turned back to offer his hand to her. She took it, allowing him to hand her down. Brogan sent the driver on his way; they'd need to arrive in Maida Hill the way those of the lower classes would or the jig would be up before it even began.

"Mr. Donnelly's sister won't think me odd for borrowing clothes?" Elizabeth sounded more amused than concerned.

"The two of them spend a lot of time working with the struggling and destitute. The people they help trust them more when they don't look like someone who'd think themselves above the work."

"Does his sister know he belongs to your club?" she asked.

"I never said he did."

She rolled her eyes dramatically, pulling a laugh from him. A keen mind, for certain.

Brogan's sister, Móirín, greeted them with her customary enthusiasm. "It's yourselves, then. Come in. Come in."

"Móirín," Brogan said. "This here's Miss Elizabeth Black."

"Oh, saints. This is the Miss Black our Fletcher's been courting, is it?"

Fletcher had nearly forgotten he'd told Brogan they were courting back when he and Elizabeth were trailing Alistair Headley. "I'm doing my best."

"Seems 'your best' is managing well enough." She winked unabashedly, her smile growing broader. "Now, I suspect you've not all come for a spot of tea and barmbrack. What is it I can do for you?"

Elizabeth answered before anyone else. "We have, apparently, come to borrow your clothing."

"What? All four of you?"

"I offered to wear trousers," Elizabeth said, "but they turned me down."

Móirín sighed as if that were a terrible tragedy. "Up the stairs with you, then. I'll find you a dress since the men are bein' so difficult."

Elizabeth obeyed. Móirín remained back a moment longer.

To Fletcher, she said, "I like her."

"So do I."

She turned to her brother next. "What precisely is it I'm to provide Miss Black with?"

"We're for Samford Street, St. George's Mews, likely Venables Street."

Her dark brow shot upward. "A pistol, then?"

"A disguise," Brogan said. "We'll all be armed. She won't need to be."

"A woman needs to be prepared to defend herself," Móirín said firmly.

"True though that is," Fletcher said, "I don't know that she's ever shot a gun."

Móirín *ahhed* in understanding. "And we'd rather she not accidentally shoot herself." She started up the stairs but stopped to look back at them. "I *am* going to give her a dagger for her boot, though."

A dagger for her boot. Did Elizabeth realize how tall an ask this "favor" really was?

CHAPTER 24

Elizabeth hardly recognized herself. The powder Móirín had applied to her hair had turned it a dark shade of gray. That, in combination with the floppy bonnet and rough-hewn fabric of her dress, truly changed her appearance.

"The lads were worried someone would recognize you," Móirín said. "They're not wanting to put your wee girls at risk. This'll do brilliantly."

"Do you often go about in disguise?"

Móirín nodded. "Brogan and I frequent rough areas of Town. 'Tis best no one knows we've a couple things worth filching, or some of the unsavory sorts would likely follow us. And regularly changing the way we look also helps us not draw attention."

Here was a woman of some degree of comfort and standing, enough to live in a neighborhood populated by the middle class, who unapologetically broke with expectations in order to do good in the world in the way she preferred. Elizabeth had only begun to give herself permission to do that. Seeing someone else navigate it so effortlessly was reassuring, encouraging, exciting.

How far dared she push it? Fletcher hadn't been entirely wrong the evening of their near-kiss. There were many who would withdraw support from her school should her name be connected with his. Not all, but some. More still would abandon Thurloe if Mr. King's identity were known. Could she find the courage, as Móirín had, to forge her own path no matter the objections, no matter the very real risk?

"Do your brother's friends often go along on your adventures?"

Móirín pulled open the door of the bedchamber. "Now and then. They all help each other with their various efforts. The lot of them are up to their brain boxes in humanitarian mischief."

Did she know about the Dread Penny Society, or had the men simply convinced her they were vaguely connected philanthropists? Fletcher hadn't given her permission to speak freely with others about what little he'd told her.

The sight that met her at the bottom of the stairs pulled a laugh from her. All three of the men were dressed precisely like struggling costermongers or bottle men, complete with smudges of dirt on their faces. Brogan had even managed to darken his hair to a less-startling shade of red.

"Don't we look quite the picture?" Elizabeth said.

Brogan made a show of strutting about, as if he was playing the part of an aristocrat instead of a street vendor. Fletcher leaned against a nearby wall, watching the display with amusement. Stone, as she was beginning to suspect was customary for him, simply waited with an expression and posture of neutrality.

Fletcher's gaze shifted to Móirín standing on the step just behind Elizabeth. "Did you have to make her so old? I'll look quite the quiz making up sweet to an ancient hag."

"Perhaps the 'ancient hag' hasn't any interest in making up sweet to a soot-covered vagabond," Móirín said. "Did you think of that?"

He looked to Elizabeth, a flirtatious gleam in his eyes. Surely his teasing and hand-holding and concern for her meant he wasn't entirely opposed to some kind of connection between them. Surely. "Do you mean to reject my attentions, dove, simply because I'm in need of a bath?"

Stone spoke before she could. "We haven't time for this."

"Stop being a grump, Stone," Brogan said. "You'll take all the fun out of the day."

"How'll we know 'tis truly him if he stops being a grump?" Móirín asked. "Best let him keep grumbling."

Fletcher held his hand out to Elizabeth. He'd done so when they'd stepped from the carriage. He'd done so the first time she'd met Brogan. They'd used their supposed courtship as a pretense for being together, but it hadn't felt like a ruse lately. It felt like a question mark.

A hired hack waited outside the flat.

"I thought we weren't taking hackneys since that would draw attention."

"The afternoon's wearing on," Fletcher said. "We can't waste time going that far on foot. The hack will drop us near enough our destination we can walk the rest of the way."

Were they not concerned that would be suspicious?

Especially being picked up directly outside the Donnellys' home?

In the moment before Elizabeth stepped up into the carriage, she caught sight of Brogan tossing a penny to the driver. A penny. Oh, these men were up to their brain boxes in more than just humanitarian mischief.

Once they were all settled, Fletcher took up the matter at hand. "Do we begin at that criminal enclave near Maida Hill, then?"

Brogan shook his head. "It'd make more sense for criminals to be congregating in that area, but I keep going back to the lad being able to hear the elephants. Those beasts are loud, but they ain't so loud that Móirín and I've ever heard them when we've been nearer that end of the park."

Elizabeth wasn't the least surprised that the fierce Irishwoman regularly made her way to dangerous areas of town.

"There're also only a few bits around St. Mark's where a criminal element could hide," Brogan added. "We'll cover ground there quickly."

"I haven't ever been on a spy operation," Elizabeth said. "You will have to fill me in on the finer points."

"Act like you belong," Fletcher said. "Act like you know where you're going. Don't look shocked by anything you see."

"How likely am I to be shocked?" She eyed the other men as she asked her question. Their silent, earnest expressions told her she was probably about to see a few things she was not expecting, things more drastic than three men who usually dressed like clerks or shopkeepers donning the rougher, dirtier attire of street folk.

"We'll none of us require you to undertake this," Brogan said. "'Tis a lot to take up without prior experience."

"I can very easily identify the man who came to my school," Elizabeth said. "I've seen him more recently than any of you. Having me nearby will help."

"It'd be helpful, aye," Fletcher said. "But we'll not force you."

"I'm not likely to be forced into doing much of anything."

Brogan grinned. "Nothing beats a strong-willed woman, Fletch. I'm glad you introduced us."

"Quit your flirting and tell us where we're headed." Fletcher did a fine job of appearing jealous. Part of the role he was playing? She couldn't help but hope at least a portion of it was unfeigned.

"We'll be let down on Regent's not far from St. Mark's Church. A quick walk'll see us to Sharpleshall Street. There's a section near there that's poorer than the rest. Not particularly crime-riddled, but criminals might go unnoticed there. A hop and a jump away is another little patch of want. If we don't find what we're seeking there, Móirín suggested trying Portland Town. 'Tis a bit farther from the zoo, but not so far as Maida Hill, and there's more struggling there."

"Near Lord's?" Elizabeth couldn't imagine the cricket pitch, frequented by the wealthy and highborn, would attract the set they were seeking. Indeed, she knew the homes nearest Lord's were quite fine.

"Not so far around the park as that," Brogan corrected. "The poor often live within the shadow of the wealthy, unseen and undetected."

That was truer than it ought to be.

"But *you* see them." She addressed all three men.

"We make it our business to see them," Stone said, his attention never wavering from the carriage window.

And here she was, making it her business as well. Apparently *inching* her way toward this new branch of her life wasn't her way; she had run at it at full speed.

As they all stepped out of the carriage, Elizabeth silently repeated her instructions: *Act like you belong. Act like you know where you're going. Don't look shocked by anything you see.* She watched the men, following their lead. None walked with perfect posture or refined step, but neither did they hunch over or shuffle.

Fletcher kept close to her, giving the clear impression of being a beau or husband. She'd be less likely to find herself harassed or importuned with his claim being made so pointedly. Somehow he managed to offer the protection without making her feel weak or suffocated or a liability.

They moved along Regent Park Street with a determination that belied their uncertainty. No one seemed to note them in the least, not even the finer ladies and gentlemen they passed as they made their way past the upper-class homes nearer the park.

"We're invisible," she observed aloud.

"It's both an insult and a relief, i'n'it?" Fletcher said.

"When I first came to London with no relations or connections and money enough for nothing but travel to the school where I was meant to work, my clothing old and worn and muted, I was invisible then, too. It was the most . . . free I've felt since leaving home."

"Do you miss it?" he asked.

"A little at times."

He nodded. "I used to belong to the streets. My future were a bit bleak and mostly out of my hands. But my present—that was all m' own."

"Is that why you undertake these missions? To reclaim some of that freedom?"

"Heavens, no. The freedom of invisibility is a miserable sort of liberty. My escape from the streets was mostly a matter of chance. Too many children who started where I did ain't got a shred of hope. Luck got me out. Now *I'm* getting as many of them out as I can."

She took his hand, touched by his goodness, grateful for his friendship, hoping for something more.

The area around St. Mark's proved unhelpful. Nothing in the poorer areas of the parish offered a single clue. They made their way back toward Regent's Park, the sound of the zoo animals following them as they wound toward the Portland Town area. That seemed a good sign.

"There's a police station on New Street," Brogan said.

"So we avoid that area?" she guessed.

He shook his head. "I'd wager our man Allen is the sort to make camp near the police so he can track their movements and know who they're watching."

"And because he thinks it's proof he's brave," Fletcher added.

Stone nodded. Brogan raised a brow in obvious agreement.

"He sounds lovely," Elizabeth said, earning a laugh from two of the three. Stone, she was coming to learn, didn't laugh often. Or speak. Or react.

Brogan motioned them off Regent onto a side street, then

onto another, then another, and another. Elizabeth was beginning to see the wisdom in bringing someone along who knew these neighborhoods. She would have been hopelessly lost.

This area was poorer than the ones they'd searched first. Elizabeth could easily picture someone like Mr. Allen making his home here without drawing undue attention. His neighbors weren't likely to be criminals—she didn't get that impression from the humble homes around her—and he had just enough manners and he dressed in worn work clothes, not rags or tatters, that he wouldn't pull anyone's notice.

Fletcher met her eye, raising his eyebrow knowingly. He, too, must have thought they'd come upon a promising area for their search.

A casual stroll up and down the streets revealed nothing of significance, but the elusive sweep could be in any one of the homes. They couldn't exactly knock on every door, asking. They needed to find them in a public setting.

"Any chance there is a pub in the area?" she asked.

"Brilliant," Fletcher said.

Brogan led them there and inside. Elizabeth had been inside pubs in the past, though mostly those attached to posting inns on the road to London. This one was not much different. It was early enough in the day that the establishment wasn't busy.

They were quickly deposited in a corner at a narrow table with full view of the door. They watched. And waited.

A man stepped inside, drawing the attention of her companions, who, she could tell, were studying him.

"That's not Mr. Allen," Elizabeth whispered.

The same thing happened several times. Weren't they

fortunate she was there to help narrow their search? They'd have lunged at every questionably dressed man who walked in the pub.

"I'm beginning to suspect Móirín exaggerated things." Elizabeth allowed a theatrical amount of innocence into her voice. "I haven't needed to use my boot dagger even once."

Brogan raised his pint of ale. "To Móirín."

They all joined in. Even Elizabeth, though she had no intention of imbibing. She knew appearing to do so would help their efforts.

As she set her glass back on the tabletop, her gaze wandered to the door just as a stout, heavyset man stepped inside.

She looked back to Fletcher. "He has just come in."

None of the men looked in that direction. After a fraction of a moment, she knew why. Strategy. Stone casually glanced toward Mr. Allen, then, eyes on his pint once more, subtly nodded. Heavens, they were good at this.

Brogan set his empty glass on the table and rose. "I'm needing another."

"You Irish know how to toss 'em back," Stone muttered.

It was an odd remark coming from a man she'd seldom heard speak and never to say anything insulting.

"Take yourself off," Brogan grumbled.

More of their act. She was beginning to recognize it more easily.

Mr. Allen sat at a nearby table. It was both helpful—they would be able to overhear more—and far more risky. The sweep knew precisely what she looked like. And the men had had their own run-in with him a number of weeks earlier.

They sat in silence, nursing their drinks, all the while listening to the conversation beside them.

"The boy won't rat us out," Mr. Allen said. "He cain't. I brought him to the flat in the dark of night. He don't know how to get back."

"Him snitching out our location ain't the biggest worry," someone responded. "He knows too much."

They were behind Elizabeth, so she couldn't see anyone. She didn't recognize the voice.

"I didn't talk 'bout none of it in front of the boy."

"Best not have." That was a woman.

Based on the sudden stiffness in Fletcher's posture, Elizabeth would wager he recognized the woman.

Brogan returned, dropping onto the bench across from her, a glass in hand. "Shame George couldn't join us. He an' the missus."

Fletcher gave a quick nod. He set his arm around Elizabeth's shoulder and pulled her in tight, quite as if they were a courting couple who didn't care how affectionate they were in public. Anyone looking on would think he was showering kisses along her throat rather than whispering information to her.

"Mrs. George is behind us. She's the woman we rescued Fanny and Janey from."

Good heavens. Elizabeth turned her head to him and whispered back. "What if Mr. Allen tells her the girls are at my school?"

"He'd have no reason to know them sisters was connected to her."

She hoped that proved true.

Brogan coughed a little, like he'd swallowed a bit of ale the wrong way. They both looked at him. He indicated the table behind them, then folded down one finger of his right hand.

"Four fingers," Fletcher whispered.

Four-Finger Mike.

It was all too interconnected to be coincidental. "Mr. Headley's been associated with him," he whispered. "But Headley ain't here. He'd be easy to sniff out in a place like this."

"Generally speaking, so would I," she pointed out.

"Aye, but you've had help."

That was certainly true.

Behind them, the voice she now knew belonged to Four-Finger Mike spoke again. "I told yous to silence the boy after he got away the first time. He knows too much 'bout how we operate. Cain't risk that, I told you. But you ain't one for listening, is you?"

Silence the boy? Elizabeth feared she knew what that meant.

Mr. Allen spoke up. "Worked three jobs with that imp in the few days he were back with me. Didn't have to teach 'im what to do like I would a new climbing boy. You weren't complaining when I shared the loot with you—with *both* of yous."

So Mrs. George was part of this criminal operation as well.

"The Mastiff ain't happy about this," Mrs. George said. "There's a boy out free what can spill a few too many secrets, and you lost 'im again. Now you ain't got a climbing boy to help you bring in your take. And them two sisters oughta be earning the Mastiff a pretty penny, but they was spirited off too. The Mastiff'll eat the lot of us alive if we don't have some good fortune to pass on."

Daniel and the Smith sisters were being discussed. How the men at her table managed to look so calm while overhearing this, Elizabeth didn't know.

Fletcher rubbed her arm, keeping her close. He pressed a lingering kiss to her temple. Though it was likely part of the disguise, she found it was comforting, reassuring.

"We can at least tell the Mastiff we've ended a threat," Mrs. George said. "Where'd you last have the boy?"

"At a girls' school near Charing Cross."

Elizabeth held her breath. Her eyes met Stone's. He was watching her, something he never did. She silently pleaded with him to recognize her worry, to share it, to help. He gave the tiniest nod. It was enough. She was still concerned, but less overwhelmed.

"Do you think someone at the school took the boy?" Four-Finger Mike asked.

"Not likely," Mr. Allen said. "Hardly noted 'im. Even helped me look for the little devil."

"Someone had to've seen somethin'," Four-Finger muttered.

How she hoped Janey had managed to disguise little Daniel well enough to not be noted.

"We'll go sniff around the place," Four-Finger Mike said. "Find what we can. We know someone helped the boy. We'll find out who. Get our satisfaction one way or another."

"They're going to my school," Elizabeth whispered to Fletcher.

"We will too," he whispered back. "Once we've a spot more information."

"These girls at the school," Mrs. George said. "They poor?"

"Ain't daughters of aristocrats, but they're grand sorts. Quality, y'know?"

"Genteel, then?" Mrs. George pressed.

The brief silence suggested she received a nonverbal answer.

"Them soft, innocent types'll fetch a higher price than the pluckings I usually get," Mrs. George said. "Might be m' boys could nip off with a few. The Mastiff'd crow about that for months."

Elizabeth dug her fingers into Fletcher's arm, too terrified to even speak. Her girls were in danger. Desperate, immediate danger.

Fletcher pulled his arm away and leaned his elbows on the table. To the other men he said, almost silently, "We need to safeguard Thurloe."

Stone nodded.

"We'll hang back," Brogan said, "then go find reinforcements."

"Get up and leave in a huff, dear," Fletcher said quickly and low to Elizabeth. "Not enough so as t' draw attention, but enough as to give you a reason for leaving."

She understood. She moved away from him as if suddenly disgusted, and stood up. With a glare and a spin, she all but stormed to the door.

She heard Fletcher sigh behind her and say, "Guess I'd best go make up sweet to the bird, else it'll be the suds for me."

He caught up to her on the walk not too far from the pub. He made a show of apologizing for an imagined argument. They turned a corner, then another.

Then, they ran.

THE VAMPIRE'S TOWER

AN URCHINS OF LONDON ADVENTURE

by Fletcher Walker

Chapter VI

"Hold!" Morris shouted at John-John and Sally.

But he was too late. A towering man stepped into the room from the stairs below, his footsteps echoing. The sound stopped the vampire's pursuit. The creature turned and looked at the newcomer.

"There's plenty enough, master," the man said. "And young. Full of vim. They'll fill you up fine. Speed you up."

Speed him? The monster was already fast.

John-John and Sally pressed the children back, away from this enormous man, while also still keeping away from the vampire.

Morris slipped over to Jimmy. "What do we do now? Two of 'em and no way out."

"The vampire wouldn't go near the window. Maybe we'd all be safer there for a time."

"But that man likely can reach us. What's to stop him from pulling us away?" Morris wasn't about to stop trying, but he didn't have the first idea how to go about the thing.

"We'd have only the one threat to contend with, though," Jimmy said. "Fighting a battle on two fronts ain't exactly a winning approach."

The vampire had done nothing but glare while they'd been by the window. He hadn't lunged or swiped at them until they'd passed into the dimness.

The dimness.

"What if it ain't the window?" Morris asked Jimmy, keeping an eye on the monster as it listened to the newly arrived man's words of reassurance. "What if he can't go in the light?"

"I've heard of that," Jimmy said. "Some creatures are done in by sunlight."

It was the only chance they had. "I'll see if I can't lure him over there. When he's near enough, shove him from behind or ram him with your shoulder—whatever you have to do. See if we can't get him to fall into the sun."

Jimmy shook his head. "He's a big'n. Don't know that I can get him down on m'own."

"Get the others to help."

"What about 'Big Bob' over there? He'll not like it."

A two-front battle weren't a good idea at all. "Just be quick. Don't give 'im time to like it or not."

Jimmy spat into his palm. Morris did the same. They shook hands, a vow of unity. They might not emerge from this alive, but they'd go into it together.

"It don't matter where you begin, master," the large man said. "You'll get around to all of them."

Jimmy motioned the urchins closer. Morris inched

toward the window, keeping an eye on the children, the monster, and the towering man.

"Start with this'n." The man pointed at Morris. "Big enough to give you pep for seeing to the others."

The vampire turned to look at Morris, his glare heavy and unblinking.

This was their chance. He steeled his resolve.

The vampire floated toward him.

Morris crept backward, slipping into the very edge of the spill of light.

The monster stopped mere inches in front of him.

"Out with you," Big Bob barked at him. "I'll only set him on the others."

Morris ignored him and spoke, instead, to the monster. "You thirsty, mate? I'm right here."

The vampire didn't move closer, but he didn't listen to his underling, either.

Big Bob came toward them. "I'll pull him out for you, master."

"Now!" Jimmy's shout rang out.

The thunder of a full dozen feet answered. In the instant before the urchins reached the vampire, Morris dove to the side. Caught off guard, the monster was knocked forward. He didn't fall, didn't even stumble. He simply shifted forward a single step.

But that step took him into the sunlight.

The vampire had been silent from the moment he arrived, but now the silence ended. A howl that twisted every organ in Morris's body tore through the air.

"Master!" Fear and desperation filled the word.

Morris rolled over in time to see Big Bob grasping at the disintegrating outline of the vampire.

"Out, out, out!" Jimmy'd kept his wits about him.

Sally snatched the hands of the nearest children and ran out with them. Jimmy and John-John herded the rest of the little ones out. Morris scrambled to his feet, rushing after the others. His eyes met Big Bob's. The anger there chilled him to his core.

"I'll find them again! You can't hide 'em away forever!"

Still, Morris didn't stop. He couldn't. The danger would follow them onto the streets of London, but it wasn't a danger he could stop in that moment. They'd warn the children, keep their eyes peeled. Defeating Big Bob would have to wait for another day.

For now, they were safe from that day's danger. The vampire was gone.

They had lived to solve another mystery, to have another adventure. And there always was another one. Always.

CHAPTER 25

The hackney Fletcher summoned rushed them toward Thurloe School. He could see Elizabeth was concerned, but she was also calm and determined. He would never have guessed when he first met her all those weeks ago that she had the disposition for this kind of work. She had portrayed the prim-and-proper schoolmistress to perfection.

"Mrs. George and Mr. Allen were both at the pub when we left," she said, brow drawn. "Surely we'll reach the school before they do."

"Aye. But we've not much time."

"Mrs. George means to snatch my girls." Fear quavered in her voice. "You made very clear the life her victims are sent to, and at my school I have twenty-three potential victims."

"I know." He'd not anticipated that particular danger when he'd first brought Janey to Thurloe. He felt a fool now, guilt eating at him. He'd only wanted to help the girl; he hadn't meant to endanger so many others.

"How do we protect my students from hired thugs? We're

only two people, one of whom is extremely new to this sort of thing."

"Brogan and Stone are sending more our way."

She rubbed at her face. "One of my girl's parents recently offered to host the students for a day or two at their country home just outside of London. I could send them a telegraph, asking if they would have the girls to stay for the next couple of days. It's not a permanent solution, of course."

"That'd give us time to make the school safer while your girls are outta harm's way. I've a mate with the police who'd help. And now we know where to find Mrs. George and Four-Finger Mike and Allen. Given a few days, they likely could be rounded up. The police'd keep a watch on your school day and night out of sheer gratitude."

"I still mean to hire a manservant to work at the school. Someone dependable and burly, who'd keep an eye on things." She didn't shrink from the challenge ahead of her. This was a woman of steel. "I would wager you know a few people who fit that mold, likely in possession of a cleverly marked penny or two."

He chuckled quietly. "Nothing slips past you, dove."

"Let us hope not." Her humor had vanished, her thoughts, no doubt, on her school and students.

A moment later, they were there. Elizabeth didn't wait for him to hand her down but scrambled out on her own. She was through the front door before he'd even finished paying the driver.

By the time he joined her in the entryway, two of her teachers and Janey were there, staring at her with mouths agape. He'd grown accustomed to Elizabeth's costume and had all but forgotten how odd she truly looked to those who knew her.

"No time to explain," she said, waving off something someone had said before his arrival. "A telegram to Penelope's parents, Ana. Tell them the girls are coming for a visit, and would they please make ready for them to arrive later this evening."

"Are they to have no more warning than that?" Miss Newport asked.

"They told me when they made the offer that they required nothing beyond a telegram ahead of their arrival." Elizabeth turned to Janey. "Fetch Fanny. The two of you help Miss Beating"—she indicated the other teacher standing nearby—"and the rest of the staff see to the girls' packing. I wish to have them on their way soon."

Janey dipped a curtsey of agreement. Her eyes met Fletcher's, a question hanging heavy in them. He gave a subtle nod and motioned her on her way. There wasn't time for explanations.

As the women left to do as Elizabeth bade, she moved into her office. He followed her, crossing directly to the windows and the view they afforded of the street. Nothing suspicious met his eye, but he wouldn't expect experienced criminals to simply walk up to an establishment they meant to target.

"Tell me what we need to look for," she said.

He turned back toward her. She'd pulled the floppy bonnet from her head and tossed it on a nearby chair, then began pulling pins from her partially powdered hair. He added his misshapen hat to her pile.

"Jimmied windows. Somthin' slipped into locks so they don't slide fully into place. Signs someone's been hanging about the place."

"Like the discarded torches at Hogg's school?" Her hair was down. She thrust her fingers through it, shaking vigorously at the bits still grayed by Móirín's powder.

"Like the torches. Except Mrs. George don't mean to burn your school down."

"She means to steal any girls her thugs can snatch."

"Your girls'll be safely away soon enough." He moved to the smaller side window, opening it to check for anything suspicious.

"What about Janey and Fanny?" Elizabeth pressed. "Should I send them away?

He shook his head. "They're safer where we can keep an eye on them."

Nothing in the window looked out of place. He snapped it shut, locking it firmly.

"Let's check the windows and doors, then," she said. "At least those not in the girls' bedchambers. I'd rather not alarm them."

They checked the ground floor, then the more public rooms above that. Meanwhile, the house was in a flurry of activity. Her students were in good spirits, speaking excitedly about the unexpected adventure of a few days in the country. It was the perfect cover, and they would be safe while Fletcher and Elizabeth found a means of securing the school more permanently.

Miss Newport arrived after a time, having received confirmation via telegraph that the girls were welcome to make their country visit. Elizabeth provided her with money enough for train tickets. Either she had just handed over most of the school's funds, or her financial situation had improved. He hoped it was the latter. Her idea about hiring a manservant was a good one, but it wouldn't come cheap.

He remained in her office while she saw the girls off. They would check the remaining rooms once the school was empty. When Mr. Allen and Mrs. George's thugs arrived, they'd find a locked and empty school. Fletcher hoped it would be enough.

He leaned against the edge of her desk. There was nothing for it but to bide his time and keep a weather eye out. A stack of parchment sat on the desk, Elizabeth's careful hand filling the top page.

He moved the uppermost sheet aside. The pages beneath were equally filled. This, he suspected, was her next silver-fork offering. He was glad of it. She'd not published anything in ages, and he knew all too well the burden on an author's soul when the work was slow or frustrating.

He spied among the words the same name as the heroine of Mr. King's story. Odd. Then he saw three more names also from *The Lady and the Highwayman.* That was more than odd—it was suspicious.

The girls' voices could still be heard outside. He had a bit of time for indulging his curiosity.

Fletcher quickly skimmed the first couple of paragraphs. Blazes. This *was* Mr. King's story. Why did she have his work here? And in her handwriting? Fletcher didn't recognize what little he'd read, so it was likely not yet published. He remembered the many times he had seen her in the area of the penny dreadful publishers with stacks of papers.

Could she—Could she *be* Mr. King? No. King's stories didn't sound like her. There was, of course, a hint of breeding and upbringing in the writing, but too much cant and lower-class phrasing. He'd never once heard her use those phrases. Of course, if she were attempting to hide her identity as the author . . .

If anyone ever discovered, she'd be done in. Too many patrons and parents disapproved of penny dreadfuls, enough that they would likely withdraw their support and their students if such a thing were true and known. He knew what her school meant to her. Would she truly risk it that way?

He glanced at the manuscript again, not to merely read but to evaluate. The lines were neat and orderly. Nothing was crossed out or written over. These were not working pages, but final ones. Maybe she was a scribe for King, recopying his words in her neat and legible handwriting.

He knew she and King were close. This only further confirmed it. His rival. The secret that sat between him and the woman he loved.

The woman he loved.

Outside, the voices had grown almost too dim to hear. Carriage doors closed. Horses' hooves clomped on the cobblestones. Elizabeth's students were gone, but she would return any moment and find him with a mind in turmoil.

He loved her. He loved how much she cared about people, how hard she worked to do the right thing, that she could be prim and proper one minute and a spy the next, that she'd never turned her nose up at him or his work, that together they were more of a team than they were competitors.

He loved her.

But King was ever there, the axe hanging over them.

A rap on the window pulled his attention. Martin and Hollis stood there, motioning for him to let them in. Reinforcements from the DPS.

He stepped into the entryway and to the front door, pulling it open.

"Brogan sent us to help," Hollis said. "Stone mostly just stared."

Fletcher jerked his head toward the entryway and made room for them to pass by him. "Did they explain the situation?"

Martin nodded. "Have you found anything?"

"Not yet. The students just left, so we ain't checked their bedchambers yet. I suspect we've arrived on the scene before the scoundrels."

"What do you want us to do?" Hollis asked.

"I want you to wait until Elizabeth comes back inside and ask her."

Hollis grinned. Martin's amusement was less obvious. Fletcher wasn't overly bothered. Elizabeth was more than capable of directing the efforts at her own school.

Something crashing toward the back of the school caught their attention.

"What's that way?" Martin asked, motioning to the corridor behind the stairs.

"Kitchen."

"Are the servants in there?"

Fletcher's pulse picked up pace. The housekeeper, Fanny, and Janey had all been outside helping Elizabeth send the students on their way. "No."

The men exchanged the briefest of glances, then moved with measured step toward the kitchen, cautiously approaching each turn and bend. A narrow set of back steps set them just outside the kitchen door.

Fletcher carefully looked around the doorframe. Two of Mrs. George's bullyboys. One had just set fire to the worktable.

"On 'em!" he barked.

Martin and Hollis rushed in. Chaos erupted. The man holding the torch dropped it, popping up his fists. It was a good thing all the Dreadfuls spent time sparring at headquarters.

Fletcher dove for the torch, tossing it in the large cooking fireplace. He stamped out the smoldering spots on the floor where the flames had been, then snatched up the suds bucket near the dirty dishes that had been abandoned by the housekeeper. He tossed the water on the burning table. The flames weren't entirely doused, so he grabbed a heavy rug from the hearth and swatted at the table over and over, beating at the flames. If the fire spread, the whole school would go.

One of the ruffians, the one giving Martin a run for his money, slipped free enough to dart to the hearth and grab for the torch. If he started a second fire, they'd be done for. Fletcher spun around and landed a bare-knuckle jab directly on the man's nose.

A crunch. Blood, some of it Fletcher's.

Martin was on the thug in a flash, taking the man down.

Across the room, Hollis struggled to keep his feet. These were big, vicious men, the sort who took down mountainous villains with little effort. The Dreadfuls weren't built like tree trunks, but they were scrappy.

"Tie 'im up and help Hollis," Fletcher barked to Martin, beating at the flames again.

Elizabeth arrived in just that minute. Her wide eyes took in the scene in an instant. She didn't cower, didn't faint, didn't do any of the things most men assumed all women did when faced with the slightest shock. Rather, she took up a towel and beat at the flames as well.

The fire, at last, was out, but the table was a blackened mess, cracked and broken in places. Much like one of the miscreant's nose.

Martin and Hollis had the arsonists tied up good and tight, thanks to the Dreadfuls' efforts in practicing knots. Bloodied lips and black eyes testified to the difficulty they'd had in the fight.

Between the lingering powder in her horribly mussed hair and the singes along her borrowed, lower-class clothes, Elizabeth looked nearly as bad as the rest of them. With the immediate crisis past, Fletcher felt sharply the pain of his split knuckles.

"You're bleeding," she said to him.

"And your school was almost on fire. Worth the trade, I'd say."

She wiped a trickle of sweat from her forehead. "Why would they try to burn the school if their aim was kidnapping?"

Fletcher hunched down in front of the man whose nose

he'd given a bit of character and grasped the man's shirtfront in his uninjured fist. "Why the fire? Tell me."

The man spit in his face. Fletcher didn't care.

"I'll break your nose a second time," he warned.

"We did what we do when someone shortchanges Mrs. George."

Fletcher shoved the man down once more and stood, crossing to Elizabeth. "The girls they came to steal weren't here."

"So their only choice was to burn down the school?"

"The likes of George and Allen ain't exactly the saintly type."

"The threats of arson at Hogg's school," she said. "Might those be this same sort of spite?"

"Hogg gives street children options other'n being enslaved to no-accounts like Allen and George and Four-Finger Mike. That'd set their blood boilin' and no doubting it."

Elizabeth grew very still. "Mr. Allen knows Daniel was in the York Place mews. That would give him added reason to be vengeful toward Mr. Hogg's school."

Fletcher looked to Hollis and Martin. "You two, keep an eye on these louts and this school." He turned to Elizabeth. "I need you to do something probably dangerous."

She didn't hesitate but nodded firmly and with conviction. She walked with him from the kitchen.

"I'm for Bow Street." He spoke as they walked quickly to the outside door. "I've a contact there what can summon enough of the Metropolitan Police to take care of these bully-boys and whatever's found at Hogg's school."

"Can they get to York Place fast enough?"

"I don't know. That's where you come in." He met her eye, needing to know she was up for what he was about to ask her. "Stone, Brogan, and some of the others are at our headquarters. I need you to go there and tell them. They can get to York Place fast, and they know how to handle themselves."

"The Dread Penny Society headquarters?"

Lud, he was treading on dangerous ground. He nodded.

"Are you allowed to tell me this?"

"Children's lives are in danger. Some things are more important than rules."

She raised up on her toes and pressed a quick kiss to his cheek. "You're a good man, Fletcher."

"And I'm hoping you're a good runner." He whispered the address to her.

"I'll not tell anyone," she swore, though she didn't need to. He hadn't the least doubt in her.

He set one of his etched pennies in her hand. "Go. Quickly. We're going to save some children today, Elizabeth."

She ran. So did he. If luck was with them, they'd be fast enough.

THE LADY
AND THE
HIGHWAYMAN

by Mr. King

Installment VI,
in which our Heroine faces great Danger and
uncovers Secrets within the Forest and beyond!

Did Lucinda dare cry out? She stood at the very place on the road where she had last crossed paths with the highwayman and his band, the same road on which he had searched her carriage all those weeks ago, yet now saw not a single sign of him. She knew not where else to search, but she needed his help. Nanette needed his help.

Beneath her thick outercoat, the necklace the highwayman had found in her carriage rested heavy against her heart. Though she still did not know the jewelry's origin, she had found it gave her courage and strength. It had, before anything else, afforded her a feeling of connection to her new home and new life. She pressed her hand to it as she stood on the deserted road, surrounded on all sides by the ever-thickening fog. She would not let her courage fail her now, not when so much depended upon it.

If the highwayman and his men were not here where she

had expected to find them, she would simply have to take upon herself the task of searching out Nanette.

Sir Frederick had, as far as she could recall, rescued Nanette the first time from within the shadows of the forest. Therefore, into the forest Lucinda must go. One step, one breath at a time, she moved further into the thick of the fog and the cold of the ever-shaded trees. Calling out the girl's name might draw the attention of the monster within the woods, but she had little hope of finding the poor soul if she did not give Nanette a chance to hear her voice.

"Nanette!" she called. "Answer me, if you can. Nanette!"

On and on she walked. Though her fears never fully abated, her courage rose to the occasion. She had grown strong during her time at Calden Manor. She had discovered in herself an inner fortitude.

"Nanette!"

Quick steps came toward her from the darkness, too heavy to be Nanette's. Ought she to run? Stand her ground? She hadn't a thing with which to defend herself, having assumed the highwayman and his men would see to the necessary weaponry.

Nearer and nearer the sound came, only slightly dampened by the fog and trees. Merciful heavens! Where was she to go? What was she to do? She swallowed and forced a breath. She raised her fists, ready to do all she could to fend off the inevitable attack. It was her only hope.

In a swoosh of thick, dark fabric, a man grabbed her about the waist and pulled her off the road. The movement was so quick and so sudden, she hadn't even a moment to react.

"You mustn't call out like that, Lucinda. The beast has acute hearing." Sir Frederick!

She clung to him, allowing her pulse to slow and calm. The air shuddered from her lungs. "I thought you were the monster."

"It cannot be far," he whispered. "I heard your voice quite clearly. It most certainly did as well."

"I was trying to find Nanette." Emotion broke in the words. She was so afraid for the girl, so overwhelmed herself.

"As am I."

"I had hoped to secure the aid of the highwayman," she said, "but I could not find him."

"We will simply have to make do on our own." He kept his arm around her as he led her through and around the nearby trees.

"You are not going to insist I return to Hilltop House?" She looked up at him, surprised by both the shake of his head and the disheveled nature of his appearance. He had, it seemed, already passed through an ordeal in his search. "Are you injured?"

"No, but I *am* worried." He looked out over the misty forest, mouth set in an earnest line. "I had hoped to find our sweet little Nanette by now."

Our Nanette. His choice of words touched her, even as his worry added to hers.

"Where did you find her last time? That would seem a good place to begin."

He kept his arm around her, its warmth keeping the cold at bay. "I began there, I assure you. The ruined cottage was empty, with no sign of having been occupied recently."

"Have you any other idea where to search? You know more of the beast than I do."

"There is a cave," he said. "My father believed it was the beast's lair."

She looked up at him once more. "If its lair has been known all these years, why has the monster not been hunted or expelled?"

"It is dangerous," he said, "and grows stronger when in the presence of our fear. Thus far, rooting it out has proven impossible."

Her throat thickened with worry. "And you believe Nanette is there?"

"I do not want to believe it, but I do."

Within the circle of his arms, she squared her shoulders. "Then we must go there. We must."

"Screw your courage to the sticking place. It must not fail you."

"I do not intend to allow it to falter."

His arm tightened about her. "Your courage has impressed me from the beginning. I have known from the moment I first encountered you that yours was a courageous soul. That I was not wrong on that score does my heart good, both in this moment and in all the moments leading to this one."

"I do not always *feel* brave."

"And yet you are."

And yet I am. She repeated those words in her mind as they walked on. The forest grew bone-chillingly cold. The fog, thicker the deeper they traveled, turned the midday sun dim as dusk. Just when she grew certain they could not possibly travel any farther without reaching the forest's far edge, Sir Frederick stopped.

"Have we arrived at the cave?" How she wished her voice were steadier. Sir Frederick believed her brave and bold. She wanted to be precisely that.

He motioned directly ahead of them. She took a step forward, slipping from his arms, and studied their misty surroundings. There was, indeed, a cave, its mouth wide and gaping and terrifying.

Her mind begged her to flee, to put as much distance between herself and the cavern as possible. But her heart, warmed by the touch of the necklace against her skin, insisted she remain.

"If Nanette is in there," she said, "we must go inside. We must find our dear girl."

Sir Frederick joined her. From underneath his heavy coat, he produced a small lantern, which he lit, and, together, they walked into the lair of the monster.

The air inside was dank and heavy. Long, pointed daggers of rock hung from the ceiling and jutted up from the ground. Water dripped, pooling in places. The cave ought to have been cold—no sunlight penetrated its interior—but it was not. The warm moistness of it was overwhelming, cloying.

Further into the dark deep, a growl echoed and bounced toward them. Lucinda's every hair stood at attention, her pulse quickening.

"The beast will sense my fear," she whispered to Sir Frederick.

"I do not doubt it already has. We must simply make certain it senses our bravery as well."

"What if all the courage I can summon is not enough?"

"If anyone's fortitude will be sufficient, I haven't a doubt it will be yours."

Another growl. Another rush of hot wind. They were drawing nearer. How many more steps before the beast was upon them?

Questions of the monster were quite suddenly swept aside at the sound of whimpering tears.

"Nanette?" she whispered.

Sir Frederick must have heard the cries as well. He slipped past her and, lantern held out in front of him, moved toward the sound. Around a bend in the cave, they found Nanette huddled against the wall, crying and shaking. She caught sight of them and leaped to her feet, rushing headlong into the strong arms Sir Frederick held out for her.

"We must move quickly, child," he warned her. "The beast will know we are here."

"We must go! Now!" Franticness added volume to Nanette's pleas.

Sir Frederick kept the girl close. He held high the lantern they were depending upon. He looked to Lucinda. They exchanged silent nods of equal relief and concern. They had found Nanette, but they were far from safe.

At a quick clip, they retraced their steps but did not get far before the growls and snarls grew even louder. The monster must have been very close behind them.

It senses and thrives off your fear. Be brave.

Nanette froze, eyes wide. Not a muscle in her body moved.

Lucinda looked to Sir Frederick. Worry filled his features. "The monster has seized her," he said.

"It is feeding on her fear?"

He nodded.

"Can you carry her out, even frozen as she is? Take her as far from here as possible?"

His gaze turned to something behind her, something that drained every drop of color from his face. "We are too late," he whispered.

Lucinda's lungs felt like stones in her chest. Her heart pounded against the heaviness. The weight seemed to spread, holding her arms still and her legs rooted to the spot. Moving felt increasingly impossible. Was the beast sensing her fear as well?

She yet faced Sir Frederick and could see that he, too, had grown unnaturally still, eyes frozen on the threat lurking behind her. The growling had stopped, replaced by the loud, steady breathing of something so near she could feel the heat emanating from its body.

If only the highwayman had found the legendary talisman! What hope had they of defeating the beast, or even escaping its clutches, without the protection of the missing amulet?

Against her chest, a warmth started, small and pointed at first, but spreading bit by bit. The necklace. The one the highwayman had found in her carriage! It was responding to the presence of the beast. Could it be the talisman they sought?

No. The highwayman had searched high and low for years. He would not have given it to her if he'd thought for even a moment it was a powerful amulet. Yet everywhere the warmth of it spread, her stiffness abated. It reached her neck. She could turn her head. Then her shoulders.

I am able to move. Only I am able. She and she alone could face the beast that had held so many captive for so many years, that had caused such pain and suffering. Only she.

Why had the highwayman not simply taken the amulet and faced down the beast himself rather than leaving the task to her? He'd not even told her what he'd actually given her.

Can I be so certain I am correct, that this is, in fact, the sought-after talisman? She was able to move enough that she could turn to face the beast if she chose. Whether or not the necklace she wore was the mystical charm destined to destroy the hideous beast, she had to at least try to save them all.

She set her hand on her coat, directly above the necklace. Its warmth spread farther, faster. *I must do this.*

Lucinda spun about. Mere inches away, a hideous face glared at her. A lion. A dragon. A demon. She didn't know what it was, only that it was horrifying. It growled low in its throat, steam rising from its wide, flaring nostrils, saliva dripping from its long, pointed fangs.

As when she had been stopped by the highwayman, and later, rushing to the forest to save her home, Lucinda held her chin up, shoulders back, and told herself she was braver than she felt.

"I—" Her voice shook. She began again. "I am not—"

The beast released a piercing, earth-shaking howl, the

heat of its breath nearly knocking her down. She ought to have been terrified, but she felt a growing calm.

"I am not—"

Again, it interrupted her declaration with an anger-filled roar. Its enormous clawed feet scratched at the cave floor. Its broad beastly shoulders crouched, glowing eyes narrowed on her.

"I—"

It crouched lower, shifting its weight again and again from one taloned paw to the other, clearly preparing to pounce.

"—am—"

It leaped for her, hooked claws aimed for her head.

"—not afraid of you."

Light poured from her necklace, so bright it penetrated her coat, filling the cave with a red glow. The beast, in mid-flight, was tossed away from her by the force of the light.

Lucinda, herself, was thrown backward. She landed on her side, skidding along the rocky surface, glowing and hurting and confused.

Complete silence descended on the cave. No claws tearing at rock, no hot, heavy breaths. She pulled herself up on her elbows. The necklace no longer glowed. The lantern Sir Frederick had been holding was extinguished. She could hear nothing and see nothing.

"Nanette?" Her voice quavered. She was concerned for the girl, yes, but not truly afraid. No longer. The fear she had felt upon first seeing the beast was, somehow, gone. "Sir Frederick?"

"We're here." His deep, steady voice proved vastly reassuring.

"I cannot see," she said. "The beast may be—"

"You've destroyed it." Nanette spoke with surety.

Something brushed against her. She flinched back, only to realize it was Sir Frederick. He pulled her into his embrace. Her hands found Nanette there with them. She clung to them both.

"You've done it, Lucinda," Sir Frederick whispered. "I knew you would. I knew it from the very first."

"The beast really has been destroyed?"

"It has."

"And I'm no longer afraid," Nanette said.

Sir Frederick helped her to her feet. As Nanette had said, the aura of fear that had filled the place, that she had fought against while facing the monster, had dissipated.

The lantern was lit a moment later. Sir Frederick held it aloft, illuminating the cave once more. She saw no sign of the beast she had faced.

"It is gone," she said in amazement.

"When the light from your necklace reached it, the monster simply dissolved." He held out his hand.

She set her hand in his. "Then the necklace really is the amulet." She wrapped her other hand around Nanette's.

"It is," Sir Frederick said.

She eyed him as they moved swiftly but carefully from the cave. "You do not seem surprised."

"I recognized it," he said.

"Then why did you not tell me? Or take the talisman yourself? You knew where the beast was and what it was and—"

"I haven't your bravery, my dear. I could not have done what you did."

She shook her head. "If you had worn the amulet, you could have."

"The necklace was important, but it was not the crucial element. Others have attempted what you just did and failed."

They stepped from the cave into the forest. She had all but forgotten it was daytime. It had been so dark and foreboding in the cavern. She looked back at the mouth of the cave. The beast was truly gone. She, somehow, had faced it and, without knowing, defeated it.

"I have never been truly brave," she said.

Sir Frederick raised her fingers to his lips and pressed a kiss there. "Your bravery was apparent from the very first. I knew then that you were the one we'd been waiting for."

Their first meeting had been tea amongst neighbors. She'd hardly been brave then; she hadn't needed to be.

They walked through the forest, hand-in-hand-in-hand.

"The monster truly is gone?" Nanette asked as they approached Hilltop House. "It won't come back?"

"It won't come back," Sir Frederick said. "Our Miss Ledford made quite certain of that." He looked to Lucinda. "You've saved us all."

He then did something Lucinda thought never to see: he smiled. A heart-melting, soul-warming, *dimpled* smile.

CHAPTER 26

 Making Street. The Dread Penny Society had its head-quarters on King Street. How had she not realized it sooner? She'd crossed paths with Fletcher on that very street more than once. She'd come across Hollis Darby and Stone, both of whom she suspected belonged to that mysterious fraternity. She might have written about great mysteries being unwound by intrepid women, but she herself was falling short of that mark.

As she turned swiftly from Garrick onto King Street, she eyed the familiar buildings. She'd passed them often with no idea the secrets one of them kept.

From the crossing of Garrick and King. The fifth door toward Covent Garden. Knock three times. She'd repeated Fletcher's instructions again and again as she'd raced toward King Street. She knew them now word for word.

"One. Two." She silently counted each door she passed. ". . . Four. Five." She stopped, out of breath but determined. She knew this door. It was the very step on which she'd stood with Fletcher and Stone only that morning. They'd been at their headquarters, and she hadn't even realized it.

She knocked at the door three times as instructed.

When the butler answers, give him the penny and tell him you require an audience with a Dreadful. He'll make you wait on the step, but someone will come speak with you.

The scraggliest butler she'd ever seen opened the door, looking for all the world as if he were barely awake. She knew better than to trust appearances. The building looked to be of little import, but was actually significant. The members of this society gave the impression of hiding nothing, but they all were doing quite the opposite.

She produced Fletcher's penny and held it out to him. "I require an audience with a Dreadful." She spoke with more surety than she felt.

The butler took her coin and promptly shut the door.

He'll make you wait on the step.

She hoped that was indeed what he was doing rather than simply taking her penny and promptly forgetting her existence. She hadn't another penny. Without one, she wouldn't have Fletcher's backing to grant her the ear of this organization. And she needed their help. Mr. Hogg and his children needed their help.

So she waited.

And waited.

And waited.

Oh, Fletcher. You had best be correct about this. I don't know what else to do.

The door opened once more. Far from relieved, her nervousness increased tenfold. She knew for a fact she wasn't meant to be on this doorstep in possession of the information she had. The Dreadfuls might not be willing to listen. Or they might lend her an audience only to later exact some kind of punishment on Fletcher for whispering their secret. What if she was about to create mountains of trouble?

On the other side of the door stood Brogan Donnelly. She ought to have realized they would choose someone she already knew had an association with the Dread Penny Society. They'd be giving away no new information that way.

"Come in." He motioned her through the door with a sharp jerk of his hand.

She moved quickly. The door was shut directly behind her. The scraggly butler sat in a chair nearby, slumped against the back, head bent backward and mouth agape, quite as one would be if asleep in a chair. But how could he be so quickly?

"This is one of Fletcher's pennies." Brogan held up the coin she had delivered.

"Two of Mrs. George's men attacked my school and attempted to set it afire. They've indicated that others are heading for Hogg's school to do the same." She spoke quickly, not wishing to waste even a moment. "Fletcher sent me here so the society could send help to Mr. Hogg. He himself went to Bow Street."

Brogan turned to the man in the chair. "Sound the alert. All hands to Hogg's."

The butler jumped agilely to his feet and rushed to the back of the corridor. An instant later, Elizabeth heard bells ringing throughout the building.

"What do you need me to do?" she asked.

"Secure your school. The Dreadfuls there will stay with you until all's well."

"Will someone send word once Hogg's school is safe? I will not be able to rest until I know."

His smile was quick but kind. "I'd wager Fletch'll call on you soon enough."

Her heart simultaneously rose and dropped. "Will he be in trouble for telling me where to find all of you?"

The Irishman's expression turned serious. "He's violated a rule. There're consequences for that."

"But what choice did he have?" she argued.

"There's always a choice, lass. He wouldn't have made this one lightly."

That was not overly reassuring. "Will he lose his membership?"

"Possibly."

Oh, mercy. "The work of this group is so important to him, Mr. Donnelly. Not being part of it would . . . It would tear him apart."

"It's out of his hands now." He motioned her to the door. "The fewer people you see here, the better chance he has, since he'll not have revealed everything. I'd suggest you go."

"New people must be told of this location sometimes, else you'd never have new members," she said as she moved to the door.

"But you're not a new member, are you? And you never could be. That's a crucial difference."

She set her hand on the doorknob. "Please argue for him. Please."

He only gave a quick nod and indicated again she should go.

In the length of a breath, she was out on the step in the diminishing light of evening. Alone. And worried.

CHAPTER 27

arkington had faith enough in Fletcher to rouse several of his colleagues to join the rush to the York Place ragged school. Many in the Dread Penny Society would be there already—Fletcher hadn't a doubt Elizabeth had delivered her message—either doing their utmost to counter the threat or waiting for it to arrive. Parkington didn't know they belonged to the DPS. They'd always explained themselves to him as merely a group of concerned citizens who did what they could where they could. Bringing the man in didn't violate any rules. Sending Elizabeth had.

He'd not worry about that yet, though. They'd far more immediate troubles.

Hogg's was a day school. The students wouldn't likely still be there. But Hogg very well might be. His partners at the school, Kinnaird and Pelham, might be as well. The school's staff also. While fewer lives were in immediate danger, the situation felt no less urgent. They'd people to warn and a school to save.

Parkington barked out orders as soon as they reached the

school, sending some of his men around the building in one direction, some in the other.

"I've a few mates who're likely here," Fletcher told him. "They've come to protect the school as well."

"Might be tough to tell who's with us and who's against us." Parkington glanced at him briefly.

"We save the school first and sort out the rest later."

A whistle pierced the air.

"One of my men," Parkington said, rushing in the direction of the sound, Fletcher hard on his heels.

The sounds of a struggle reached them before the sight of it did. Brogan and Stone were fist-to-face with two brawny men, neither of whom Fletcher recognized. Three of Parkington's men were rushing on other unknowns, all of whom held the very type of torches they'd been finding around the school the last weeks and that George's bullyboy had tried to use to set fire to Thurloe.

Parkington rushed into the fray. Fletcher spotted Kumar, another of the Dreadfuls, swatting at smoldering flames among a few of the bushes that were dangerously close to the school.

"The staff?" Fletcher asked.

"We got them out," he said. "Hogg and Kinnaird were here. They've taken the servants to a safe place. This lot"—he indicated the men fighting and shouting and attempting to get their torches to the walls—"were on us almost the instant the staff were out. It was a close-run thing, my friend."

"And we ain't clear yet." Fletcher swatted at the bushes. It was the second fire he'd fought that day.

One of the policemen blew on his whistle again. Everyone

who'd come would soon be there to join the fight. With any luck, they'd vastly outnumber the ne'er-do-wells.

Fletcher and Kumar managed to extinguish the glow in the shrubbery in time to spot the telltale amber of new flames not far distant.

"These blokes'll burn the place down yet," Fletcher growled.

"Not if we've a say in the matter." Kumar was on the move before finishing the declaration.

Fletcher's attention was caught by a stout man tossing a torch and running from the fray. Oh, he'd not be getting away so easily as that. Fletcher rushed after him, catching up easily. With a leap, his arms outstretched, he tackled the would-be arsonist, slamming him hard against the ground. The man struggled, surprisingly strong. Fletcher held fast, managing to turn his quarry enough for the dim remaining light to reveal his identity.

"Allen," Fletcher spat.

"You. You were one of 'em who stole the boy." Anger. Pure, unsheathed anger.

"I'll steal a hundred children from the likes of you," Fletcher said.

Even pinned to the ground, Allen's arrogance didn't abate. "And Four-Finger'll steal 'em back. You'll never save 'em all."

"Watch me." He shoved the man hard against the ground again.

"Rough me up all you like. I already have what I came for."

Fear seized Fletcher's chest. Daniel. Had Allen abducted him again? Fletcher refused to believe he'd failed the child again. But the Dreadfuls might not've thought to evacuate the mews.

"Parkington!" He had to shout twice to catch the policeman's notice. "I've a lowlife for you here. Caught him tryin' to run off."

"You'll be too late." Allen sounded gratingly sure of himself.

Fletcher tried to hold back his own doubts and worries. He'd not lose Daniel again.

One of Parkington's colleagues soon took Fletcher's place. Ignoring Allen's heckling, Fletcher rushed toward the stables a fair distance away. Joe would be guarding the boy, but he needed to know the danger was higher than it had been.

The stable door was open. Fletcher didn't pause, but ran directly inside and nearly collided with Joe. He ducked before the man could land him a hard facer.

"It's Walker," he said, slipping out of the way of a second punch.

Joe lowered his arms and took a tight breath. "Thought you was Four-Finger Mike."

"You know, then?"

Joe glanced over his shoulder into the dim interior of the stable. "Miss Black told us there was like to be trouble tonight."

"She was here?"

"*Is* here." Joe motioned with his head in the same direction he'd looked only a moment ago.

Was she daft? "Elizabeth?"

"I was afraid for Daniel," her beloved voice answered. "I knew Joe would stand guard if only he knew."

"Keep an eye out," Fletcher told the stablehand, then crossed to where Elizabeth was. His eyes adjusted as he moved farther inside. By the time he reached the backmost stall, he could see her sitting there, holding Daniel to her. "You took a mighty risk."

"I've taken quite a few today, in fact," she said. "I'll keep taking this one until I know the boy is safe."

Fletcher crouched down on the ground in front of them. "Your school's secure. My mate at the Metropolitan Police sent some men over to keep watch. We might do best to take Daniel there until we know he'd be safe here."

Elizabeth thought on it a moment. "I don't think he'd like being away from Joe. But it wouldn't be permanent. I imagine he would be back here tomorrow."

"Likely." Fletcher's senses were on edge. He had the strongest suspicion the danger was growing, though he couldn't say why he felt that so keenly. "Joe," he called over his shoulder. "Would you object if we took the boy to Miss Black's school? He'd be safer there."

"Whatever'll keep him safest."

Fletcher tucked Daniel up against him. Elizabeth kept close at their side. Together, they moved swiftly from the stables, pausing long enough for Joe to tell the boy to be brave and that he'd come for him the moment it was safe to do so.

Out into the night they stepped. It was nearly completely dark. Perhaps they'd best call for a hansom cab. They'd only just crossed in front of Hogg's school when pounding foot-steps approached.

"Guard the boy," Elizabeth called out the instant before

a looming figure pounded into Fletcher, sending him to the ground, Daniel with him.

The assailant reached for Daniel. Enough light remained to reveal his four-fingered right hand. This was the man they'd feared would come.

Fletcher rolled away, hopping to his feet and setting himself between Daniel and Four-Finger Mike. Elizabeth slipped behind him, guarding the child. "Leave the boy be."

"Cain't do that. He knows too much."

"I know a few things, m'self." Fletcher was stalling, hoping Joe or one of the Dreadfuls would pass and tip the scales in his favor. "I know you're being watched by the police."

"That ain't news, friend."

"I know you have dealings with Mr. Alistair Headley."

Four-Finger snorted in derision. "That gentry cove? Small beans, that one."

Headley was involved in something shady, then, but not this. "He's not one for arson or kidnapping, then?"

"Ain't kidnapping if I'm taking back what's already mine."

"The boy's not yours—or anyone else's." Fletcher stood firm.

"I say he is." Four-Finger brandished a dagger.

Blimey. Without a blade, he was doomed in a knife fight. This situation could get bad quickly.

"The boy stays with us," Elizabeth said, moving to stand beside Fletcher. She'd changed up her voice in a believable version of a street accent. Enough of Móirín's disguise remained that Four-Finger wasn't likely to know who she was.

"No bird's gonna thwart me."

Elizabeth shrugged then pulled a knife from her boot.

One of the largest knives he'd ever seen hidden on someone's person. She brandished it like an expert. Her show of confidence brought the first hints of doubt to Four-Finger's face.

"Drop your wee knife," Elizabeth said. "Save me the trouble of cutting it out of your hand. I ain't looking to make that kind o' mess."

"You're bluffin'," the man spat.

"Try your luck, then."

Directly behind Four-Finger Mike, Fletcher could see a tall, broad-shouldered silhouette stealthily approach. Elizabeth kept her knife pointed menacingly at their foe. Fletcher assessed their situation. Where could they run? What makeshift weapons did they have? How likely was it this new arrival was one of Four-Finger's comrades?

The figure addressed Four-Finger Mike by a less-than-flattering name. The thug spun about and was, almost too fast to be seen, leveled by a punch so hard, so perfectly placed, that Fletcher swore he could hear teeth and jaw and nose all crack at once. Four-Finger hit the ground, hard. A kick was delivered, causing the man to curl up in pain. He'd not be going anywhere.

"Danny." The figure was Joe. Of course it was.

Daniel rushed to his friend and guardian and was promptly scooped up and carried away without a backward glance.

"That was impressive," Elizabeth said.

Fletcher eyed her sidelong. "As was your expert knife brandishing."

She pushed out a rush of breath. "I'm a better actress than

I thought. I was also doing my best to appear unafraid, which was absolutely not true."

Fletcher crossed to the prostrate form of Four-Finger Mike. He would eventually feel equal to standing. Fletcher would be ready when he was.

"The other Dreadfuls'll come 'round soon enough," he quietly told Elizabeth. "It'd be best if you weren't here when they arrive."

"Because then I'd be able to identify them?"

He nodded. The more she learned of the Dread Penny Society, the harder it'd be to keep his membership.

"You ain't likely to get credit for all you've done today," he said. "But I thank you for it."

"I didn't do it for the credit," she said. "I suspect you didn't either."

He eyed the man still curled up on the ground and holding his hands to his bleeding face. "There're too many men like this'n in the world."

He could hear someone approaching. Telling her the location of the Dreadfuls' headquarters, giving her the ability to identify a growing number of them . . . he'd broken a lot of rules. There were always consequences for that. If another of the Dreadfuls were to appear, it'd be best if she didn't see him.

"Rush off," he told her earnestly. "It's for the best."

She hesitated only a moment before leaving swiftly. Watching her go, he realized something. Losing his membership in the Dread Penny Society would hurt and sting and frustrate him. But losing Elizabeth was a tragedy he'd never recover from.

THE LADY
AND THE
HIGHWAYMAN

by Mr. King

Installment VII,
in which our Heroine seizes her Happiness!

Lucinda casually mentioned over tea the next afternoon that she meant to take a walk in the woods and do all she could to find the highwayman. She hinted that she meant to tell him all that had happened the day before and that the necklace he had given her was the amulet he'd been searching for. Sir Frederick had shown only minimal interest, nodding and expressing his relief that the forest was now a safe place.

She knew she was not wrong about him. His smile had given him away.

Thus, when she saw her highwayman sauntering down the forest path toward her, she could not entirely contain the excitement she felt. All that she had come to admire and enjoy about this mysterious man of daring and intrigue, and all she had come to love and cherish about Sir Frederick's generous and caring heart, were found in one remarkable gentleman.

"Miss." He tugged at his bedraggled hat. "Fine thing seeing you here."

"I looked for you in this very spot yesterday," she said, "but it seems you were occupied elsewhere."

His mouth tipped in a smile. "I was, in fact, in the forest yesterday."

She bit back a smile of her own. "I know."

Curiosity tugged at his mouth. "You do?"

"And, by the end of the day, I understood why I couldn't find you."

He tucked his hands into the pockets of his outercoat. "Did you?"

"I also discovered why Sir Frederick told me that he knew I was brave from our very first encounter, when that encounter involved no degree of courage."

The highwayman grew noticeably uneasy. "Because he misremembered?"

"No." She stepped up to him and, rising onto her toes, reached up and took hold of the brim of his hat. "Because he is you." She pulled his hat off. Sir Frederick. Her Sir Frederick. Her highwayman. "Why the ruse?"

"The amulet was found during my father's lifetime, but it did not work as it was meant to. We had the talisman, but not the one intended to wield it. Our only hope was to find someone inherently brave."

"So you held up carriages to gauge your victims' reactions?"

"I severely disliked the necessity of it. It felt cruel and was certainly not kind." All the bravado of the highwayman melted away, replaced by uncertainty and heaviness of heart.

"I wished again and again I were in a position to be truthful with you about all of this. That day when we saw each other in town, I was discussing my work as a highwayman, which necessitated my dismissal of you; I could not risk you over-hearing."

So many things were making sense to her at last.

He took her hand as he'd done the day before, but this time with an aura of pleading. "I will understand, my Lucinda, if you cannot forgive me for deceiving you. The secret was simply too vast and the consequences too potentially devastating."

She understood fully and deeply. "My darling Frederick." She set her arms about his neck. "My dear, brave highwayman."

In true dastardly fashion, he bent and kissed her, declaring his love and devotion through the earnestness of that very personal gesture. Lucinda clung to him, reveling in the certainty she felt within his arms, and in the promise that they could weather any storm.

Together.

The lady and the highwayman.

CHAPTER 28

The Metropolitan Police stationed two men outside Thurloe, agreeing to keep them there for the time being. Mr. Allen and Four-Finger Mike had been apprehended, and they knew where to look for Mrs. George. All in all, it had been a fruitful night.

Elizabeth lowered herself into the armchair nearest her office fireplace, utterly spent. The school was completely silent, which was both reassuring and unnerving. Her girls were safe; that was what mattered most.

Fletcher stepped inside, the skin under his eyes marred with the shadow of exhaustion. He also bore the telltale bruises of one who'd been in a few too many brawls back-to-back.

"You look a tad worse for wear," Elizabeth said, hearing the weariness in her own voice.

"Always do after a night like this'n." He pulled the ottoman over to her chair and sat on it, facing her.

"You do this often, do you?"

"Saving children like Daniel and Hogg's students and yours ain't always a small ask. Sometimes it requires a fight."

She reached out and took his hand. "The sort of fight Morris and Jimmy undertake in your stories?"

"Aye."

"Is that why you write what you do? A parallel of your own efforts?"

"I started fighting for urchins while I still was one. Tried feeding m' fellow street children while I was hungry m'self. Fought to free little'ns from violent masters while I was still bein' beaten. Life ain't always been kind to me, Elizabeth."

"I know."

Contrition touched his tired expression. "I hadn't meant to make life harder for you, endangering you and your girls the way I did."

Keeping his hand in hers, she rose and led him to the front-facing window. "The school is safe," she said, motioning to the policeman patrolling the street. "I will have a brawny, capable manservant in place before the girls return. We will be safe, and no one, other than you and I and a small handful of your very trustworthy friends, will be any the wiser about my less-than-prim role in all of this."

He wrapped his arms around her from behind, holding her tenderly. "You saved a few lives tonight. Though few know of it, I hope you feel how blasted remarkable that is."

She turned in his arms, looking up at him, her hands on his chest. "Brogan said you might lose your membership in the Dread Penny Society."

"Might." He tucked a stray strand of hair behind her ear, then set his arms around her again. "Tellin' you where to find the Dreadfuls breaks some mighty big rules."

Whether her heart pounded from worry over him or the

comfort of his embrace, she didn't know. "You *had* to send me, though. Everyone at Hogg's school was in danger."

"I intend to argue m' case, I assure you. But it won't be an easy-won battle," he said.

"Was it worth it?"

"In this moment, dove, I cain't think of a thing these past weeks that ain't been worth it."

He tucked her even closer. She slid her arms around his neck. His pulse picked up pace.

"You know I ain't the sort society's sticklers are likely to approve of."

She interlocked her fingers behind his neck. "That is a risk I am excessively willing to take."

His gaze narrowed. "Even if it costs you support for your school?"

"I have enough faith in us to believe we can weather whatever storms may come."

"And if your Mr. King objects?" he asked hesitantly.

Mr. King. That still stood between them, the secret she kept, the literary rival he chased.

"Does Mr. King bother you a great deal?" she asked.

"A bit at least, but not on account o' his success." Fletcher lowered his voice. "He's close to you in ways I can't claim. How am I to compete with that?"

Of all the responses she might have received, jealousy was not one she'd expected.

"I can tell you truthfully, Fletcher Walker, that the closeness we're sharing now is something I have *never* shared with Mr. King."

"Truly?" The corner of his mouth tipped upward.

"Truly. Furthermore, I have every intention of introducing him to you."

That pulled his eyes wide. She couldn't help a laugh at his surprised amazement.

"King won't object?"

She shook her head. *Mr. King* most certainly wouldn't. How she wished her nom de plume was a real person so she could send him traipsing into the Dread Penny Society headquarters demanding both membership and Fletcher's reinstatement.

"My heart aches that you might lose your place among the Dreadfuls." She rested her head against him, relishing the lingering embrace. "I will think of a way to help; I swear I will."

"You're helping more than you know, dear."

She tipped her head enough to look up at him once more. "We can still be a team, even if the DPS tosses you out."

"I've every intention of always bein' on *your* team."

She could feel herself blush even as her smile grew. "I suspect you like me, Fletcher Walker."

"I *love* you," he said. "With every breath, every heartbeat, every thought. I love you, Miss Elizabeth Black. I love you, and I always will."

She swallowed back the emotion rising unexpectedly in her throat. He loved her. He truly did.

"No matter that I make my living with words, I'm at a loss to express how very much I love you," she said.

"I don't need words, dove."

He bent, his arms holding her close. His kiss was not tentative, not questioning, but sure and reassuring. Theirs was not a love that had taken the direct route, but they'd found their way to this solid foundation all the same.

Fletcher kissed her cheek, then her jaw.

"I do like when you call me 'dove.'" A sliver of pleasure slid down her body as his lips brushed her neck.

"It ain't exactly a high-class pet name." He kissed her right temple, then her left. "It's something street people say."

She shifted her hand to his face and looked into his eyes. "It is perfect because it is the name *you* gave me."

"You've fallen in love with an overgrown urchin, you know."

How she loved when he smiled at her in just that way.

"If that overgrown urchin knows what's good for him, he'll kiss me again."

"My great pleasure." He leaned his forehead against hers and added in a whisper, "Dove."

He kissed her slowly and deeply, holding her in his strong, gentle arms. He kissed her in the peaceful silence of her beloved school, quite as naturally as if they'd been doing so from the very beginning.

She loved him and knew with absolute certainty he loved her. The moment was utterly and absolutely perfect.

CHAPTER 29

A letter sat on the table, sealed in black wax under the mark of the Dread Master. Fletcher sat in a spindle-backed chair in the empty aisle between the rows of seats his comrades occupied in the Dreadfuls' parliamentary chamber. Ahead of him, just beyond the table and the letter, his usual chair sat empty, as the bylaws required when a member was on trial. This ritual had been enacted only twice before, and never with Fletcher in the position of scrutiny.

He'd been explaining his actions for a full five minutes now, and there was little else to say. The situation was not truly so complicated. "Dozens of children's lives was at stake," he said, bringing his testimony to its conclusion. "If saving their lives meant losin' my membership, that was a trade-off I's willing to make."

He took a breath and steeled his resolve. He would face the consequences of his decision.

"My membership had already been guessed at," Brogan said. "Seeing me here didn't reveal anything new to her."

"It revealed our society's location," Doc pointed out. "No one's ever spilled that secret before."

"Certainly we have," Hollis countered. "Every time we have determined someone new was worthy and eligible for membership."

"Which Miss Black ain't," Martin said.

"She is most certainly worthy," Brogan said. "As much as anyone we've brought in among us."

"But she ain't eligible." Doc didn't speak unkindly, but neither was he wrong.

Elizabeth didn't write penny dreadfuls, though she was closely connected to King, who *did*. And Fletcher himself had told her all the members were male, though he'd jokingly explained it as a requirement to wear trousers.

"There weren't anyone else I could send," Fletcher said. "But I also knew she could be counted on to keep mum."

"Why not send Janey or Fanny?" Milligan pressed.

He turned in that direction. "They don't know where headquarters is, and they ain't any more eligible than Miss Black. Less so, truth be told. She, at least, is a writer and a do-gooder."

Doc nodded his acknowledgment of that truth. Nothing about this debate had been unkind or even personal. They were, as was required, arguing all aspects of his decision and the impact it had on the group. He only hoped those continually reminding the others of the rules he'd broken didn't actually wish to see him tossed out.

"You might've sent Martin or me," Hollis said. "We were both at Thurloe."

"If I had, that would've left Miss Black and only one of

you to keep them two men subdued, a difficult task for three of us Dreadfuls to manage. That would've been dangerous in the extreme."

The others looked to Hollis and Martin. Both nodded.

"None of us'd argue that you weren't in a fix," Irving said. "But neither can we overlook that you laid out our location to someone who ain't approved to know it. You're aware that's against the rules. So are we."

"So is *she*," Brogan said. "Told me as much. Worried, she was. Afraid Fletcher would lose his membership. Someone as concerned as she was wouldn't go blabbing about what she knows."

"But she's not a member," Irving said. "And can't be. We've never revealed our location to someone who wasn't coming here to join up, having already been fully scrutinized."

Fletcher remembered how he had, for a moment, once wondered if Elizabeth might have been the pen behind Mr. King's stories. If only that had been true. He'd have a firm argument in his favor, and she'd be able to join the Dreadfuls. Almost.

"We're arguing the same things over again," Stone muttered. "Time to vote."

It was a mercy, really. No point prolonging the pain.

A knock sounded immediately on the council chamber door. That almost never happened. All eyes turned in that direction. Not a word was spoken.

Nolan, the butler, stepped to the threshold. "A visitor, gentlemen."

The silence among the Dreadfuls echoed Fletcher's confusion.

Fletcher might've been on trial, with his membership on the line, but he was still the acting head of the organization.

"You never allow visitors," he said to Nolan.

"This'n placed a penny right where one's meant to be placed."

Intriguing, but not reason enough. One need only look at the pile of coins on the entryway table to know that much. "We don't let people wander in, declarin' themselves interested. That ain't how this works. You know that."

Nolan was unmoved. "For this'n, you'll want to make an exception."

"What makes you so certain?" Fletcher asked.

A smile slowly spread over Nolan's face. "Would I be interrupting if I weren't certain?"

They all knew Nolan too well to think he'd get up off his bench for anything that wasn't worth their time or the risk he was taking interrupting the meeting.

"Who is he?"

Nolan dipped his head. "Mr. King."

Fletcher was on his feet on the instant. Half the room was as well, the other half staring in disbelief. King? They'd been searching for him for weeks. *Fletcher* had been searching for him. Elizabeth knew him, knew him well. Still, she wouldn't have told him where the Dread Penny Society made its headquarters.

She *wouldn't* have. Yet King was here.

He didn't know how both things could be true, but he

knew they were. Fletcher met each of the Dreadfuls' eyes. One nod after another. His gaze fell last on Stone.

The often-silent man spoke. "Looking for King started this whole muddle. It's best we see it through."

True as the day was long. Fletcher turned to Nolan. "Let King in."

Nolan slipped out. All eyes were on the empty doorway. From the darkness beyond, a walking stick tapped against the floor. The clack of shoes joined, both growing louder.

A shadowy silhouette appeared where Nolan had been. King wasn't very tall, even with a stovepipe hat on his head. Fletcher could make out little beyond that. Too much darkness shadowed the entryway.

King took a single step into the spill of light from the council room lanterns.

"Bung your eye," he breathed.

Elizabeth—*Elizabeth*—quirked an eyebrow beneath the tall hat sitting at a jaunty angle on her head, her hair pulled up in a loose bun. Her high-polished walking stick tapped against the floor once more as she took another step, her heeled, pull-button boots echoing their earlier sound as well. She was not merely wearing trousers, she was *wearing* trousers. And a shirtwaist and tailcoat precisely in the style of a man's but tailored quite perfectly to her.

Fletcher attempted to swallow and found it took more effort than it ought. He didn't bother trying to look away; he knew he'd never manage that. No one else in the room had either.

Elizabeth eyed them all, chin at a confident angle, her expression one of patience and expectation. She continued her slow, steady walk into the room and up the aisle directly to him. She stopped just out of arm's reach and met his gaze.

He cleared his throat. "Mr. King?"

A hint of a smile pulled at her lips. "Surprised?"

"By a few things."

"You said members have to wear trousers." She shrugged a single shoulder. "Fortunately, I know a very talented tailor."

"That tailor is either my new favorite person or my new archenemy."

She pulled her hat off her head and, with an expertise that matched his own, tossed it, brim down and spinning, onto the throne-like chair he usually occupied. She then faced the room of shocked, amused, and stunned-into-silence men around her.

"I am Mr. King, reigning monarch of the penny dreadfuls. I give my time and effort to the causes of the poor, the oppressed, the afflicted. And I am wearing trousers." She added the last bit with a flourish to indicate her unexpected attire.

Brogan didn't bother suppressing his laughter. Hollis let his grin blossom as well. Martin hid his smile behind his hand.

"I am here to apply for membership in the Dread Penny Society, having met all the requirements."

"This is highly unusual," Kumar stated the obvious without true disapproval.

"And highly risky," Fletcher said quietly to Elizabeth. "Should word of this—you dressing as a man and petitioning for membership in, essentially, a gentlemen's club—reach the ears of Society, you could lose everything, dove."

She met his eye and, for the first time since her breath-catching entrance, her surety gave way to the tiniest hint of doubt. "I told myself I'd find a means of salvaging your membership. Revealing the location of headquarters is only tolerated when the person being told is applying for membership."

"You mean to exploit a loophole?"

"I mean to save your skin," she said.

Even Stone allowed a glimmer of appreciation in his usually unreadable eyes.

"You took an enormous risk coming here as you did," Fletcher said.

"No fear. I still have Móirín's knife in my boot." She turned back to the others. "Vote, then. In or out."

"First, though," Hollis jumped in. "We have an opportunity to settle our previous matter quite quickly. Fletcher revealed our location to someone who, technically, *was* eligible to receive that information. He hasn't, if one is being fully honest, violated any of our rules."

"Is she eligible, though?" Irving asked. There was no mistaking the hope in his tone and expression.

"Our bylaws don't specifically ban women from joining," Stone said. "I say she's eligible."

"Then I'm calling for the vote on Fletch," Hollis said. "All insisting his membership be revoked, make yourselves heard."

Not a soul spoke.

"All finding no cause to dismiss him?" Hollis continued.

A chorus of "ayes" filled the large room. Relief surged through Fletcher. Relief. Gratitude. Exhaustion. The sealed letter on the small table nearby contained the Dread Master's vote, one that carried the weight of two of theirs. Enough to break a tie. Enough to create one. Not enough to overthrow a unanimous decision. As custom dictated when the Dread Master's voice was not needed, Fletcher would take the parchment to the fire after the meeting and burn it, unopened.

"Resume your place, Fletcher Walker." Brogan jerked his head toward the throne.

Fletcher crossed to it. He took up Elizabeth's hat, then sat in the familiar spot. Ah, but he'd missed his chair. When his eyes met hers, she smiled softly, dipped her head, and turned to go.

To go?

"Mr. King," he called out.

She turned back, eyeing him with confused curiosity.

"Did you not wish for a vote on your membership? That is why you came, after all."

She leaned on her walking stick. "That's not why I came, Mr. Walker. I've done what I came for."

She'd saved him.

Stone, of all people, burst into the momentary silence. "I'm calling for a vote. All feeling Mr. King hasn't shown herself worthy to be counted among us, make yourself known."

"And then take yourself off," Fletcher added for good measure.

Chuckles and headshakes were all that answered.

"All feeling Mr. King belongs here as much as any of the rest of us?" Stone continued.

With "ayes" as enthusiastic as those cast in Fletcher's favor, the Dreadfuls welcomed a surprising, brave, remarkable woman among them. They'd turned a would-be rival into an ally. An ally who'd saved his skin at great risk to herself.

"Welcome to the Dread Penny Society, Mr. King," Fletcher said as he languidly stood, her hat still in his hand. He crossed to her and set it on her head.

"You're not angry with me for keeping this secret?" she asked.

"On the contrary." He wrapped one arm around her. He turned his head ever so slightly to address the membership. "I'm breaking with tradition, lads, and sealing this vote with something more than a handshake."

"Go on, then," Brogan called.

"No objections," Irving tossed out.

Fletcher looked to Elizabeth once more. "Any objections from our newest Dreadful?"

"None whatsoever."

Fletcher tugged Elizabeth close enough to entirely close the gap between them. She tossed her walking stick to Hollis, who caught it with a laugh. Elizabeth held Fletcher's face in her hands, her eyes fixed on him.

"I do love you, you know," she whispered.

"I know it, and I'm amazed by it."

Her mouth twisted saucily. "I think you'd best show me a bit of that amazement."

"My pleasure, dove."

He kissed her. He kissed her in that room full of the odds and ends of the literary world, in the council chamber of the group she'd confronted in order to save his hide and give him back his future. He kissed her with all the emotion in his heart and the love he'd struggled with for weeks.

Then he held her in his arms, marveling that she was here with him, with *them*. He'd found the other half of his very soul, and they had an entire lifetime ahead of them to weave tales, to rescue children, and to fall further and further into love.

ACKNOWLEDGMENTS

I could not have hoped to make this story half as authentic and accurate without the invaluable information and insights I gained from the following:

- Susie Dent's many brilliant books on dialect and etymology.
- Normanby Hall's exhibit on Victorian-era clothing.
- The Charles Booth archive at the London School of Economics and Political Science.
- The United States Library of Congress's "WPA Slave Narratives" project archive.

I could not have hoped to survive the crafting of this tale with half so many functioning brain cells without the following:

- Jolene Perry, the first person with whom I shared this story in detail and who responded with such unabashed enthusiasm I finally began to believe that maybe I could pull this thing off.
- Lisa Mangum, whose invaluable editorial feedback included a not-so-subtle reminder that a romance ought

to have at least a *few* romantic moments tossed in the mix somewhere—advice I apparently require often.

- The Bear Lake Monsters writers' group, who kept my spirits and confidence up while life gleefully beat me to a pulp during the writing of this story.

- My family, who, despite being quite bored of hearing about these characters who reside in my head, continued to nod and smile vaguely each and every time I began expounding at length about Fletcher, Elizabeth, and the gang.

- Pam Victorio, who is not afraid to tell me when my expansive plans for my brilliant future are neither brilliant nor verifiable, and who expertly sets my feet back on solid ground, pointed in the right direction.

- Twisted Mango Diet Coke—both my liquid joy and my Achilles' heel.

DISCUSSION QUESTIONS

1. The Dread Master's identity is never revealed. What are your theories about who the secretive leader might be?

2. Is Fletcher justified in keeping the Dread Master's identity a secret from Hollis, his closest friend and confidant? Is Hollis justified in his frustration over Fletcher's refusal to share that information with him?

3. Victorian London was a more ethnically diverse place than is often acknowledged. The members of the Dread Penny Society, to a degree, reflect that diversity. How do you think their diverse backgrounds help their efforts? What complications might it cause?

4. Each of the Dreadfuls has a personal passion—an area of injustice, inequality, or lack of opportunity—that he is particularly determined to address. If you were a member of this band of philanthropists, what would your passion be?

5. Elizabeth and Fletcher both acknowledge that their upbringings and careers will make a relationship between them difficult, with potential consequences for Elizabeth's school, specifically. What problems might await them in

the future? How do you think they will weather those storms?

6. In what way do you think Elizabeth's actions in the final scene of the book will impact the future of the Dread Penny Society? How will it impact her career as a secret penny dreadful author?

7. Quintin Hogg is a real figure from history who founded the York Place Ragged School in London, where the poorest of that city's children could receive an education. While the events surrounding that school are fictionalized here, the education of the poor and destitute faced significant opposition at this time. Why do you think that was?

8. At this time, a child's opportunity for education and the type of education he or she might receive depended almost entirely on that child's wealth, ethnicity, and gender. In what ways has educational inequality improved since the nineteenth century? In what ways could it still improve?

9. What Victorian-era issues and problems could you imagine the Dread Penny Society tackling? What future adventures do you think await them?